I0618978

THE PERFECT WITNESS

A gripping psychological thriller full of suspense

SUSANNA BEARD

JOFFE BOOKS

Joffe Books, London
www.joffebooks.com

First published in Great Britain in 2022

This paperback edition was first published
in Great Britain in 2022

Cover art by Stuart Bache

ISBN: 978-1-80405-262-4

For Charlie

PROLOGUE

A boy's face, contorted with pain, his mouth stretched wide. The same every time, haunting, persisting. The image doesn't fade, the boy never ages. Any time, day or night, anywhere, he shows up.

Other memories break through sometimes. A boat, rocking on murky waters, ripples escaping from its heavy bow. A serpent, yellow eyes accusing, sinuous body tensed, ready to strike.

A dark bundle sinking.

Memories are important — they keep us anchored, tell us who we are. We remember the good times, and the bad. We recall the date of our first kiss, or the day we got our driving licence. The exact time, day and date someone important died, and where we were at that moment. Even, perhaps, the clothes we were wearing, or our first thought on hearing the news.

It's when we can't remember that we begin to feel frightened. When our memories vanish, we fear we're losing our minds.

But not Daniel. What frightens Daniel is that he can't forget.

CHAPTER ONE

Friday, 9 March 2018 started as a normal day. He took the Underground as usual, squeezing into the crowded carriage along with a swarm of dark coats and jackets, people staring blankly, earphones firmly in place. Hunching his shoulders against a chill wind, he walked from the station to the nondescript building where he'd worked for almost two years, forcing his feet to take him through the front door into the dusty lobby and on into the creaking lift. At the third floor, the lift deposited him in a gloomy stairwell, opposite the double doors that led to the open-plan office where he worked. As usual, he made his way to his desk next to the window, avoiding eye contact with Rachel at reception, James at the desk next to his, and the girls across the way who always seemed to be watching him.

But today something was different. Someone had already been here. A neon-pink Post-It note sat jauntily on his computer screen. It wasn't there when he'd left yesterday. He glanced over at James, but his colleague was frowning intently, jabbing with stiff fingers at his keyboard.

Removing the slip of paper in a single swipe, Daniel studied it in the palm of his hand. The message was friendly enough: *Hi D — need a chat. 5.00 my office — thanks. J.* But his stomach did a tiny flip, his shoulders tensing as he crumpled the note into a ball and dropped it into the plastic bin under his desk. It lay there, pulsating with rude colour, a silent reminder.

As he fired up his computer, he remembered that colour on another day. A summer holiday when he was fourteen, Lauren twelve, on the beach at Lyme Regis. Lauren in her pink costume that shone like a beacon as she picked her way across the pebbles towards the sea. It was a Thursday — 24 July — the first day of a two-week camping holiday, their regular summer break. It wasn't quite raining, though the clouds on the horizon were gun-metal grey and plump with unshed water. They'd ventured to the beach anyway, because that's what you did on a summer holiday. Daniel had been—

No, he mustn't drift. With a sigh, he began to work through his emails, taking his time. He knew he should be getting on with that report, but he needed to work up to it, prepare his unruly brain to study the numbers, tease out the important points, develop a perspective.

How had he ended up here, in an office, in a job he had no passion for? Although in truth, he had no passion for anything. There was too much going on in his brain. It was too fast, too unpredictable, too—

His mind flipped back to the Post-It note.

A chat? What did that mean? Another reminder that he was floundering, another motivational talk? If only he'd slept well. That would have made all the difference. As it was, it took all his energy just to keep his focus on the screen in front of him.

* * *

"Come in, come in, Daniel." Jeremy rose from his desk and gestured expansively to an empty chair. "Sit down, sit down."

Daniel smothered the urge to reply, *OK, OK, I will, I will.*

His boss was forty-something with a patchy bald head, wire-rimmed glasses and a burgeoning paunch. He favoured pinstripe suits with pink shirts, and was never seen without a tie. All this might have given a good impression, but somehow the overall image was of dishevelment. Nothing fitted well. Jeremy's body didn't seem right for him and the result was a clumsiness that made everyone feel awkward.

As he sat down, his chair rolled away from the desk, leaving him paddling his feet and pulling at the desk with his hands to return to position. He cleared his throat and shifted a few papers around. "Where was it? Ah, yes . . ." He pushed his glasses back up his nose, a habit Daniel found profoundly irritating.

In the long pause that followed, Daniel glanced around him. The window looked out over another unremarkable office building, relieved by the presence of a large chestnut tree. He watched as clusters of leaves danced in the wind. It reminded him of his childhood, the house in the country where he grew up, and the tree he used to climb with Lauren, in the local farmer's field. One day — also a Friday — Lauren fell and broke her arm. She was only seven. Daniel had been scolded and punished for not looking after her better. He still felt angry at being blamed. He'd only been nine himself, and Lauren had a way of insisting on doing what she wanted.

"Daniel?"

He dragged his mind back with difficulty. Jeremy had been talking — or had he?

"Sorry," Daniel said. "I was distracted."

Jeremy kept his eyes on a sheet of paper he was holding, lifting it to his face as if having difficulty deciphering the writing on it. The light shone through it from the window. Daniel tried to read the faint lines from behind, without success.

"You see, Daniel, that's exactly the problem." Jeremy removed his glasses, placed the sheet in a folder and closed it. He gazed into Daniel's eyes.

Daniel wilted under the scrutiny, shrinking into the back of his chair. "I'm sorry, Jeremy, I don't quite—"

"There you go again. You don't quite what?" His boss sat back in his seat with an air of frustration.

Daniel stared at him. He had no idea what was going on.

"We've had this conversation before, remember? You're not . . . engaged . . . with this job. Never quite with us, always one or two steps behind. You show no enthusiasm for your work whatsoever. Now, I know the industry can be a little dry — no, don't pretend you find it fascinating, we both know that wouldn't be true." Jeremy stood up and strode over to the window. "I'm afraid, Daniel, it's time for you to find a position you feel more affinity with. I'm going to have to let you go. We'll give you your full notice, of course — no need for anyone to know you haven't resigned — but that's it, you've had your warnings. It's time for you to go."

For a moment, Daniel heard the words but their meaning escaped him. *Let you go. More affinity.* He felt his jaw slacken.

Jeremy returned to his seat, knocking his thigh on the corner of his desk. Rubbing the spot distractedly, he continued, "One month from today . . . human resources . . . holiday owing . . . contents of your desk . . . confidential . . . references, of course."

Daniel nodded and smiled, letting the voice drift over his head. The boy's face began to materialise, that same expression, the fear in his eyes—

"Well, I'm glad you're taking this so well." Jeremy fixed him with a fatherly gaze. "You must have realised it's not a good fit."

The boy disappeared.

"Not a good—?"

"Fit. You and us. The organisation. The job." Jeremy drew breath, still staring intensely at Daniel's face, as if searching for something deep inside him, but not finding it. "Right. Well. I wish you luck." He stood in a rush, his chair rolling away again as if in a hurry to leave the room. He held out a fleshy paw. "I'm sure you'll find the perfect job, Daniel. Good luck."

Because Jeremy seemed to be expecting him to stand as well, Daniel rose and shook the clammy hand. He closed his mouth, nodded in Jeremy's direction and walked slowly to the door.

* * *

Amber was sitting on the top step, a bulging supermarket bag beside her. She'd been resting her head against the banister, motionless, and he failed to notice her until she moved her head. He'd been focusing on his feet, watching their dejected journey up the staircase. He almost tripped over her.

"Danny!"

"Oh, sorry, Amber, I was miles away." He fumbled in his pocket for his keys.

"You always are. Did you forget?" She pushed past him as he opened the door, the bag of shopping bumping against his shins.

"Forget?"

"You forgot." She almost spat the words out at him. "God, Danny, what's wrong with you? We only talked about this yesterday! We were going to get away from work early, have a nice supper and watch a film. I've done all the shopping on the way here, nearly killed myself carrying it up the stairs, and you don't even have the grace to apologise for being late."

Dumping the bags on the worktop in the tiny galley kitchen, Amber gazed into the fridge, scowling. "Sometimes, you know, I think you wouldn't care if you saw me or not. And you haven't got any wine." Slamming the fridge shut, she stomped to the sofa and sat down hard on his Xbox controller. She threw it to one side. "Shit."

He felt his shoulders slump, his head drop. He'd done it again. She was right — there was something wrong with him. There always had been. He was just not like other people.

"I'm sorry, Amber, I really am. I know, I'm hopeless. I do care, honestly, but I get distracted . . . I can't explain it . . ."

Amber grabbed a cushion and held it to her chest like a shield. Her mouth was set in a grim line. "That's what you

6

said last time, and the time before. Honestly, I don't know why I bother."

"Sorry."

She shook her head, her dark curls bouncing. "Sorry isn't enough. You need to sort yourself out. Go to see a doctor — or a shrink. Get yourself checked out properly."

"You're right." He hung his head, unable to find the words to appease her.

"Is that all you have to say?" She glared at him, her eyes flashing.

But what could he say? If he tried to placate her, he'd only end up annoying her more. If he tried to deny his hopelessness, she'd know it was a lie.

She waited a moment, her eyes on his face, but before he could open his mouth, she sprang to her feet, hurling the cushion at him. "Do you know what? I've had enough. I'm off. And I'm taking this with me." She grabbed her coat and the bag of shopping in a single sweep and stamped to the front door. After a second grappling with the latch, she swept out, leaving Daniel with a tailwind of fury that electrified the air.

CHAPTER TWO

Daniel had never been much good with women. Even now, approaching thirty, he was tongue-tied and gauche. He had never felt anything but out of place and awkward.

As a teenager, he'd grown into his body gradually and it had been a surprise to him when suddenly he was no longer a boy. At nearly six feet tall, he was slender, with unruly dark hair that seemed to grow faster than anyone else's. Or maybe that was his impression — he hated going to the hairdresser, preferring to let it grow to his shoulders.

When Daniel had started to get attention from girls, he was far too shy to do anything about it, except wonder what they saw in him. He'd studied himself in the mirror, trying to look objectively at his image, to see what they saw. Staring back at him was a serious-looking teenager with a spotty forehead and an intense gaze. He'd tried smiling. The person in the mirror smiled back, and for a split second he could see that his smile had a certain appeal. But it didn't help. He still had no idea how to behave around girls, and whenever one made it clear that she liked him and wanted to get to know him, he shied away, angry with himself for ruining it yet again.

He could hardly believe it when Amber pursued him. They'd bumped into each other on a crowded Tube a year ago. The journey had been almost unbearable that day. The platform was full when Daniel reached it, people lining the walls from end to end, the narrow space in front of them filling all the time. Though it was a fresh autumn day outside, deep beneath the streets of London, the air was stale, tinged with an unpleasant fusion of human sweat, singed metal and ancient dust.

By the time the train arrived, Daniel was engrossed in the depths of a vivid memory. He was jolted into the present by the impatient mass of people surging forward and he found himself carried onto the train, shuffling hard to keep his footing. More and more people tried to squeeze on, and those inside were forced into the narrow space between the seats. Briefcases bashed painfully into shins, handbags caught between shoulders and ribs, unfortunate people with suitcases grew hot with the effort to move them into the smallest spaces. The doors opened and closed three times before clicking shut securely.

When the train finally lurched off, the entire line of standing passengers stumbled forward. Daniel lost his balance, the crush having pinned him in position. His foot shot forward, stamping down hard as he tried to right himself. There was a muffled cry and the girl ahead of him swivelled her neck around, a curse on her lips.

"That was my foot!" Her face crumpled with pain. The top of her head barely reached Daniel's shoulder.

Still struggling to stay upright, Daniel mumbled, "I'm sorry . . . so sorry. Are you OK?"

Somehow she managed to turn her shoulders, then the rest of her body, towards him. "Don't worry," she said. "I've got another one. Somewhere around here."

Despite himself, Daniel smiled. She was pretty. Perhaps mid-twenties, with a mass of curls and a Cupid's bow mouth painted red. They were standing uncomfortably close, and he tried to inch his head away from hers, but the rocking of the train forced them together.

When the train emptied out at last, they sat down together and she rubbed her bruised foot. He felt compelled to apologise again, but she waved his apology aside and started to interrogate him — at least, that's how it felt. He was relieved when his stop was announced, then alarmed to find she was alighting with him.

He couldn't have made too much of an idiot of himself because she suggested he buy her a coffee to compensate for the injured toes. Two hours later, he got back to his flat, never expecting to see her again.

But they had swapped numbers — more, he thought, from politeness than interest on her side. He was surprised when she texted him, and stunned when she suggested they met for a drink one evening. He wanted to say no, but every excuse he thought of sounded so lame, he deleted the hastily drafted messages immediately. So he agreed to meet her at a local bar.

It was one of the hardest things he'd done. He'd never been on a proper date. He'd had girlfriends, if you could call them that, but before this, he'd always fallen into a state of 'togetherness' through school or work. None of them had lasted. He couldn't even say, if he was completely honest, that he'd had a proper girlfriend.

He went into a state of panic just thinking about it — was it a date, really? Perhaps she was just being friendly. He tried to work out what indications she'd given him when they met, but went round in circles wondering what kind of signals a girl might make. What should he wear — should he dress up, or down? Should he kiss her on the cheek or hug her when she arrived? Should he get there early, to make sure she didn't have to sit on her own, or would that look too keen? He had no idea what they would talk about, whether he should offer to pay, or if that would insult her. It was all such a minefield.

As he always did when he was in trouble, he called his sister. Though Lauren was younger than him, she was far more streetwise. She'd had boyfriends since she was fourteen. He felt an idiot for having to call on her, but he wanted to make a good impression on Amber, and he needed all the help he could get.

To his relief, Lauren took the situation in her stride. She didn't laugh at him, or make fun of him for needing advice on dating. "Wear clean clothes — things you like and feel good in — just your normal, everyday stuff. Kiss her on the cheek when you get there. Smile. Buy the first drinks, then let her get the next round. Be yourself, try not to worry, and listen to her. Listening is the best thing. She'll appreciate you for that. If you run out of questions, repeat the last thing she said with a verbal question mark after it. Then she'll carry on." There was a pause. "Do you like her?"

"Yes. I think so . . ."

"Good. She obviously likes you, so you don't need to try too hard. Just take it as it comes, she'll warm to you if you're a bit vulnerable."

Somehow Daniel had got through the first date, and the next one, and soon they were seeing each other regularly. There were many hurdles to cross, and every time he suffered terrible self-doubt, but Lauren coached him through without mocking him, listening patiently to his anxieties, his never-ending stream of doubts.

At last he was 'in a relationship'. It felt strange but comforting to know that someone liked him. Of course he worried. Most of the time, in fact. Was he good enough for her? Would she tire of him and dump him unceremoniously? What were her expectations?

Amber was very different from him. She didn't seem to worry about anything. Maybe that was why he didn't open up to her, even though she was closer to him than anyone — except his sister. He couldn't bring himself to tell her his innermost fears or about the barrage of memories he dealt with every day. He didn't know how she would react. Would she think he was weird, as the kids at school had done? They had made him clam up, and for years he'd hidden the things that made him different, forcing himself to behave like other people. Maybe she'd think he was making a big fuss about nothing, as his father had when he'd gathered the courage to talk to him. "Nothing to worry about, Daniel," his dad had said. "You'll grow out of it."

But he hadn't. If anything, it had got worse.

He hadn't wanted Amber to see him as weak, as a victim. Or even as a worrier. As it was, he couldn't see why she was interested in him, a bit of a loser, lacking ambition, just about managing to keep his act together. When he thought about it, which was often, he couldn't see a future for them. He knew in his heart they weren't right together. But he didn't want it to end, either.

He decided not to call her that night, to let her simmer down, but he wanted to say sorry, to make up for it somehow. This had happened before. She'd lost patience with him — and he felt doubly stupid this time for not seeing it coming. But he had lost his job, and that surely was a good reason for forgetting their arrangement. He hadn't even had the chance to tell her.

He texted with clumsy fingers. *So sorry. Lost my job this afternoon, not thinking straight. X*

Then, thinking she might not respond to that, *Let's do it tomorrow night? X*

He waited a few minutes for her response but nothing came. The screen remained stubbornly empty. With a sigh, he picked up the Xbox controller and pressed *Start*.

CHAPTER THREE

It was four in the morning before he realised the time, and when he stood up to go to bed, his back ached. The muscles in his shoulders were stiff and sore.

This wasn't unusual for Daniel. He'd got into the habit of distracting himself with gaming, and now it seemed the only way he could escape. He knew it wasn't doing him any good. He was in a permanent state of sleep deprivation. It wasn't surprising that he'd lost his job: he'd been functioning at about a third of his capacity for months.

But the games gripped his brain in a way that stopped its manic delving. The memories would stay away for a few hours, giving him respite from the constant flow of images, sounds, smells, feelings.

He imagined his brain as a kind of circular library, curving like a mollusc's shell, slowly turning. Shelves and shelves of books, each holding a capsule of his past. Events, details, colours, sounds. Dates, days and times. Things he'd learned, too, of course, but their corner of the library was insignificant compared with the never-ending lines of memories, each one slotted into its place, indexed with precision, but rising to the surface without warning, at random. Triggered by a word from a stranger, a touch on a smooth surface, a tantalising smell. There were a few that needed no trigger, like the boy's face.

Something in his brain had gone wrong, he was sure of it. The switch that retrieved memories was frozen in the 'on' position, its messages constantly on 'send'.

As he fell into bed, a dull pain in his stomach reminded him that yesterday, he'd lost his job. And possibly his girl-friend too. With a groan, he turned his head into the pillow and prayed for sleep.

* * *

The light seeping through the gap in the curtains was flat and grey. The patter of rain on the window did nothing to raise his mood as he drifted towards consciousness.

An image of Jeremy's face, oddly coupled with Amber's parting words, jerked him awake. He threw the covers aside with a curse. He needed to rouse himself or what happened yes-terday would flatten him all day. There wasn't much he could do about the job, but he might just be able to placate Amber.

He checked his mobile. Nothing from her, not even an acknowledgement that she'd seen his message. He'd better call her, try to make it up to her. Perhaps he should take her out to dinner, make a real effort. Buy her flowers? No, that was too much — he didn't want her to laugh at his pathetic efforts towards reconciliation.

Why did he never know what to do?

After a breakfast of buttered toast and black coffee, he felt more able to face the day. He badly needed to go to the supermarket. He was down to the last few slices of bread, a small chunk of butter and some spongy potatoes. Otherwise, the cupboard was bare.

Daniel hated shopping. If he steeled himself and went soon, before it got too busy, he might be able to cope with the small Sainsbury's on the corner. They wouldn't have everything he needed, but the idea of a major shop at the megastore was unbearable. Without a car, he'd have to stagger back a mile or so, weighed down by bursting bags, before navigating the sixty-four steps up to his flat. Not to mention the panic attack he might have, surrounded by Saturday shoppers and too much choice.

He left before he could change his mind and was back in record time, relieved that he'd dodged a panic attack. But in the middle of unpacking, he was startled by the buzzing of the entry phone. Nobody ever came to see him. His few friends were not in the habit of dropping in, and his parents wouldn't dream of it, frightened by what they might find.

He grabbed the handset. "Amber? Is that you?"

"Sorry to disappoint," said a male voice. "Can I come up?"

"Who is it?" he said, trying to place the voice. It was familiar, but for a moment he was confused.

"Malcolm. Malcolm Brown."

Daniel tried to remember who that was.

"Your landlord?"

His landlord. *Christ.* "Of course, come in." Daniel slammed the handset back in place and looked around the room in a panic.

It was a mess, but not as bad as it could have been. He darted around, clearing the kitchen surfaces of plates and bowls and dumping them in the sink, wiping the coffee stains with the cloth that itself needed a good wash. He cleared Xbox controllers and wires, stashing them behind the TV unit, and plumped a couple of cushions. That would have to do. He could already hear the stamp of Malcolm's heavy tread on the stairs outside.

Organising his face into a smile, he opened the door. Malcolm stood there panting, in his usual beige raincoat, a briefcase in his pudgy hand. They had only met a couple of times before — when Daniel had looked around the flat that first time, and when he'd moved in. Otherwise, all contact had been by email. Daniel wondered what had brought him up the stairs today, especially given how unfit he seemed to be.

"Come in, Malcolm." He opened the door wide. The entrance to his flat was tiny and with two of them, it felt far too intimate, so he hurried ahead into the sitting room.

"Would you like a coffee?" he said, to fill the pause. Malcolm had yet to say anything, his chest still heaving after the ascent. Daniel regretted his offer straight away — the last thing he wanted was for Malcolm to hang around, inspecting the less-than-clean corners of his property.

But Malcolm shook his head, fiddling with the lock on his briefcase. "No, I'm not stopping." He removed an envelope and handed it to Daniel. "Just wanted to let you know in person that I'll be needing the flat back. I'm giving you notice from today. My niece will be moving to London in the summer, and I've promised the flat to her."

Just like that. No apology, no apparent sympathy for the person he was effectively evicting from his home. In one or two sentences, Malcolm was removing the one thing he had left in his life here.

Daniel didn't open the envelope. He felt the blood drain from his face. He managed to part his lips but nothing came out. He waited for Malcolm to make eye contact, to show some sense of humanity, but the man just closed his bag and turned to go.

"I — wait!" His voice was hoarse, but it was working. "You can't . . . you can't just—"

"Check your contract." Malcolm turned one shoulder in Daniel's direction. "It's all in there — one month's notice, as agreed. I'll be sending someone round to do the inventory nearer the time. Goodbye."

CHAPTER FOUR

Poppy poked her head around the door to her grandmother's room. These days her gran lived downstairs, in what used to be the dining room, though now Poppy could barely remember what the room had looked like without the single bed with its pink candlewick cover, the circular rug, and the family photos dotted around the room. Her gran could no longer manage the stairs on her own, so the downstairs toilet had been converted to include a shower, though she was under strict instructions not to lock the door. Just in case.

"Gran, breakfast's ready!"

The curtains were closed, but Gran answered straight away. "OK, love, be there in a minute. Having a lazy start today."

"Are you OK, Gran?" Poppy went to the window and drew the curtains, allowing a shaft of golden sunshine to flow through, making patterns on the carpet as it slid through the apple tree in the garden.

"I'm fine, thank you, dear. Just enjoying the birdsong."

Poppy's father had hung bird feeders from a bracket outside the window, and birds flitted to and from the apple tree. A robin seemed always to be nearby, blue tits flashed from branch to feeder, pigeons waited below for the fallout.

Though Poppy's gran was in her eighties now, her sight was good with glasses and her hearing as good as ever. But she was getting increasingly wobbly on her feet, hence the installation of rails at the front and back doors to help her manage the steps, and the wheelchair in the porch. And her memory was fading — rather fast.

Poppy loved her grandmother with every beat of her heart. Not that she didn't adore her mum and dad, but her gran had a special place in her life, and always had done. Her gran had looked after her often when she was little, while her mum was out at work. Always smiling, Gran was generous, never cross, though when she wanted, she could be scarily firm.

These days Poppy was working part-time, spending as much time as she could looking after her grandmother, taking her for walks in the wheelchair, brewing endless cups of tea and helping her with complicated jigsaw puzzles. Gran could always find a way to make her laugh, even on the odd occasion when she felt down.

Poppy didn't often feel that way. She was doing what she loved, working with animals, despite the terrible money. The job at the animal rescue centre suited her, and it meant she could spend more time at home. The Alzheimer's diagnosis two years ago had saddened them all, but Poppy had decided to forgo the chance to move in with friends in favour of staying with her family. It meant her mum could continue to work, and her parents were grateful for all the time she put into caring for her grandmother.

"It's a lovely day, Gran." Poppy dropped a quick kiss on the pale forehead. "Don't rush. See you in the kitchen!"

"I'm coming, love. A couple of minutes."

In the kitchen, she laid out two places at the table. Her parents had already eaten their breakfast and left for work — her mother at the local grocery store, her father heading for the Royal Mail sorting office in Banbury. Poppy liked to eat with her grandmother. They would listen to the radio, chat about the news and plan what they would do for the day.

Neither of them got bored or lonely while they had each other. But in the back of her mind, Poppy knew that the day would inevitably come when her gran would no longer be around. The thought was almost unbearable.

* * *

By the time Poppy's mum got back from work, Gran was asleep in her chair in the living room, white curls framing her face against the worn fabric of the seat. Poppy placed a blanket gently across her knees, taking care not to wake her. She looked small and frail, her hands folded neatly in her lap, her thin legs encased in robust opaque tights.

"Looks like you've worn her out today, Poppy," her mother said as she unpacked a bag of shopping in the kitchen. Poppy went to help her, stacking tins of beans and tomatoes in the corner cupboard while her mum pushed packets of fish and chicken breasts into the freezer compartment.

"I hope not. We didn't go far, and it was a lovely day. She seemed to enjoy it."

"I'm sure she did. But perhaps let her rest tomorrow, eh?"

"I'm working tomorrow, anyway," Poppy said. "She can have a lie-in and a peaceful day without me."

"That's good then." Her mum dropped her voice and glanced towards the sitting room door. "She runs out of energy more quickly nowadays. Sometimes even talking seems to exhaust her."

"OK. I'll be careful not to tire her out."

Poppy crept back into the sitting room and stole a look at her grandmother while she slept. That dear, lined face was so precious, those delicate hands with their sprinkling of age spots so beautiful. Now that she thought about it, the rings on her fingers looked quite loose. She had never been particularly overweight, but her body had definitely shrunk. She'd lost height as well as girth and, as she slept, she looked fragile, like a fine piece of porcelain. Her time was getting nearer.

CHAPTER FIVE

Daniel sank onto the sofa, the envelope fluttering to the floor. What had he done to deserve this? The sad thing was, he'd done nothing, and that was precisely the problem. Doing nothing was probably the only thing he was really good at.

A sharp clenching of his stomach brought him to his feet. Anger rose up inside him. He strode from end to end of the tiny room. A grim voice in his head yelled, "*Loser! What are you? This is all your fault! Twenty-nine years old and what have you achieved? Nothing! Why can't you be normal? Why can't you just sort yourself out? You're a grown man, not a child.*"

Everything piled in on him, images of the past, incidents where he'd gone wrong, failed, disappointed his parents, lost his friends. He thumped his forehead against the door jamb, once, twice, on and on until his neck ached and tears of pain prickled at his eyelids. Only then did his mind stop whirling.

Breathing hard, he stumbled to the sofa and collapsed, cradling his pounding head in his hands. Blood trickled over his temple towards his ear. He wiped it with a shaking hand. In a few moments, his breathing settled and the crashing in his head dwindled to a rhythmic thud. His brain was clearer, the memories retreating to their places in the library of his mind.

It took quite an effort to get to his feet. Still clutching his head, he shuffled to the bathroom to inspect the damage. It wasn't the growing lump on his forehead or the oozing cut that shocked him — it was the haunted, ghoulish look on his face that made him recoil. Dark lines beneath his eyes seemed to pull his eyelids downwards, giving his face a monstrous droop. His skin was a blotchy mix of grey and white, his hair hung thin and greasy, sticking to his neck in places. He had the look of a desperate man.

To his horror, tears threatened, and this time they were not tears of pain. The face in the mirror grimaced, a flush spreading angrily from its neck towards its ravaged cheeks. He bent over the basin and ran the cold water directly onto his face, through his hair. It was freezing, but he forced himself to stay there until his scalp felt numb and the lump in his throat faded away. Burying his head in a towel, he returned to the sitting room.

He sat for a long time, the towel draped over his shoulders, his mind still empty, a welcome relief, though he knew it would be short-lived. He practised breathing slowly, in for ten beats, out for ten, in for ten . . .

But at last, he had to face what was happening to him, and he felt the immediate stab of fear. How was he going to sort this out? He had not one huge problem, but three, and in the vital parts of his life — his job, his girlfriend, his home.

He reached for his mobile. There was only one person in the world he could bear to confide in.

She sounded breathless, traffic noise in the background blurring her voice. "Hello, you."

"Where are you?"

"Just finished my run. Be home in a minute. Call you back?"

"Can you be quick?"

"You OK?"

"Not really. Go on, call me when you're home." He cut the call.

Sitting with his damp head in his hands, waiting for her to call back, a new feeling crept over him. At first he didn't recognise it, but the heaviness slowly taking hold of his neck, his shoulders, his stomach, his legs, revealed its true nature.

Desolation.

It was as if someone had placed a huge burden, a chunk of solid rock, on his back, and he knew — really knew, for the first time in his life — that this horrible situation was of his own making.

Since the age of ten, he'd fudged everything. School, work, relationships — everything, always, was a fudge. There was not a single thing he'd focused his energies on, nothing that gave him inspiration, joy, or satisfaction. Always the fact — no, the excuse — that his brain was different, the memories were distracting, he couldn't help the way he was.

The perilous, paper-thin structure of his life had finally collapsed. It had never been real, any of it, not really. He'd scraped through school, fallen into a job. There had probably been no other applicants. Even his girlfriend had struggled to create, let alone sustain, a relationship with him.

So what now?

He couldn't go to his parents. Yes, his mum would be kind, she would welcome him home and try to help in her own way. But she'd never really understood him, and neither had his dad. He was disappointed in him. He'd never actually said so, but the look in his eyes told Daniel all he needed to know.

The only person he had left was Lauren.

* * *

The jangle of electronic music from his mobile felt like a stab in his temple. His heart began to race and he fumbled with the handset, dropping it twice before he was able to press the right button. "Lauren?"

"It's me. You sound terrible — what's going on?" Her voice was calm and close now. He imagined her in her cosy flat, the cushions and rugs of her living room softening any noise from outside.

"Lauren." Even to him, he sounded wrong. Choked, gruff, throaty. "I've fucked up. *I'm* fucked up." The effort not to cry was suddenly too much, and tears rolled down his cheeks unchecked. "I don't know what to do." The words came out in a rising wail of despair.

"Whoa, Daniel. Come on, it's OK. It will be OK. Get yourself some water, it's fine, I can wait."

Scrubbing the tears from his cheeks, he stumbled to the kitchen and grabbed a mug of water. A deep gulp, two, three, and he put the handset back to his ear. "Are you still there?"

"Of course I am. Come on, tell me. What's happened?"

"Everything's happened. I'm just a fuckhead. A waste of space, a useless piece of shit."

"Stop it, right now, and tell me what's happened."

He took a deep breath and told her. His job: the endless boredom, his inability to find enthusiasm, energy, the constant need to pretend. Jeremy's efforts to encourage him, to involve him in team social events, bolster his self-confidence, all to no avail. How exhausted he was by the simple act of pretending to be present. The flat, and being ousted without apology, like a piece of broken furniture.

He did his best to describe his relationship with Amber, to explain why it had been doomed from the start. His inability to *engage* — Jeremy's favourite word — to find it in him to focus on a person, a job, a task. On anything.

He found himself talking about the memories. The relentless barrage of images and feelings, the never-ending, exhausting, debilitating, mind-numbing non-stop nature of a brain that never, ever stops retrieving and presenting scenes and images and senses and emotions.

He stopped short of talking about the boy. That was a step too far.

She knew about his memories, of course. As a child, before they had turned in different directions as teenagers, he'd tried to describe to her what it was like to remember everything about his life. The time, the date, the day of the week of every single event. Not only to remember it, but to have it emerge over and over again. His brain stretched to the limit. The triggers, the distractions, the never being present. But she had only been a child, younger than him, and though she tried, it was clear she didn't get it, and he hadn't wanted to burden her. He'd mentioned it a few times since, but had never really confided in her.

Afterwards he realised the depths he must have reached to unburden himself so completely to his sister. In the moment it seemed as if he couldn't stop talking, the words tumbling over themselves — the need to get them out, for her to understand.

She let him talk, interrupting only when he stumbled over his words, or to get clarification. When the torrent petered out, there was a long pause and he began to worry that she'd gone away. Then she took a deep, ragged breath and let it out slowly. A kind of emotional expulsion.

"Lauren?" His hands were shaking, his palms clammy with sweat.

"Yes, sorry, I'm just — absorbing it all. Wow, Daniel. My God. I knew you struggled sometimes, but — this!"

"Yes." A sense of relief washed over him. Even if she understood only a fraction of what he had said, the unburdening was cathartic.

There was another long pause. He swallowed. "The thing is, Lauren . . . I don't think I can bear it any longer." As he said it, he knew it was true. "I'm twenty-nine years old, and I'm finished. I've tried to control it but it's obvious I can't. It's ruining my life — it's already ruined it. There's nothing I can do about it. I've had enough."

"Don't even think about it." She almost shouted down the line. "Daniel, do you hear me?"

Was that a sob?

"Oh, Lauren, I'm sorry. I'm not thinking about that, not really. But I can't ignore it. I'm never going to have a proper life if I can't find a way to deal with it. I've tried controlling it, ignoring it, pretending — look where that's got me. It's tied me in knots until I'm ill with it. Therapy was a fat lot of good."

"I didn't know—"

"Oh, there's been a series of therapists. None of them had a clue. Nothing they said did anything whatsoever. I don't think they'd ever come across someone like me. Nobody has."

"There must be other people like you, I can't believe there aren't. Have you—"

"Yes, of course. There are stories online — anecdotal, I think — about people who have recall a bit like mine. But not to this extent. Not overwhelming, exhausting, sapping the life out of you—"

"Stop. There has to be something we can do."

He felt the tears threaten again. "I don't think there is."

"There always is."

He had to respect her certainty. Helpless as he was, he felt a surge of emotion for Lauren.

"Listen, this is what we're going to do," she said. "I'm going to come and see you — no objections."

He'd taken a breath to demur. His sister lived on the outskirts of London, and without a car, the journey involved a train, then the Underground, plus a walk at the end, a journey of at least an hour.

"I'm coming as soon as I've had a shower and grabbed some overnight things. We'll start with the practical stuff, and find a way to deal with the rest. No arguments. This is a crisis, and we'll sort it out."

* * *

It was mid-afternoon now. Still no response from Amber. He checked his mobile again — no new messages. The reality of his situation began to dawn on him. Things couldn't be much worse, really.

It would be a couple of hours at least before Lauren arrived. He was too jumpy to watch TV or play computer games, and anyway, he didn't want to get embroiled in a long game and lose track of time. There had to be something he could do until his sister arrived.

Amber. His finger wavered over the button to speed-dial her number. Should he keep trying? She was clearly angry with him, but knowing his situation, surely she would come round? She'd been angry with him before, and forgiven him — but then, all the more reason not to forgive him this time.

Forcing the questions from his mind, he made himself press the button. He felt his anxiety grow, his breathing become fast and shallow, his hands clammy. This was ridiculous — he was ridiculous. All he was doing was calling his girlfriend and his stress levels had gone through the roof.

She didn't answer. After a few moments, the call went to voicemail. He wavered. Should he leave a message? He still hadn't decided when the beep echoed in his ear, and he was left stammering, unprepared. "Ah, hi Amber. Sorry, I was hoping to speak to you . . . I — Look, I want to apologise for yesterday. I lost my job and I wasn't thinking, and I know that's how I always am, but this time it was for a good reason, I hope you understand. Anyway . . . sorry. Please — can you just call me? Or message. Anyway . . . bye."

He cut the call, still wracked with nerves. He should have told her he cared, he didn't want to break up. Should he call back? Should he have told her he loved her? No, that would make her snort with laughter. He'd never said it before and he'd look even more of a fool. Anyway, he didn't know if he did or not.

But he didn't want to break up with her. Whether this was for the right reasons or not, he didn't know. He knew it would be pretty difficult to find another girlfriend willing to put up with him, but that wasn't a good reason.

The last time she'd been angry with him — 1 June, a Friday — he'd done almost exactly the same thing, but without the excuse that he'd lost his job. They'd arranged to meet after work at a tapas bar close to his flat, have a drink and some snacks, then get a takeaway. He'd completely forgotten, gone home and only remembered when she'd called him.

Her voice had a cold edge to it. He remembered immediately. "Oh my God, I'm so sorry. I'm coming, right now."

"You forgot." It was a statement, not a question.

"I — Yes, but I can be there in five minutes. I'll run." He heard a sigh as she cut the call. Dashing down the stairs, he hoped she'd wait, but he knew there was no guarantee. She took no nonsense from anyone. He wished he were more like her.

That time, he was lucky. She waited, and though he got a frosty reception and a reminder that she had better things to do than wait alone in a bar for forty minutes, he managed to turn the evening around by buying her dinner at the French restaurant nearby. It was expensive, but she was mollified.

This time, he wasn't convinced he could find a solution at all, let alone one so simple. Each time he let her down, he knew he was being judged — he knew, because he was judging himself every time, too. Bit by bit, her respect for him was being eroded by his behaviour. And at the same time, his self-esteem moved in the wrong direction.

He was lost in the memory of the last time he'd let Amber down when the phone rang. He saw her name flash on the screen and tried to calm the thumping in his temple.

"Hello, Amber." He hoped his voice sounded calmer than he felt.

"Daniel." There was that cold edge again. His anxiety ramped up another level.

"Listen, I am really sorry about last night. I know it's happened before but I was pretty devastated yesterday, losing my job and everything and I just—"

"I've heard it all before, Daniel. I'm sorry you lost your job, but to be honest, I'm not sure if this relationship is going anywhere."

"Wait, I . . . Please can we meet and talk about it?" He could hear himself pleading, and his self-esteem took another lurch downwards.

"I don't know, Daniel, is it worth it? You're not going to change, are you? People don't change, do they — not really. You don't seem able to help yourself. We're so different, Daniel. I want to get out there, experience things, challenge myself, do something with my life. You do nothing but avoid commitment and play computer games — I'd even say you're addicted. Even when you're not doing that, you're in a world of your own. You've never really opened up to me, and that doesn't work for me. I'm sorry."

This wasn't going the way he wanted. He didn't blame her for being harsh, but he had to defend himself. "I'm not addicted, Amber. I'll give up gaming, I promise. We'll plan some things, weekends away, days out, whatever you want. Just give me a chance."

There was an ominous pause. Daniel held his breath. Had he done enough?

"No, Daniel, I'm sorry, I've given you plenty of chances. You and me — it's just not working out. It's not what I want."

He swallowed. The lump in his throat had grown again. *Don't cry, just don't cry.* "Amber . . ."

"I'm going to go now. Look after yourself, Daniel. Bye."

CHAPTER SIX

"Perhaps I should go to Mum and Dad's."

"Don't be stupid. That's going backwards."

"I know. But I don't have many options. You can't have me to stay, there's no room." He half-hoped he was wrong.

"No, there isn't. You can sleep on the sofa for a few days, but that won't solve your problem long-term."

He shook his head miserably. It was still throbbing from the abuse he'd subjected it to, the lump on his forehead now a deep purple, its centre a gash of dark blood. Lauren had been horrified when she saw him. Her mouth had set in a tight line and she'd pulled him to the bathroom, where she'd bathed the wound with warm water and applied a layer of antiseptic cream.

She made tea for both of them, then sat down with him, her legs curled under her.

They started with the practicalities of his situation. A job and a place to live.

"Look, you've got a full month before you have to move out, and a month's notice at work," Lauren said. "Do you have any holiday owing?"

"I think so. Yes, I'm pretty sure I've got a week or so."

"Well, find out as soon as you can. You can use that time to look for a job."

He nodded, but the burden on his back pushed him down another notch. He wanted to seem positive for Lauren, but looking for a job, finding a place to live — each of these felt like a huge mountain to climb, while he was at the very bottom, facing an insurmountable task, unable to take even the first step.

"Daniel. Daniel, look at me."

He raised his head and glanced at his sister's face. But he couldn't look her in the eye for long.

"What is it? I know this is hard, but we can — we *will* sort it out."

"Oh, I don't know." He started to pace again. "I know what you're saying and I'm grateful to you for coming here and helping, I really am. But it's not about the flat and the job, not really. It's me. I can't — I just can't go back to the life I've been living. Don't you see? It's a lie, an utter lie. Mentally, emotionally, I can't pretend any more. I think — I don't really know what I think. But I've got to change things. Change myself."

It was the first time he'd said that to himself and he was terrified. He stopped pacing and looked directly into Lauren's face. He could see his own fear reflected in her eyes.

"I have to know what's going on with my brain. It's what's stopping me, holding me back. If I don't do something about it now, I'll end up a nobody for ever, scratching out a life in the background, never experiencing anything new. Living in the past, on memories that repeat and repeat and spiral and never leave. It's unbearable, Lauren. I don't know if they're real memories at all, half the time. I don't know if my brain is making them up, imagining things, terrible things, that have happened in the past . . ."

Lauren's eyes filled with tears. She held her hand out to him. Like a drowning man, he grasped it and allowed her to draw him towards her.

"Sit down," she said, her voice wobbling a little. "I'm so sorry, Daniel." She took both his hands in hers and rested her forehead against his shoulder. His chin dropped onto her head and he felt a fleeting moment of relief. Lauren cared for him, and that helped, a little.

* * *

Lauren's flat was tiny. She didn't own it but Daniel knew how proud she was of it. Decent places for one person at an affordable rent were hard to come by, so she was lucky to have it.

He remembered how hard she'd found it, living with other people. She would arrive home, tired from a long day's work, to find her flatmates had cooked supper between them, leaving all their mess in the kitchen. The bathroom was always crammed with make-up, face cream, bath oil, *stuff*. The hallway would be full of coats and shoes, strewn all over the place, tripping her up when she came and went. She had dreaded going home each day.

She'd lasted nine months, then told them she was going. There was no bad feeling, fortunately — they could remain friends, see one another often. She just couldn't live with them.

Her new flat was perfect for her. She could walk to work rather than take the Tube, which saved her a lot of money and was the only reason she could afford the flat on her own. It was small but sweet. You stepped from the pavement into the tiny lobby and turned immediately left to climb the stairs to the first floor. There was one reasonably sized bedroom, a living room about the same size with a kitchen area in one corner, and a small shower room. It was newly redecorated, the kitchen well equipped, despite the lack of space, and it was light and airy. There was just enough room for her books.

It wasn't perfect for guests though, and Daniel couldn't stay long. Lauren had made it very clear this was a temporary arrangement. She was happy to help, but she'd chosen not to have flatmates, so he knew it wouldn't be long-term. During his time there, she expected him to find something to do, somewhere to go, and then she'd maybe let him stay until he could move. As long as she knew he would be going.

Lauren had always been like this. Fiercely independent, fiercely territorial. As a child she'd put large notices on her bedroom door: *Keep Out Or Else!* And later, *Enter At Your Peril, All Who Approach.* Even their mum wasn't allowed in. Lauren cleaned the room herself, changed her own bed and kept the door shut. Once, Daniel had ventured in while his sister was at her music lesson. He only wanted to see what was in there, what was so important that nobody was allowed in. In fact, it was nothing special — neat and tidy, as he expected, with unremarkable posters on the wall and a pristine desk. There were books everywhere. Books on floor-to-ceiling shelves, the authors in alphabetical order. Typical Lauren. Books piled on her bedside table, in a line against the wall at the back of her desk. He knew she was a bookworm, but hadn't realised how many she actually owned. It was quite impressive.

She could tell he'd been in there, of course. He might have known — she'd booby-trapped the door. She'd found the piece of invisible tape out of place when she got home. She was furious with him.

"You *know* I don't want you going in my room," she fumed, her eyes flashing, her entire fourteen-year-old body fizzing with anger. "Why do you think there's such a big sign on the door? Can't you read? I'll spell it out to you. K-E-E-P O-U-T. That means never go into my bedroom. Ever. I hope you didn't touch anything — I'll know if you did. Loser!" She slammed the door then, in his face, leaving him nonplussed.

"I don't know what all the fuss is about," Daniel said later to his mum. "There's nothing in there, anyway. Just a load of books."

"I know, darling," his mum said. "But you know what she's like. Now don't go in there again, you'll only wind her up."

After all this time, she hadn't changed. Twenty-seven-year-old Lauren still loved her books, still guarded her space fiercely. And didn't want him in it. He was grateful to her for allowing him to stay. He tried to keep his stuff to a minimum. Much of it had gone back to the garage at their parents' house.

"I don't want to find this here in three months' time," his dad had said. Even though he never used the garage, except for storage. He just didn't want Daniel's stuff there. Still, three months was longer than he'd expected. His dad must have mellowed.

Daniel could tell Lauren was stressed by him being in her flat when she got home each evening. The weather was wet and miserable, and she worked long hours in a difficult job. He tidied up as best he could, made sure the washing-up was done and all his things hidden behind the sofa, but just the fact of him being there, he could tell, was difficult for her. She would try her best to be cheerful when she came in, popping her head round the sitting room door with a hello before she disappeared to her bedroom to get changed. But he knew she'd rather he wasn't there, even when he cooked for her, even when he bought wine with his dwindling savings, even when he made himself absent for hours at a time, walking around the local streets to give her some space.

This couldn't go on much longer.

* * *

At the end of the first week, she said, "Right." This, with Lauren, indicated business. It was a Saturday morning and they were finishing breakfast, sitting side by side on the sofa, their cereal dishes on the coffee table in front of them.

"So, what have you done this week?" Lauren said.

So businesslike. So *not* the question he wanted to hear.

Resisting the urge to put his head in his hands, he sat back and decided to try the positive angle. "I've registered with five recruitment websites and given them all my info."

"What are you looking for, exactly?"

Another incisive question. She knew the answer already. He didn't really know. "Look, I'm doing my best." He didn't want this to get heated in any way, so he added, "I'm willing to take pretty much anything that'll pay enough for me to get a room somewhere. If I can get the job first, I'll find somewhere to live nearby, so I can walk to work. I'll share a flat or a house if I have to, for six months or something. I just need to survive for the moment, while I make up my mind what to do about — all this."

Lauren nodded. There was a pause while she sipped her coffee. "Define 'all this'."

She didn't pull her punches, his sister. Straight to the nub of the thing. She didn't have a degree in psychology for nothing.

"Me. My head. My mental condition, if you want to put it like that. I know I've got to do something about it. I just don't know what, yet."

"Start now."

He was startled by the firmness of the statement, flashing a glance at her to gauge her mood. "Sorry, I'm not with you . . ."

"Start now. Make a list of the things you can do to help yourself. Explore all the avenues." She turned to him, her eyes full of concern. "Listen, I know it's hard." Her voice softened. "I can help, you know. I come across all sorts of people in my job, many of them needing support. Some of them make huge changes for the better through talking therapies or by getting help from charities. Even small changes sometimes make a massive difference. Here, let's start a list." Jumping up from her place on the sofa, she gathered up the breakfast things and took them to the kitchen before reappearing with paper and a pen, which she put purposefully on the table in front of him.

Daniel hung his head, his stomach twisting. This was exactly what he didn't want to do, here, right now. The boy's face rose again, unbidden as always. He pushed it back down and tried his best to focus on Lauren's earnest face.

"Lauren, I know you're trying to help and I'm grateful, but I'm nowhere near understanding what I need to do," he said. "I don't . . . I can't even describe what goes on in my brain. I don't know where to start."

Lauren took a deep breath and took the pen in her hand, moving the paper in front of her. She crouched down on the floor, looking up at him. He couldn't bring himself to meet her gaze.

"But you do want to sort it out?" she said.

He nodded. "I really do, yes."

"Let's just write a few things down, then," she said. "In no particular order. Just some things that you could do for a start, then some things that you might want to do later on. We'll write them down, then look through them one by one and whittle them down. There may be something you feel you can try, you never know. You don't have to do anything, just stay with me, OK?"

"OK," he said. The rock on his back grew heavier.

* * *

He'd first gone to a therapist when he was nineteen. It was Wednesday, 27 February, to be precise. By then he was convinced that his brain was different from other people's. It had gone into overdrive when he was ten, and it hadn't stopped since. At first he liked being able to remember every day, every date, every event from his life. He thought the other kids must be stupid when they couldn't do the same thing. But the feeling of superiority didn't last. When they started to call him weird, avoided him at break times, laughed at him in class, he stopped saying anything, though it didn't stop the memories, the days and dates, the events playing out in detail like a film, always in his mind. Even his family got fed up with him correcting their vague recollections, or interjecting with the day and the date when they were trying to remember. It didn't pay, always to be right.

He got away with it at school by not verbalising what was in his head. This took some effort, but it became a habit. Nonetheless, he had made some friends who accepted him as he was. They knew he had this strange ability, but they didn't judge him for it. Still, he didn't mention it often, and he became 'the quiet one' in the group. Three of them hung out together in school and in their spare time, and school was OK as long as they were around.

He didn't excel at maths, or science, or even at history, with its emphasis on the passing of time and the recording of dates. He thought about this often. His brain didn't retain those facts and figures in the same way as it held onto memories of his life. It seemed strange to him that his brain could retain some things in such detail and with such power, while being rather average at retaining the information he needed to take exams or complete his homework without looking things up. In fact, he was in the bottom half in most subjects, a fact that bothered him mostly because of his father's barely hidden disappointment.

He'd scraped through his A levels with less than average results and had no idea what to do with himself afterwards. University didn't appeal, even though his friends had all applied and most of them had been successful in getting a place. His results weren't good enough, and anyway focusing his unruly mind would be doubly hard without the discipline of the school day. But what next? Over the summer break, before the results came in, he'd found a temporary job with a garden design firm. It was hard, physical work, digging new flower beds, laying paving stones, creating ponds in rich people's gardens. It was good to have the work, but he dreaded each day. His boss and the team were strong, silent types who told him what to do and left him to it — there was very little banter or conversation. His mind was free to wander. And man, did it wander.

As his mind was increasingly invaded by random memories, his anxiety grew. He wondered how he would ever get a proper job if he was unable to control the never-ending slide show in his brain.

His mum sent him to the doctor. The harried GP, who he'd never met before, asked him a set of standard questions, taking rapid notes. *What makes you feel anxious? Have you ever harmed yourself? What kind of diet do you follow? How is your sleep?*

Daniel answered with monosyllables, waiting for the moment to talk about the real issue. But with no more than a slight pause, the doctor wrote out a prescription for an anti-depressant and suggested therapy. He scribbled a name and number on a piece of paper, handed it to Daniel and turned back to his desk, effectively dismissing him.

CHAPTER SEVEN

Daniel paced Lauren's tiny living room, trying to focus. But the memory was back again, the image like a painting in his mind — the bright green of the grassy field, the dark water of the canal, Tattoo Man's back as the narrowboat eased away. The bag on the deck, the white flash of the trainers—

No, that wasn't what he was supposed to be thinking about. He needed a job, a place to live. He had to make some really big decisions about his life. Otherwise . . . He couldn't bear to think what might happen if he didn't sort this out. His mind was tricking him, malfunctioning, like a computer glitch, a virus affecting everything, so you couldn't get any of the software to work properly. He liked the analogy, it helped him to see his brain as a machine. It could be a single tiny element that had gone rogue, some hidden pathway that had twisted, or split, or whatever pathways in the brain do.

Golden Serpent. At the time, at only ten years old, he hadn't understood what it meant, so he'd asked his mum. "Mum, there was one of those long boats on the canal the other day. It was called *Golden Serpent*. What does it mean?"

His mum smiled. "A serpent is an old-fashioned word for a snake. I don't know why a narrowboat would be called that, they're long and straight. And canals don't twist and turn much."

Like a snake. Maybe it didn't mean the boat was twisty and turny, but the man who owned it.

This wasn't getting him anywhere. He had to get out of here. Grabbing his jacket and keys, he ran down the stairs and out into the street. Without thinking where he was going, he stuck his hands in his pockets and walked, allowing his feet to lead him.

Perhaps he needed to get therapy, as Lauren suggested. It was first on her list, unsurprisingly. But he cringed at the thought — it had been such a waste of time before. A picture of the therapist's room popped into his brain: the woman sitting there, a soft smile on her face, waiting for him to speak. Daniel, tongue-tied and miserable, unable to find words to describe what was going on in his head. He had learned from bitter experience that therapists hadn't the skill or the understanding to help him. Only someone who had studied the human brain in detail, who knew how it connected, how memories were formed and retrieved, could help him. Someone who knew what happened when part of the brain goes wrong. Or never starts out right, more like.

He'd gone down that path before, more than a decade ago. He'd researched psychiatrists, psychologists, scientific studies. But every time he'd become more confused and, in the end, had stopped looking for the Holy Grail. It just made him feel worse, more alone than ever. There seemed to be nobody else like him.

But surely there must be other people suffering as he did? Surely now, years later, someone with a similar condition would have materialised. The scientists would be more experienced, the research deeper, the expertise greater. Still, he balked at the prospect of finding out. Because if he found there was nobody in the world with a brain like his, how on earth was anyone going to help him? There would be no hope for him.

His hands broke out in a sweat as he walked, nervous energy driving him further and further into the labyrinth of roads around Lauren's flat. He tried to think differently. If his brain really was that unusual, surely there would be some professor somewhere in the world who would be interested? Someone would want to know why this happened to him, what could be done, if anything, to help him, and what the implications might be for others? It was at least a route he could pursue, if he could find the courage.

It could all result in disappointment and despair. But he couldn't think that way. He was close to despair now. If nothing else was driving him on, it was that. He needed to find that courage, to delve deep into his unruly mind, to confront the devil in his head.

At the end of a particularly long street, lined with Victorian villas, cars parked in every possible space on both sides of the road, he realised how far he had walked. A main road crossed the end of the street. It was a stark contrast to the quiet roads he'd been wandering along. He turned onto it, intending to cross to the other side, but found himself distracted by the energy of it all.

He passed charity shops, displaying racks of clothing on the pavement, cafés, a bike shop, a hardware shop with mops and buckets and washing-up bowls stacked alongside stepladders and gardening tools. A melange of spices, herbs, garlic and chilli drifted across the street. It was an assault on his senses, disconcerting and exciting.

Here he was invisible. Nobody paid him any attention as he headed south towards the centre of London, pausing every so often to avoid prams, groups of kids with skate-boards and hobbling senior citizens. For a while he enjoyed the distractions, the stimulus to his senses, the unfamiliar sense of being out of his comfort zone. But it didn't last long — soon it became overwhelming. His mind flashed back to other cafés, other smells and other noises from months and years ago.

Time to go back. He wanted to make progress before Lauren came home. She'd be impressed and encouraged by his idea, and that could only be good.

* * *

He opened his laptop. The last time he'd tried to research his specific condition, he'd suffered a terrible panic attack that had sucked his breath away and left him on his hands and knees, thinking he was going to die. It had taken days for him to recover. Though that was a few years ago now, he'd been too frightened by its catastrophic effect to put himself through it since.

Hesitantly, he searched 'constant memories' — and sat open-mouthed when he saw the flood of results. Things had moved on, a lot. The very first item on the page was an article from *Psychology Magazine*, dated 2013, entitled '*Involuntary autobiographical memories*'. Could this be what he was suffering from? His scalp fizzed with anticipation as he read. The first paragraph gave him hope:

Involuntary autobiographical memories (IAMs) seem to pop up into consciousness more easily and more frequently than voluntary memories. Occurring without any deliberate attempt at retrieval and often during undemanding everyday activities, IAMs also appear to be more resistant to ageing and dementia. Newly developed laboratory paradigms, such as the free word association method or a vigilance task, could be used along with neuroimaging to help describe the functional anatomy and pathways of IAMs in the brain.

This seemed hopeful, but as he read on, his excitement turned to disappointment. The article suggested that most people had involuntary memories, and that they were a normal part of people's mental make-up, occurring only three to five times per day. Three to five times a day! Daniel's heart sank. His brain would release more like three hundred memories a day, although admittedly he'd never attempted to count them — how could he? They were like a swarm of locusts, ravenous, picking away at him, out to bring him down. Other people, the article said, experienced IAMs when they were engaged in automatic, regular activities like driving or eating. Daniel's memories occurred all the time, whatever he was doing.

But that was just the first item on a list of results that went on for pages. Although there was little else to do in Lauren's flat — she'd banned the idea of him setting up his Xbox — he almost gave up. A feeling of panic began to grow — his hands sweating, a knot forming in his stomach. He stood up and took a few deep breaths, struggling to quell the fear that had stopped him doing this before. He sat down again, squared his shoulders and clicked on the next item, feeling as if he was entering a deep, dark hole, packed with dangerous secrets.

CHAPTER EIGHT

"Hi, Daniel." Lauren's face was pinched, dark smudges beneath her eyes. She closed the front door and took off her coat with limp arms.

"Are you OK?" Daniel said. "You look exhausted. I'll put the kettle on." He jumped up from the sofa, where he'd been engrossed in his research. His head ached, his eyes were beginning to feel strained and dry, and yet he'd only confused himself.

"Thanks. It's just . . . my job can be very challenging. Full on. Today was worse than usual."

Lauren was a probation officer. In her work she saw more of life than most people ever would. Though she had done all the training and was by nature robust and positive, the issues she dealt with were often heartbreaking, sometimes shocking. The satisfaction she gained was occasionally overwhelmed by the misery of people's situations, and that's when the strain showed.

"I don't know how you do it, honestly, Lauren. I couldn't even start to manage a job like yours. I'm proud of you."

"Thanks." Lauren sank down on the sofa, resting her head on the back cushion. "I love my job, but on days like today I wish I could take a break, just for a few hours, when

I need to. God, I'm shattered. And I'm hungry. Have you eaten?"

Daniel returned from the kitchen with two mugs of tea. "Not yet. I'll rustle something up if you like."

Lauren's face relaxed. "Would you? Just something quick would be great — soup, or cheese on toast."

"I'm sure I can manage that."

As he rummaged around the kitchen, Lauren glanced idly at his laptop, still open beside her.

"What were you up to? Searching for jobs?"

"No, actually."

Lauren's face fell. "But Daniel—"

"I know, I know. I will, I promise. I was looking for someone who could help me with . . . you know, my brain. I thought if I could just find the top expert in memory, and what happens when memories go wrong, like they do for me, maybe I could find a way."

Lauren sat up. "Daniel. I know you want to help yourself, and you need support to do that. It's a good idea, I'm not denying it. But practically, and to be honest, from a selfish point of view—"

Daniel, stirring a bubbling saucepan, nodded miserably. He knew she needed him to leave her flat. The feeling of helplessness silenced him.

"When I was walking to work this morning, I noticed two places advertising for staff," Lauren continued. "One was a bar–restaurant called William's, the other was more of a café. I know they won't pay much, and it's catering work, but it would get you some money, and you might meet some new people. That's the way to find somewhere to live."

"Right. Thanks, I'll have a look." The sinking feeling was back. How could he work in a bar, when he got overwhelmed walking down a busy street?

"Here's William's." Lauren held up her phone. "And the café is only a few doors down. You'd be able to walk there, and it'll be shift work, so you can look for something better at the same time. I'll send you the link."

"Thanks. I'll walk over there tomorrow."

"Good. Just going to change." Lauren smiled at him as she passed. Her efforts to help had cheered her up, even if they'd had the opposite effect on him. He turned back to the cooking, glad of the chance to hide his face.

After Lauren went to bed, he resumed his research. He read until his back ached, his shoulders stiffened with tension, his vision blurred. When he looked at the time at last, he was surprised to see that it was one o'clock in the morning. Lauren had been in bed for hours, but he wasn't tired. The opposite, in fact — his brain was fizzing, his muscles tight, his stomach in knots. There was no way he could sleep yet.

Lauren's bedroom door was firmly shut. No light seeped from beneath. He listened carefully, but there was no sound from her room. In his bag behind the sofa, he'd stashed his Xbox and it was calling him. Perhaps he could just get it out for tonight, and put it away when he went to sleep? Lauren would never know. He understood why she didn't want it cluttering up her sitting room, but surely it was OK if he used it while she slept? It was the only thing he knew would help his hyperactive mind right now.

* * *

"Daniel? What's going on?"

He jumped to his feet, guilt flushing his face. "Lauren, I . . . Sorry, I couldn't sleep. Did I wake you up?"

"Yes, you did. It's three in the morning and you're playing on the Xbox. We agreed you wouldn't, didn't we? You promised." Her face was pale and rumpled and she squinted against the dim light of the table lamp. Her forehead crumpled into a frown.

"I know, I'm sorry." He hurriedly packed up the Xbox. He unplugged the wires from behind the TV and wound them round the handset. "I got really anxious doing all that searching. There was no way I was going to get any sleep. The Xbox takes my mind off it."

"The Xbox is bad for your mind. You admitted you might be addicted. And anyway, you promised. Just . . . stop. I'm going to try to get back to sleep. I don't need this. I've got another heavy day tomorrow. If I feel like shit, it'll be your fault."

She turned and stomped back into her bedroom, closing the door behind her. Not quite a slam, but with the same energy, the air rushing into the space she left.

He felt terrible. She was right, he should be sticking to their agreement, and he really must spend his time looking for work. He promised himself to look for a job in the morning, to do his best for his sister. After all, she was the only person he could rely on right now. He didn't want to upset her, of all people.

When he woke the next day, Lauren was already gone. He hadn't heard her leave, though there was evidence in the kitchen that she'd grabbed breakfast before she left. He fumbled for his mobile, which had fallen behind the sofa cushion. He couldn't believe his eyes. It was four thirty in the afternoon! He flopped back onto the pillow with a groan. How did that happen? He hadn't done that since he was a teenager. He worked out when he'd finally got to sleep. Probably about five thirty in the morning, so it wasn't surprising he'd slept through. It was already getting dark outside and he'd wasted the entire day. What a loser.

Forcing himself to get up, Daniel looked around. The flat was in a bit of a state, with his things strewn around, the kitchen sink full and the bathroom needing a clean. If he spruced it up for Lauren, perhaps she'd forgive him. He remembered the places she mentioned last night, the ones advertising jobs. He'd give them a try, or she'd be even more angry with him. Perhaps he'd go out around the time she was due home from work. Then she'd come back to a clean, orderly flat without him cluttering up the sitting room. He could buy her some supper and maybe some flowers while he was out — maybe that would help.

But when he got close to William's bar, his heart began to race, his hands broke out in a clammy sweat and his breathing quickened. He stopped short and leaned against an empty shop window, focusing on a count of five to breathe in, eleven out. It wasn't working, and he could feel the panic rising even more. He could barely see or breathe, and he bent double as his stomach churned. People hurried past but he was hardly aware of them. He certainly didn't want anyone to stop and try to help him. That would be humiliating: a man of almost thirty having a panic attack, unable to control himself.

It seemed an age before he felt the signs of recovery — his breathing slowing, his heart no longer thumping in his chest. At last he was able to straighten up, wobbly but no longer panicking. Could he force himself to carry on? Perhaps he could walk past, just to see what it was like, check the ad in the window. Perhaps they'd left a phone number: that would be so much easier than going in right now, feeling so vulnerable.

After a few deep breaths, he stuck his hands in his pockets, hunched his shoulders and walked along the glazed frontage of William's. It was bright inside, most of the tables occupied. A knot of people at the bar were drinking and laughing. Loud music blared from the doorway as people came and went, and as he paused to look at the notice in the window, he spotted a waitress in a black apron hurrying around. She looked harassed.

Waiting staff needed, Wednesday to Sunday, shift work. Good pay and conditions. Apply within.

No telephone number. Could he steel himself to go in? He felt the tension in his shoulders deepen as he stood there pretending to read the notice. His hands were still shaking and he stuffed them back into his jacket pockets as he turned towards the door. He would ask the girl behind the bar — she looked nice, and she wasn't busy at the moment.

But as he approached, a group of noisy young people pushed past him, laughing and elbowing one another. "Sorry," a lad said as he pushed him out of the way, smirking as Daniel stumbled. The door closed in his face.

* * *

At Lauren's front door, he hesitated. How could he face his sister, when it looked as if he hadn't even tried? He didn't want to lie to her, pretend to have spoken to them — she would know immediately from his body language, as she always did.

The soft sounds of her favourite music drifted into the hallway. For a moment he thought about going out again, but it was cold and raining outside. Anyway, he'd bought flowers and he didn't want to carry them around. He closed his eyes for a moment, then turned his key in the lock.

She was in the kitchen, turning with a smile when she heard him come in. "Daniel, the flat looks great! Thank you so much — I wasn't looking forward to coming back and having to clear up. And flowers, too! You shouldn't spend your money on me. But they're lovely, thank you."

"I'm sorry, Lauren," Daniel said over her shoulder as she hugged him.

"What for?" Lauren was searching in a cupboard for a vase.

"For waking you up, for being hopeless, for not finding a job. For having to sleep on your sofa because I'm such a loser."

Lauren stopped what she was doing and gave him a hard look, a frown deepening between her eyes. "Stop it," she said. "That's not going to help you one little bit. You're not hope-less. You have a few problems, sure, but you'll beat them, I know you will." She turned back to the flowers and started to strip the leaves from the lower stems, putting them one by one into the vase. "Did you go to William's?"

Daniel hung his head. She glanced up, her shoulders droop-ing when she saw his expression. "You didn't go? Honestly—"

"No, I did go, I really did. But when I got there, I had a panic attack. It was really bad. I tried to go in, but it was so busy."

"That's what a good place is like. People go there because it's fun and the food's good. If it was empty, it wouldn't be successful."

"Yes, but I can't . . . I can't be around all those people, all those strangers looking at me, I'll go to pieces, I'll panic.

It's no good, Lauren, I'm never going to be able to do a job like that."

Lauren opened her mouth as if to reply but sighed instead. She shook her head. "Well, what are you going to do?"

Daniel flopped onto the sofa, tears gathering. He bit his lip. What was happening to him — a grown man, close to tears? He put his head in his hands so Lauren couldn't see.

"I know I can't stay," he said when he'd regained control. "You've been so good, letting me stay. I know you hate having flatmates. I appreciate it, I really do. But—"

"But what?" Lauren sat next to him, her hand on his back.

"I'm sick, Lauren. Mentally, I mean. How can I get a job when I'm like this? I can't even tick one thing off your list. It's hopeless." Lauren's list had been taunting him, sitting on the coffee table, waiting to be dealt with, like a pet waiting to be fed.

"Oh, Daniel. It's not hopeless, really it's not. You'll get past this. I know you will. Look, how about you go to Mum and Dad's for a while? Not for ever, obviously, but while I'm so busy at work, I really need some space when I get home. Otherwise I'm going to go nuts."

Daniel shook his head. "I know, I do understand, I really do. But Mum and Dad's? How is that going to help me? You said it yourself — it's going backwards, not forwards."

"Just for a couple of weeks. Could you manage that? See it as a break, to help us both sort ourselves out. In the meantime, I'll see if I can find someone who can help you — a brain expert, a psychologist, or whoever might understand what's going on with you. I can ask at work, they have loads of contacts. You'll have to keep looking yourself, too."

He didn't trust himself to speak. Two weeks with his parents — perhaps he could cope with that. He could use the time to keep researching, decide what to do next. It was doable for a couple of weeks.

Looking at Lauren's pleading face, he knew he had no choice.

CHAPTER NINE

When Poppy had first got the job at the animal rescue and told her friends, they'd assumed she wouldn't stay long. The work would be menial, unpleasant even. Lots of mucking out filthy cages, mopping up after dogs and cats, measuring out feed. Not something you'd want to do for the rest of your life.

To be fair, she did all those things, and there were tasks she liked more than others. But they all needed to be done, and once she was in a rhythm, it became a habit — she barely noticed the smell and the bad jobs got done quickly, giving her more time with the animals.

Poppy was made for the job. Nobody was better at entertaining animals, especially the dogs. When they were in the exercise field, it was Poppy who ran with them and threw balls for hours. She set up an agility course with tunnels and jumps and zigzag posts and seesaws and all the other challenges she'd seen on TV dog shows. Poppy's boss, Karen, was delighted, and gave Poppy a Dogged Devotion Award for her ingenuity. Her prize was a big bar of chocolate.

Unsurprisingly, Poppy was Karen's favourite assistant. Nobody worked harder, or longer hours than she did, even though she was officially a 'part-timer'. Often Karen had to insist she left when the new shift started, because she'd take everything on without complaint, and the other workers had a tendency to take advantage.

Poppy owed her love of animals to her grandparents. When her grandfather was alive, there had always been pets in their house. As a little girl, Poppy had longed for a pet of her own, but with both parents working, it was never going to happen. Visiting her grandparents was the next best thing, and sometimes her mum suggested that she loved their house more than hers. She didn't — but it was fun, with ready-made playmates who loved her as much as she loved them.

Now things were different. When her grandfather died quite a few years ago, her gran hadn't wanted to live alone, so she had moved in with Poppy's family. It was hardly believable that she was to be eighty-five in a few days' time.

"Mum," Poppy said as she dried the dishes. "What can we do for Gran's birthday? I want it to be really special."

Her mum smiled. "That's kind. But don't overdo it. There's nothing she really wants or needs, and she'd feel bad if you spent your money on her."

"But I want to! I like looking after her — you know that." Poppy reached up to put the dinner plates away in the upper cupboard. "You will join us for tea, won't you?"

"Yes, of course."

"I'll make a cake."

"She'd like that."

"It's a bit boring though, tea at home with just us. How about we invite some other people over?"

Putting a dish down, her mum turned to Poppy. "Listen, love, I'm not being funny but Gran's not up to much. You don't want to tire her out. The tea will be great, she'll love it — but don't bother with anything else."

"But, Mum, Gran loves a celebration!"

"No, listen." Her mum took her by the shoulders.

Poppy was surprised at the tone of her voice. "What is it?"

Her mother sighed. "Gran's getting worse quite quickly."

51

"What do you mean, worse?"

"Her memory's failing more and more. We need to recognise her age, make allowances . . ."

The lurch in Poppy's stomach was like stepping off an invisible pavement. "She's not going to die soon, is she?" Her eyes filled with tears.

Her mum hesitated. The lurch turned into a slow sinking.

"I'm not saying — oh, I don't know what I'm saying. I am worried about her. It's hard to know what's normal forgetfulness, and what's caused by the Alzheimer's. Oh, look — come here . . ." The tears rolled down Poppy's cheeks as her mother put her arms around her. "I'm sorry to have scared you. I'm sure it's nothing to worry about. We all love her so much. Nobody wants her to get old, but there's not much we can do about it, except make sure she's as happy as possible. We'll make her birthday special, OK?"

Poppy nodded, only partly reassured. She couldn't bear to think of life without her gran. "Thanks, Mum. Not too exciting, I promise."

She'd noticed, of course, that her grandmother had been getting more confused, even before her mum had mentioned it. But now that Mum had pointed it out, Poppy knew she was right. In the back of her mind she understood that this kind of forgetting was different. Her gran had always been so sharp, so quick with facts and figures, so clever at puzzles and jigsaws. Lately, though, she seemed less inclined. She gave up after a few minutes, staring into space with her pencil in her hand. At times, she struggled to remember names — her friends and family, even. It seemed odd that she remembered the names of her school friends from decades past so easily when last week she struggled to recall her doctor's name — a man she knew well. More often than not, she said "Whatshisname" or "Thingummyflip — you know who I mean, Poppy dear."

There was another thing that Poppy had noticed. Sometimes, when she was tired, her gran would repeat a question she'd asked only minutes before, one that had been answered properly. Poppy told herself that she was distracted, not focusing. But it was more than that. Her gran would use exactly the same words the second or third time, without any sign that she remembered. And the answer could be exactly the same, too, and she'd respond as if she'd never heard the words.

* * *

The next few weeks saw a dramatic change in the old lady. She became confused, repeating things to herself. She got agitated about the slightest thing. If something was in the wrong place, she thought the house had been burgled, her possessions stolen. She became incontinent, too, and when she understood what was happening — in one of her more lucid moments — she sobbed.

"I'm becoming a smelly old woman," she said to Poppy. And to Poppy's mum, "You'd better put me in a home."

Poppy was anxious about leaving her alone while she was at work. She reorganised her shifts and took more evening and weekend work so that someone was always home.

They went to the doctor, who confirmed their worst fears. There was little they could do about the worsening effects of Alzheimer's, and she would soon need proper nursing care in a specialist home. Poppy's mother came back from the doctor's with red eyes, doing her best to hide her upset.

"I'll give up my job," Poppy offered.

"No, I'll stop work for a while, if it comes to that. You must keep your job, you're learning your trade. I'll look after Gran. Let's hope it's a slow process. The best thing we can do is make sure she enjoys what she has left of her life." This was said with tears in her eyes. Poppy's own eyes were already spilling over.

CHAPTER TEN

From the moment he arrived, Daniel knew this wasn't going to help. It was months since he'd visited, years since he last lived at home on a permanent basis. He felt awkward and out of place. His parents looked happy to see him, but it didn't change his mind.

"Hair's grown a bit, then," his dad said. "Have to tidy that up if you're going to get a job."

"Ron." Daniel's mum chided her husband, hugging her son fiercely. "He's not even through the door yet. Give him a break." She fussed around him, ushering him up the stairs to the spare room.

She opened the door for him. "I hope this is OK for you. I made some room for you in the wardrobe and cleared a couple of drawers out. There's a spare dressing gown behind the door if you need it."

"Thanks, Mum." He put his bags down. "I don't have a lot of stuff, and it won't be for too long."

She smiled, patting him on the shoulder. "You mustn't mind your dad," she said. "He doesn't know how else to be. It's just his way."

Daniel nodded. His father would never understand him. He didn't blame him, but it didn't make it any easier to see his disappointment.

"You're a bit thin, sweetheart," his mum said. "You haven't been looking after yourself. Never mind, you'll eat well here."

"Don't worry about me, really. I can feed myself. I don't want to be any trouble. I'll try to get out of your hair in a couple of weeks. I just need a bit of time to decide what to do with myself, then I'll get a job and find somewhere to live."

"No rush," she said.

"Well there is for me. I'm an adult, living back at home when I should be moving on — I know that, so we might as well admit it. But it'll only be for a short while, I promise, and I'll do my best to keep out of your way."

His mum shook her head. "I want you to feel welcome here. Your dad wants the best for you, you know that. He's worried about you, that's all."

As he unpacked his meagre possessions, Daniel wondered how long he would last here. Being back with his parents was bad for him in more ways than one. He'd been dreading the effect it might have on his memories, and he wasn't wrong. There were so many triggers in the house — the furnishings, his mother's ornaments, even his dad's voice conjured up pictures of his childhood, his tortured teens.

There was one memory that Daniel had never mentioned, not even to Lauren. It stalked him, at his shoulder wherever he went. The tiniest of triggers prompted it — he was helpless to stop it. He avoided those triggers whenever he could, but they found ways through his defences, pressing their needle-like claws into his subconscious, summoning the scene with cruel regularity.

Now, back here, with all of his past focused in one place, it returned with a vengeance.

* * *

It was Saturday, 11 September 1999, when Daniel was ten, around the time he'd begun to realise how different he really was. Daniel and Lauren had recently started the new school year. The weather was good, the sun warming the air, the trees still in full leaf, the countryside lush and green. Daniel and his dad had decided to go to a car boot sale while his mum and Lauren went clothes shopping.

The local football ground provided a perfect venue for fêtes and car boot sales. Sellers would set up early, spreading their wares onto trestle tables in boxes labelled by price, or simply laying their possessions out for passers-by to haggle over.

This particular sale was a regular one, not far from their house. It was huge, with cars and tables spread around three sides of a large field that backed on to the canal, dense hedges shielding it from the water. There were regular sellers, often the ones with the best spots. Sometimes there were specialists — jewellery, pottery, children's toys — and between the ranks of cars were booths selling hamburgers, coffee and ice creams.

As a family day out, the sale did well. It took a good hour or so just to walk around the field, and if you wanted to stop and talk to the sellers, bargaining for an item, you could easily while away a few hours on a warm day. Daniel's dad enjoyed the challenge of haggling, and would often return home with items that sent his wife's eyes rolling. A hideous tea set once caused a rift for a full two days. But he also liked the scene, the banter and the bumping into people he knew, and often Daniel would be left to his own devices to wander around, as long as he kept in sight and returned to 'base' every half an hour. 'Base' was usually the ice cream stand in the centre of the field, with its pastel colours and plastic ice cream cone on top standing out against the trailing lines of vehicles.

On this day, things started out pleasantly enough. They wandered along one side of the field, browsing through boxes of books on one table, picking through old-fashioned tools on the next. Daniel's dad started to haggle with the seller of an iron sander he thought would be useful if he ever got round to restoring Granny's old chest of drawers, currently languishing in the back of the garage. Daniel always felt embarrassed when his father haggled, hating the counter-play between seller and buyer, so he wandered on, drawn towards the next pitch by a display of copper bric-a-brac that shone in the sunlight. But it turned out to be mostly kettles and pans, which looked good but didn't interest him.

He glanced back to see where his dad was. There was an energetic conversation going on with the seller, with plenty of arm-waving and smiling — his dad was clearly in the thick of an important transaction. Daniel wandered on, past the next couple of tables. He was delighted to see a big pile of comics on one of them as well as some hardback annuals laid out in a fan. This was more like it — he loved old comics, especially the ones in series that he could immerse himself in. The seller was an old man with a woolly hat and fingerless gloves, dressed for winter while most people were in T-shirts. He sat with an empty stare, not bothering to try to attract custom.

Daniel plucked up the courage to catch his attention. "Excuse me," he said. "Can I look through these comics, please?"

"You can," the man said. "Especially since you're such a polite lad. Help yourself. If you want anything, ask me and I'll give you a price."

"Thanks." Daniel flushed.

He took a handful from the top of the pile. *Beano* and *Dandy* were favourites of his, and he was delighted to find a couple in the first batch he looked at. He put them to one side and nodded at the man, who was keeping a watchful eye. Further investigations revealed an *X-Men* comic and a couple of *Hulk* magazines. By the time he'd looked through the whole pile, he'd found twelve he wanted to buy, some of them dog-eared and stained but readable, and a couple that looked as if they'd only been read once, if at all.

"How much for all these?"

The man hauled himself to his feet with a groan and held out his hand. "Let's have a see. *Beano* — good choice,

Dandy, yes. *X-Men*, *Hulk*. OK." He seemed to have made a decision. "As you're buying a job lot, I'll let you have them for nine pounds. How does that sound?"

"It sounds a lot." Daniel's dad said from behind him. "Look, that one's got tea stains all over it, and that one's ripped. We'll give you three pounds."

Daniel stiffened. He didn't want his dad to help, but he didn't have nine pounds. He'd been about to put some of the comics back. But if his dad could get them all for three pounds, that would be great. He glanced at the seller. His jaw was set, and he was shaking his head.

Another man hovered close by, listening to the negotiations, craning his neck to see the subject of the haggle. He was thin, with a face like a weasel. A strange tattoo wound itself around his neck: a snake with a zigzag pattern on its back, like an adder. More tattoos decorated his sinewy arms, in blues and greens, with splashes of dark red, like blood. Daniel had never seen so many tattoos on a person before. He was fascinated and more than a little scared, both at once.

All of a sudden, he had to have the comics. He pulled at his dad's sleeve. "Dad."

"It's OK, son, this is how it's done." He turned back to the seller with a smile. "What's your best price, then?"

"Can't go below seven. Those are collectors' items, mate. I could get more, I just liked your boy's face."

"Rubbish — you won't get anything for those damaged ones. We'll go up to four."

Daniel kicked at a dusty dip in front of the table. He had seven pounds in his pocket, money he'd saved for just this kind of thing. There was nothing else he'd rather buy and he didn't want his dad to ruin it for him. The tattooed man was still hovering, his eyes on Daniel's comics. If his dad failed to negotiate a winning price, they'd be gone in a flash.

"Six fifty, last price." The seller made a move to put the comics back on the pile.

"Dad, please? I've got—"

"Six quid, cash," his dad said.

Daniel looked longingly at the seller, whose hand was still hovering over the pile.

"You drive a bloody hard bargain," he said, but there was half a smile on his lined face as he handed the comics over to Daniel. "Go on, then. Enjoy them, lad, they're good ones."

As they left the comic stall, his dad clapped him on the back so hard he stumbled. "There, you see? You'd have ended up with nothing, or at least with just a couple of the ones you wanted if I hadn't come along." His dad grinned proudly at him.

"Thanks, Dad." He'd never been more embarrassed.

But he was happy with his comics. He'd brought a plastic bag in case he bought anything, and he put them into it carefully. Lauren would like them too — she was just as keen as he was, though she wouldn't spend money on them. He looked forward to sharing them with her.

"Ice cream?" his dad said.

"Yeah, OK." It was worth staying for an ice cream, even if it was his dad's excuse to lengthen their stay. They wandered over to the ice cream van and surveyed the field while they licked their ninety-nines. When they finished, his dad said he wanted to go back to a stall in the far corner, and despite his protests, Daniel got dragged back to a boring table where a couple of people were selling pewter beer mugs and military paraphernalia. He fingered some medals while his dad got chatting again, but he soon lost interest and wandered to the next table along.

"Into comics, are you?" A voice behind him startled him. "Saw you buying the *Beano*s. I love *Beano*s, too."

The tattooed man was peering at Daniel's bag. His T-shirt was pockmarked with holes, his grubby jeans fraying at the hems over heavy boots.

Taken aback, Daniel clutched his bag with both hands. "Yes. Sorry, I need to get back to my dad." He tried to push past, but his path was blocked. Daniel was trapped between the table and the man, his only escape to push through on

59

one side. But he was much smaller than Tattooed Man, who stood over him threateningly.

As Daniel backed up and bumped into the table, the woman behind it turned towards them. "Can I help you with anything?" She looked from Daniel to the man and back again, realisation dawning.

"Are you OK, mate?" she said to Daniel.

"Yes, thank you," he stammered, ducking away. He ran to his dad, glancing back when he reached safety. Tattooed Man glared after him while the woman seller waved him away. Daniel wished he hadn't looked and retreated out of sight, sheltering behind his father while he rummaged among the items on the table. When he looked again, the man was nowhere to be seen.

When they were reaching the last few tables, his dad was distracted by another seller. Waiting impatiently close by, Daniel was startled by a tap on his shoulder. He whirled around. His schoolmate, Ryan, stood grinning at him. Daniel breathed a sigh of relief.

"You're jumpy," Ryan said. "Find anything good?" He stuffed a wine gum into his mouth. "There's a wicked sweet stall over there. Got these for next to nothing. Want one?"

He held out the crumpled bag of sweets. Daniel liked wine gums, particularly the black ones, and the offer was hard to resist. He managed to single out a black one without rummaging too much.

"Hah, you like the black ones, too." Ryan laughed. His hair was long, curling to the neck of his T-shirt, and he wore loose trousers, like skateboarders did, low on his hips. On his feet were muddy white trainers, the fraying laces loosely knotted.

Ryan had joined the school four months ago in the middle of the academic year, which was unusual — if he'd been a different boy, this would have set him apart. It didn't seem to bother him though, and he'd soon joined the group of boys who kicked a ball about in break times and were always getting into trouble with the teachers. He wasn't in Daniel's class but they'd got talking recently when Ryan had offered him a handful of crisps and plonked himself down on the bench where he was sitting. Daniel liked his easy manner and was fascinated to learn that he lived with his dad on a narrowboat on the nearby canal. He hadn't mentioned a mum, and Daniel didn't like to pry, but assumed her absence might explain Ryan's grubby appearance, his ill-fitting, worn clothes and his sparse lunchboxes.

He asked him what it was like to live on a boat, and Ryan had described his life on the water, the regular moving around, the school holidays spent chugging up and down the canals, negotiating locks, mooring in a different place every night. But when Daniel had asked if he could come and see the boat, a shadow passed across Ryan's face. "It's my dad," he said. "He don't like people coming back." He had changed the subject abruptly.

But today seemed to be different.

"Want to come and see where I live?"

Daniel couldn't conceal his surprise. "But — what about your dad?"

"Oh, he's out and about somewhere. If we go now, we'll be able to go in. Just for five minutes, like."

"I can't — sorry." He really wanted to go, but the incident with the tattooed man had spooked him.

Ryan followed Daniel's gaze. "That your dad?"

"Yeah. I've got to stay nearby. Sorry."

"Come on, it's right there, just behind the hedge."

Daniel craned his neck but the hedge was too dense to see anything. He hesitated.

"C'mon." Ryan started to take his arm, but Daniel held back. It was tempting, for sure.

"I don't know . . ."

To his surprise, Ryan dropped his arm, walked over to Daniel's dad and tapped him on the back. "'Scuse me," he said.

Daniel's dad turned. "Oh, hello." He looked from one boy to the other.

"Can Daniel come and see my dad's boat? It's over there, just behind the hedge. It's called *Golden Serpent*. Just for a couple of minutes?"

"*Golden Serpent*? OK, why not? But don't be too long, we're going soon, Daniel."

Ryan grinned and pulled Daniel's sleeve. "C'mon! Let's go!"

As they stepped through the hedge onto the towpath, Ryan pointed towards a row of narrowboats sitting along the canal, their brightly painted sides standing out against the green of the fields behind.

"That one with the bikes on top." He pointed at a dark blue boat with gold lettering on the side.

Daniel was surprised to see how long the boat was. And how thin — no wonder they were called narrowboats. The paint on the sides was flaking off in places to reveal a lighter blue beneath, and as well as the bikes, there were bags of chopped wood, rope and boxes scattered about on the roof, giving the boat a dishevelled look. A golden snake was painted on the side, its body curving up and down, a zigzag pattern along its back. A forked tongue flicked from beneath flaring nostrils and its eyes were yellow, giving it an evil, threatening look. At the front of the boat, at the head of the writhing snake, someone had used the same gold paint to write the boat's name: *Golden Serpent*.

They climbed on at the front, where the boat was moored to the verge. The doors nearest them were locked, so they had to walk along a narrow ledge at the side to get to the other end. There was a rail along the roof to hang on to, and Daniel clutched the bag with the comics tightly to his side, just in case. It was exciting feeling the boat tilt as they moved along it, seeing the water ripple around the solid hull.

At the other end, the doors stood open. Daniel held back, but Ryan beckoned him down the steps. "It's OK, he's not here. Probably in the pub."

The walls inside were lined with wood, reminding Daniel of his father's shed. He stepped down into a tiny kitchen with a stove, a sink and what looked like a toy fridge, it was so small. There were mugs hanging from hooks screwed into the walls, and the sink was piled high with dishes waiting to be washed. Beyond the kitchen area was a table with benches against two walls. A narrow corridor led from there into a dark interior.

"Come and see my room." Ryan opened a curved door into a space so small it would barely take the two boys. A thin mattress lay on a platform to the side, with a window at the opposite end overlooking the water. The other wall was only a couple of feet from the bed. A muddle of bags and clothes hung from hooks along each side and Daniel had to step carefully over piles of belongings on the floor in order not to get entangled.

"This is so cool." He leaned over the window as a pair of ducks swam past. "It must be great living here, right on the water."

Ryan shrugged. "It's OK. Pretty small, and cold in winter if the stove's off. But when it's on, it's really cosy."

Daniel felt a pang of jealousy as he followed Ryan back to the kitchen. It seemed so adventurous, so exciting, to be constantly moving around. He was full of questions, but as they reached the steps, the boat moved alarmingly. Heavy footsteps reverberated on the wooden deck.

Both boys froze. "It's my dad," Ryan whispered.

"What do we do?"

"Quick, up the steps. Here, take these." Ryan shoved some playing cards into Daniel's hand. "We'll say we came to pick them up."

They raced up the steps. As Daniel reached the top, a thin figure was leaning over the side of the boat, one hand on the tiller. Above the hand, the arm was covered in garish tattoos. As the man turned, Daniel recognised the writhing serpent on his neck.

Tattooed Man.

Daniel stepped back, glancing over his shoulder. There was a gap of about two feet to the bank — he could jump if he had to.

Ryan, oblivious to Daniel's horrified reaction, hurried past his dad, pulling Daniel by the arm.

"Hey, Dad," he said over his shoulder. "We just popped in to get some cards." The boys readied themselves to jump.

The man straightened up, his eyes narrowing. Before Daniel had a chance to jump, the back of his T-shirt was grabbed by a sinewy arm. He stumbled backwards.

"It's you again," Tattooed Man said. "Got you now! How about those comics, then? I'm sure you don't mind giving them to your friend, do you?"

He reached for the bag, but Daniel held it as far out as possible, wriggling and twisting away.

"Hey, Dad, what are you doing?" Ryan cried, wrestling with his father, who pushed him away with his free hand. "He's my friend. He just came to—"

"Give me that bag!" Tattooed Man yelled, hanging onto Daniel while trying to shake Ryan off. They wrestled on the tilting deck for a heart-stopping moment, Ryan shouting, "Get off, Dad, leave him alone!" while Daniel struggled, off-balance, desperate to get to the towpath and away.

Just as he thought he would end up in the water, Daniel pulled free with a twist and jumped for the bank, stumbling and falling to his knees, the bag of comics still grasped firmly in one hand. Scrambling to his feet, he risked a look back at the boat, expecting to see Ryan's dad right behind him. But Ryan leaped onto his father's back, yelling, "Run, Daniel!" as Tattooed Man cursed and roared with fury.

"I know where you live!" he shouted after Daniel. "I'm coming for you!"

Ryan clung, limpet-like, for a moment — but as Daniel watched, horrified, the boy's dad turned and crashed his body backwards towards the jutting roof behind. There was a chilling scream and Ryan's body slipped slowly to the ground.

Terror made Daniel turn, his feet flying in time with his racing heart. Expecting the thump of boots at his shoulder at any moment, a heavy hand grasping his arm, he swerved abruptly, scrambling through a thin part of the hedge, the twigs scratching his arms, raking at his clothes. Was Tattooed Man following him? He landed in a heap on the other side, thorns still clutching at him. When he looked up, he could see the cars lined up not far away, the trading going on as if nothing had happened.

Still crouching, he listened intently, peering through a hole at the bottom of the hedge. But there was nothing moving, just an ominous, muffled thumping from nearby.

His mind raced. What was that noise? Was Ryan's dad beating him up right now? He imagined him being kicked and thrown about in the small space on the boat, out of sight, blood spraying, bones cracking. He should go back to help him . . . but what could he do against a grown man? He was half the size of Tattooed Man and shaking with fear. He didn't want to get into trouble. He turned this way and that, torn between fleeing to safety and turning back to help his friend.

Holding his breath, he pushed halfway through the hedge and risked a glance towards the boat. His heart drummed a painful beat in his chest, so loud he was scared it could be heard from the towpath.

There was no sign of Tattooed Man or of Ryan. But the boat rocked ominously against the bank, the movement slowing as he watched. That was a good sign, surely? Perhaps Ryan was all right after all, resting in his tiny cabin, waiting for his father to calm down.

Guilt tugging at his insides, Daniel jogged back towards the lines of cars. In a couple of minutes he was back at his father's side, pulling at his jacket. "Dad—"

"Just a minute, son." His dad was mid-conversation with a stallholder. He hated to be interrupted.

"But, Dad, Ryan needs help—"

But his dad wasn't to be distracted, holding up his hand to stop Daniel from speaking. He seemed oblivious to Daniel's rapid breathing, his hanging head. Daniel hopped from foot to foot, glancing anxiously back towards the canal.

After what seemed like an age to Daniel, his father turned to him. "What is so important that you have to hang on my coat like that?" he said, not unkindly.

"Ryan and his dad had a fight — we need to go and help — Ryan's in trouble . . ." Daniel tugged at his sleeve, trying to pull him back towards the boat.

"Wait a minute, Daniel. We can't just wade into a family argument."

"It wasn't a family argument, Dad. Ryan was getting a beating. I have to go back. I — we need to help him."

Daniel's father stopped and held Daniel by the shoulders. "Look, son, what goes on between father and son is none of our business. We don't know what Ryan might have done to deserve it, but it's best we don't get involved."

"But, Dad—"

His father shook his head. "No buts. He'll be fine. Let's go, shall we? I'm done here."

Daniel hesitated, kicking his feet. He opened his mouth to object, then closed it again. He could see his dad was immovable.

Perhaps he was worrying too much. Ryan was probably inside, watching TV, if they had one. Relief at leaving started to wash over him.

"Come on, then, let's go." His dad ushered him away.

Back at home, he went to his room and kicked off his trainers. He felt a rush of anticipation as he held the bag of comics upside down, letting them slip out onto the bedcover. He was looking forward to getting absorbed in them.

But then he stopped. The garish colours, the dramatic pen strokes, the speech bubbles — these were the same as every other comic he'd seen. Why was Ryan's dad so keen on these particular comics? What was it that made them worth fighting over? Daniel had picked them out at random, choosing the ones he liked best, so they weren't even a set. What could a grown man want with them? He looked at them properly, held them up and shook them, one by one, in case something was hidden between the pages . . . a bank note, a letter, a mysterious photo? But there was nothing. As Daniel's dad had pointed out, most of them were pretty well-used, even damaged. What possible value could they have?

"Dad?"

His father was settling down to watching sport on the TV. He always did on a Saturday afternoon, and the familiar shouts of a football crowd already filled the living room.

"Yes?"

"You know those comics we bought?"

"I do — what of them?" His dad was settling into his chair, his eyes glued to the screen in the corner of the cosy living room. A mug of steaming tea sat on the small table next to his chair.

"Do grown-ups buy them sometimes? Like, collect them or something?"

"I believe so — why, are you thinking of starting a collection?"

Daniel was intrigued. "Maybe. So, not just for their kids — for themselves?"

"Yes, I think so. People will collect anything, especially if they think they can make some money." There was a roar from the crowd and a young footballer fell to his knees. He was soon hidden from view by a mass of football shirts falling on top of him. Daniel wondered vaguely if footballers ever got injured celebrating a goal. That would be pretty stupid.

"Even comics like *Beano* and stuff?"

His dad was getting impatient now. "Yes, I said. The older ones, if they're in good condition, can be collectors' items, worth quite a bit. Now, can you give over with the questions please and let your dad watch the football?"

Back in his room, Daniel stared at the comics strewn around his bed. So that was it. Ryan's dad must have known something about these comics. There must be one, or more, that was worth money. Maybe the oldest, or perhaps the one in the best condition. He fingered one of the *Beano*s. The front was a little crumpled, and there was a small rip in one of the inside pages, but otherwise it seemed quite new.

Or maybe the *Dandy* was the important one? Impossible to know. Daniel decided to find out, somehow. But not now. Now he would dedicate the afternoon to reading his new purchases.

But after flicking through the first couple of magazines, he realised he wasn't concentrating. His mind kept returning to the scene on the boat — Tattooed Man yelling and trying to get at him, Ryan helping him to get away. He felt bad for leaving him there. That scream of pain . . .

Ryan could be badly hurt. The silence that had followed the struggle on the deck could mean a number of things, but he was pretty sure it wasn't good for Ryan. He could have been knocked out — dead, even, if he'd banged his head.

Daniel tried to reason with himself. He was being silly. Ryan would be fine. The boy's dad was harsh, but surely he wouldn't harm his own son. Ryan was a nice person, friendly, cheerful — not the kind you'd imagine had a dad who beat him up. But what did Daniel know? His dad could be strict, and sometimes got angry, but almost always for a good reason, when the children misbehaved or something. He never hit them.

The more he thought about it, the more guilty he felt. He shouldn't have abandoned Ryan like that. He should have left the comics with his dad and gone back, even just hung about nearby, to make sure Ryan was OK. That's what you do for friends, isn't it? You check they're OK. You look after them. You have their back, like Ryan did for Daniel.

He should go back now. It was only a ten-minute walk to the field from their house. Could he do it? His heart beat at the thought. If his dad realised he'd gone without telling him, he'd be angry, that was for sure. And his mum would be really worried if she got back and couldn't find him.

All the more reason to go right now. He wouldn't rest until he knew Ryan was OK. It was late afternoon. Though the boot sale would be finished, there would be people around on the towpath, walking their dogs, perhaps other boats coming and going. What harm would he come to?

He tiptoed down the stairs and opened the front door, closing it quietly behind him. Stage one — success! He ran down the front path and out into the street, sticking to the pavement, hoping he looked nonchalant, without a care in the world. He didn't want any of the neighbours to stop him — they might suspect a ten-year-old boy shouldn't be out on his own as dusk approached.

He arrived at the field without incident, panting. The cars from the boot sale had all gone, the only remains a few scraps of litter blowing in the breeze. Apart from the marks in the dust from car tyres and table legs, you wouldn't have known it had been there. As he walked towards the canal, the sun dropped behind dark clouds, casting a shadow across the field. A sudden gust of wind made him glance towards the sky and he felt a single drop of rain on his cheek. He'd need to be quick if he wasn't going to get soaked. Finding the gap in the hedge, he peered through, making sure he stayed out of sight. Ryan's boat was still there, though all the other boats had gone, the water turning black under the gathering clouds, a pale moon rising in the distance.

Daniel glanced around. There was nobody else there, no dog-walkers, no boats, just a dull rumble from the main road in the distance.

In the near-silence, an engine started up. It took him a moment or two to realise what it was. Ryan's boat was leaving. He could see the name, painted across the back of the boat, just below the platform. He ducked beside the hedge, his heart racing. Tattooed Man must be around if the boat was being readied to leave. Luckily Daniel was behind it, so anyone steering would have their back to him, but he wasn't taking any chances. A muffled *chug-chug* turned into a roar and Ryan's dad was at the helm, craning his neck over the canal ahead. Daniel stood, straining to see if he could make out Ryan at the other end of the boat, a movement from inside. But there was nothing — no sign of anyone else. He crouched down again, keeping his body low and still, watching the boat move steadily away.

Then it happened. Tattooed Man looked over his shoulder, glancing up and down the riverbank. Seeming satisfied, he bent, his head disappearing out of sight. He was grappling with something down by his feet — a black bundle, like a large bin bag, close to the edge of the platform. It wasn't fully closed and he had to push the contents back inside. Some faded clothes, jeans perhaps, and a flash of white from some old trainers. Whatever it was seemed strangely resistant, and Ryan's dad had to push hard to get it all in. He straightened up, took the tiller again — and kicked out, a single, powerful shove with his foot. The bundle landed in the murky water with a splash as the boat chugged smoothly on.

It all happened in a microsecond. Daniel felt the blood drain from his face, the thump of his heart in his chest even louder now. Suddenly breathing was much harder. He stood, his eyes scanning the churning water as the boat pulled away, watching Tattooed Man's back as he guided it along, hoping that at any moment Ryan would appear beside him. But there was still no sign of his friend. A few moments more and a slight bend in the canal hid the boat from view. Daniel stood dumbfounded as the last ripples reached the banks beside him.

What had he just seen? It must surely have been a bag of rubbish. Mustn't it? Ryan's dad was being lazy, dumping his waste in the water instead of taking it to a proper bin. But the bag had been heavy, lumpy in a way that normal rubbish wasn't.

Surely it couldn't have been — Ryan's body?

He shook his head. Was he seeing things? Perhaps he was going mad, the excitement of being out without permission getting to him. He was being ridiculous, making things up. He'd been some distance away, not close enough to see properly. Why would someone dump a body in clear sight? Wouldn't they take it somewhere remote, where people never went?

He told himself firmly that he was being melodramatic. Letting his imagination run riot, because he'd had a fright. Still, he ran along the towpath, his eyes searching the water, hoping the bag would float to the surface and prove him wrong.

But there was only an echo of movement left in the water, a tiny rise and fall indicating that something had recently passed through. The grassy bank with its clumps of weeds revealed no secrets, the last damselflies of summer hovering aimlessly at the water's edge. He rounded the slight bend. There was nothing, only a blank stretch of silvery water reflecting the rising moon.

* * *

The incident at the canal marked the beginning of a slow slide into self-doubt that lasted into adulthood.

He never saw Ryan again. At school, they said the family had moved on, Ryan had gone to a new school. Could that be true? It was impossible to find out. At night, he imagined Tattooed Man breaking into their house, attacking him, stealing his comics, and for months he struggled to sleep.

He relived the scene over and over, as if it were a trailer for some horror film he would never get to see. Each time he suffered the same fear, the same agonies of indecision. The guilt got worse and worse. He suffered bouts of self-hatred, sudden plunges into depression. Many times, in his teens, he wondered if he was going mad. At best, he kept himself in check, constantly vigilant, holding his tongue in case he made a fool of himself. It was deeply debilitating.

His parents, bemused by his failure to thrive, put it down to hormones. 'Teenage angst.' Even at that time, mental illness wasn't something people were prepared to acknowledge, and certainly Daniel's parents would have balked at the suggestion that their son had a psychological problem. They were quite old-fashioned in many ways. Their attitude, like their parents before them, was 'Get on with it' and 'Pull your socks up.' They were confused by him, and their way of dealing with their unhappy son was to rely on him growing out of it.

Meanwhile Daniel suffered in silence. It was only when Lauren began to mature — early, even for a girl — that he had found someone who listened without making fun of him.

CHAPTER ELEVEN

Three steps led to the door. Glass panes, reinforced with a grid of wire, revealed very little of what was behind them. Daniel stood outside and breathed. In fast, out slow, in fast . . .

Forcing himself to come here had been hard, even harder than he'd expected — especially with all the other worries he had. Every bone, every muscle in his body had resisted walking the short distance to the police station. But he'd known for a while that he had to do something — he had to make his memory real. To achieve that, he needed to tell the police. Once he'd made a statement and it was written down, then the incident existed in the wider world, not just in his brain. So here he was. And now he was here, he had to see it through.

The door swung open abruptly and a couple came out, talking in low voices. They passed without a glance. He took one last breath and climbed the steps with heavy feet. *Keep breathing. You'll be fine.*

A young policeman behind the desk looked up as he approached. "Morning," he said. "How can I help?"

"I want to make a statement." He'd rehearsed this sentence many times in his head. What happened next, what he needed to say, were unknowns. His hands were shaking, a cold sweat forming on his palms. The urge to run was almost irresistible.

"OK. Can I take some details, please?"

He gave his name and — reluctantly — his parents' address, hoping there would be no need for the police to contact him there. His father would jump to conclusions, assume the worst, and he would never be able to tell him the truth. None of this was helping his anxiety.

"What's the nature of the statement?"

"Ah . . . I witnessed something . . . an incident. A long time ago."

"Right. What kind of incident was this?"

"I was just a child. But—" He dropped his voice. "It looked like someone was disposing of a body." Daniel was grateful there was no one else in the reception area. Even to his ears, it sounded far-fetched, in this banal, grey environment.

The officer gave him a quizzical look. "A body, you say? When was this, sir?"

Daniel could feel the man's scepticism rising. "I was ten. Nineteen years ago. It was 11 September, a Saturday."

"Local?"

"Yes, on the canal."

"Right." The policeman gave him another searching look.

"I'm not wasting your time. I know what I saw. I remember every detail." He wanted to explain it all, how different his memories were, how vividly he remembered the scene, how it had haunted him for so long, how it gave him no peace. But the words wouldn't come. This man wasn't going to believe him anyway.

"I'll see if someone's free." The officer picked up a phone and muttered into it, turning his back. Daniel could only imagine what he was saying. *Some nutter's just come in, saying he saw a dead body being disposed of. Yes, nineteen years ago. Ha — yes. Says he remembers it clearly.*

"Take a seat, sir. Someone will be along shortly to take your statement." The sardonic smile said it all.

Daniel almost went back through that door. He could feel the panic, so close to the surface. He sat, placing his feet squarely on the floor, his hands on his knees. He closed his eyes and breathed. *Focus*, he ordered himself. *You can do this. You must do this. You've got this far. Don't stop now or you'll never be able to do it.*

The wait was unbearable, though only a few minutes had ticked by on the plastic clock above the reception desk before a man in jeans and a dark T-shirt arrived. He waved Daniel through a door to one side.

"I'm DC Broad," he said, without offering a hand. They took their seats in a sparsely furnished room, the walls unadorned. A blind shaded the interior from passing traffic, painting slashes of sunlight on a grubby grey carpet. From the grime around the frame it looked as if the window had never been open, and the air in the room was dusty and stale. The detective placed a folder on the table and removed a form, clicking the top of a pen on, off, on, off. Daniel could see his details had been filled in at the top.

"I understand you want to report a crime?" The man's eyes were still on the form. One of his legs jiggled, the movement reverberating through the metal table.

This wasn't going to be easy. Daniel closed his eyes for a moment, leaning back in his seat. Under the table, he wiped his clammy hands on his jeans. *Relax*, he told himself. *You can do this.*

"I was ten. The date was 11 September 1999. It was a Saturday. I went to a car boot sale in a field near my house. I was with my dad . . ."

He kept his voice level, his sentences short, pausing often for DC Broad to write, using the spaces to breathe deeply. To his relief, the detective let him speak, transcribing his every word in a spidery scrawl, his eyes on the paper. It was slow and laborious, but at least Daniel could keep going. He feared that if he stopped, he'd clam up.

When he got to the part about Ryan's body and the heavy-looking bundle, the officer looked up for the first time, his eyebrows slowly rising. Daniel braced himself for a sarcastic comment, but DC Broad nodded and carried on writing. Gradually the words filled one page, then another, and at last, Daniel's story petered out.

The detective took a deep breath and sat back, holding the pages in one hand, reading. The silence seemed endless.

Daniel hoped the sweat that had broken out on his forehead wasn't too obvious. He was pretty sure the police would assume some kind of guilt rather than a state of anxiety.

DC Broad dropped the statement onto the table, startling him. "Why now?" He gazed into Daniel's face intently.

"As I said, I get these memories—"

"You said. Did you tell your parents at the time?"

"No. I — I didn't know what to do. I thought . . . I was frightened."

"You're what? Twenty-nine? Nineteen years after the event. What's the reason for telling us this now?"

"I thought . . ." Daniel's voice trailed away. He could see the scepticism in the detective's face.

"You seem to remember every detail about this incident. But you can't remember this man's last name?"

"I never knew it. Only the boy's first name, as I said."

"And you're hoping we can find his father now." DC Broad made a show of placing the statement into the thin file. He closed it and stood up. "Well, we'll be in touch. Thanks for coming in." He strode to the door and opened it wide. Dismissed.

As he followed the detective to the front desk, Daniel could almost hear the mocking comments, the laughter that would follow. He was pretty sure he'd never hear from them again.

CHAPTER TWELVE

His legs felt weak, no longer able to carry the weight of his thoughts. He sank down onto a damp, ramshackle bench not far from the police station, ignoring the cold creeping through the thin fabric of his trousers.

The detective hadn't believed him. In a way, Daniel didn't blame him. If nobody else had a memory like his, how could he expect other people to accept what he told them? Perhaps he was wrong, and his memories weren't so special after all. But if his memories were not to be trusted, then what was he? Did that make him a useless piece of junk, as he called himself in his darkest moments?

He went back to the scene that repeated itself over and over in his mind, but this time he allowed it to unfold. The car boot sale, Daniel and his dad in quiet companionship on the way there. The comics and his excitement at finding them. Then the strange, tattooed man and Ryan. The boat, *Golden Serpent*, with its painted snake and the pile of kit on the roof. Then the horrible scene with the bag.

If only he'd been brave enough to stand up to Ryan's dad, maybe the boy would still be alive. They could have appeased him or fought him off together and escaped into the field until he'd calmed down. Even better — Daniel could have simply handed over the comics. Why hadn't he just done that?

This was stupid. Ryan was probably still alive, and all these years Daniel's memory had been tricking him. He didn't know what he'd seen.

But if his memory was tricking him, then things were even worse than he thought. In the back of his mind, he'd always held a nugget of pride. His memory of his own experiences, for so many years the root of all his troubles, was without doubt exceptional. Much, much better than other people's. A gift as well as a burden. Only recently, he'd started to think that it was far too weighty a burden to bear.

If his memories were wrong, then everything was in question. His entire essence — who he was — was worthless.

He took a deep breath, let it out slowly, and forced himself to be logical and objective. Acknowledging the emotions, he put them to one side. He needed to focus on solving his problem, rather than avoiding or bemoaning it.

Since he was unable to rid himself of the memory, perhaps he should face it head-on, he reasoned. If he could only find out what had really happened that day, he would know for certain if his recollections could be trusted. Maybe he could even find out if he really did have an exceptional brain.

If the memory was right, but the ten-year-old Daniel hadn't understood what he was looking at, then it would prove nothing about his abilities. But at least he would have tried, for Ryan's sake. It was growing in importance, the need to find out and to get justice, if justice needed to be done. Perhaps then the memory would leave him alone. Was it worth a try?

It began to drizzle, the moisture forming a sheen on his jacket, chilling his skin on his neck and his bare hands. But he hardly noticed. The germ of an idea was beginning to form in his mind.

What if he could track down the boat? *Golden Serpent* might still exist — those boats looked pretty solid, and he knew they lasted a long time. Some of the old working narrowboats were still around, albeit transformed into bijou holiday cruisers.

For the first time in years, Daniel felt the tiniest thrill of excitement run through his body. It was an odd feeling after so long. Was it possible that he could actually find the boat and, somehow, through amateur detective work, discover whether Ryan really was killed that night and dumped in the canal by his dad?

His plan gained speed like a hunting animal. He needed to get away from here, take time out, distract himself. That meant a break, away from stress, away from work. A walking trip on the canals would be perfect — peaceful, far from the hustle of cities, from computer games, close to nature. Time to think, away from the stresses of work and family. Good for his body and for his mind. And while he was on his journey, he would find out what had happened to Ryan. He could start at the field where the car boot sale had taken place and work his way north, in the direction the boat had been heading.

That was it. That was what he was going to do.

But how could he go on a trip with no money? He couldn't ask Lauren — *wouldn't* ask Lauren, because she'd say yes, and he would never forgive himself if he couldn't pay her back. There was no way he could ask his parents. They probably had the money, but he would never live it down. Even mentioning it would cause a flurry of concern.

His mind flipped back to Ryan and that crystal-clear memory that wouldn't leave him alone.

The answer to his problem was right there.

* * *

It was all about the comics, after all. They were the reason for everything — possibly even the reason Ryan had approached him. Ryan's dad could have suggested inviting Daniel on to the boat, without telling the boy his ulterior motive — to take the comics from him. Ryan had seemed genuinely shocked when his dad had grabbed Daniel. He probably hadn't a clue what he was up to.

Daniel hadn't found out what the comics were worth. He'd read them cover to cover, many times, then lost interest as he grew older. But he made sure they didn't get thrown away. When his parents moved house, he took care of them himself. He wrapped them in newspaper and put them in a box with some other precious items he didn't want to lose. On the lid he wrote: *Not To Be Thrown Away Under Any Circumstances.* He carried it up to the attic in the new house and placed it in a far corner, out of the way, where nobody could claim it was a nuisance.

But when he left home, he pretty much forgot about the comics, what with the pressure of his brain, living in London and trying to hold down a job. Now would be the perfect time to unearth them. If he could sell them for a decent amount of money, it might be enough to live on while he carried out his plan. It could be a start, at least. Walking the canals wouldn't in itself be expensive. If he went over the summer months, he could camp at least some of the time, so he would only need money to support himself.

Daniel was suddenly impatient to find those comics, so he pulled his collar up tight against the rain and set off for his parents' house. He hoped his mum would be out and he could get up to the attic without her noticing. It was too early for him to share his plans. If, for some reason, the comics turned out to be worth nothing, he'd rather she didn't know. It was best to keep the whole thing to himself.

His mum was at home, in the kitchen listening to the radio at full volume. She waved distractedly at him as he climbed the stairs.

In the dusty space above the bedrooms was the usual muddle of boxes, suitcases and zipped bags filled with unused belongings, Christmas decorations and spare bedding. Daniel went straight to the place where he'd put the box. It was still there.

Lifting it clear of the sloping roof, he made a small space in the clutter and sat on a hard-sided suitcase to look through the contents. It looked like things had been disturbed. A folder of photos had been moved, his books put back in a different order. A football shirt, an old favourite, was no longer folded neatly. His heart sinking, he took everything out, piling it on the floor beside him. At last, in the dim light of the bare electric bulb in the centre of the roof, he made out the yellowed newspaper at the bottom of the box.

He opened the package and counted the comics, twelve in all. They were all there, looking even more yellow and dog-eared than he remembered them. Shoving his belongings back into the box in any old order, he picked his way back to the trapdoor and climbed down.

Now all he needed to do was find out what the fuss was about.

In his bedroom with the door closed, it didn't take long to do the research. One or two clicks in a search engine and he was engrossed in the world of comic collectors. He was stunned when he saw that some of the earliest comics from the 1930s and 40s could sell for hundreds of thousands of pounds — he even found one that was sold for more than two million. Incredible, but unlikely that the comics he had in front of him were worth anything like that much.

Carefully he laid them out in date order on the bed. When he'd bought them, he was only ten years old, but that was nearly twenty years ago. They — or at least one of them, he had no idea which — had been spotted by Ryan's father as potentially valuable even then. Now they could be worth more. He only hoped that Ryan's dad, unpleasant though the encounter had been, was right.

Hurriedly he wrote down the publication dates, the titles and his own assessment of the condition of each. There were some *Dandy* comics, a couple of them dating from the 1940s, and a few *Beano*s from a similar era. Two were in decent condition, the others damaged to some degree, but he was going to check them anyway. You never knew with collectors. They seemed to be excited by the most peculiar things, pristine or not.

He picked up one of the *Dandy*s, dated 1949. He'd not even registered the dates on any of the front covers as a boy — he'd only been interested in the characters and the storylines. They were pretty old, that was for sure. This one was a bit tatty, but could it be the one that had attracted so much attention? He picked out another one at random and decided to see if he could get both valued, as a start.

He found a site that valued comics, then another, and another. He filled in some information, including the condition of each and the publication dates, attaching photos taken on his mobile. When he clicked 'send' he experienced a small but significant thrill of anticipation.

He lay back on his pillows and enjoyed the feeling. He had no idea how long it would take to get a response. Tomorrow he'd dash off some more queries, to see if he could sell them all. Perhaps together they could send him off on his adventure.

* * *

He could hardly believe it when, the following morning, an email dropped into his inbox from one of the websites specialising in comics. The two editions he'd queried were valued at over five hundred pounds. The valuation was tempered by plenty of caveats: mostly regarding the condition of the items, but Daniel reckoned he'd got that about right, though it was hard to say when this was all so new and unfamiliar.

But it was a great start. The two comics were not in the best condition. He still had the best ones to try. Without bothering to change from his pyjamas, Daniel entered details for all the comics into three websites that promised to value them honestly and generously. Though he wasn't convinced by their promises, he had to give it a try. After all, these strange, flimsy, childish possessions could be the ticket to the rest of his life.

He didn't mind selling them all, if they got him enough money, though as he studied them again, he got caught up in his ten-year-old self and became engrossed in the stories and the characters.

At ten, he'd been quite innocent — happy, even — in general. He remembered the good times with his dad, the trips out, the games of football in the garden. He'd join him in the garage, tinkering with his bicycle or his car, or in the garden, planting spring bulbs or hoeing the flower beds. It felt like such a long time ago.

The emotions attached to this memory were pride, to be helping his dad, satisfaction in doing a task with his hands, the feeling of being secure in his family. Contentment, even. When had he felt like that as an adult? He couldn't think of a single occasion when he'd felt either secure or contented. Could he hope for anything like that for himself, now that he was determined to change his life? As always, the doubts were there, crushing the hope.

Until he got his mind under control, he didn't have a chance.

CHAPTER THIRTEEN

One morning when Poppy went to wake her gran, she was no longer there. Her body was in the bed as usual, the window slightly ajar, the air fresh. Birdsong drifted through the room, the sun shone through a crack in the curtains. Nothing to indicate anything amiss. But Poppy knew immediately. Swallowing hard, she leaned over the pillow. There was hardly a dent where Gran's head rested in a halo of soft white curls. The skin on her face was almost as white as the pillowcase, her frail hands clasped together as if in prayer.

Forcing herself, Poppy reached a hand to the fragile neck, feeling for a pulse. She'd done this a few times before, reassuring herself that her grandmother was still with them, so she knew for sure when she felt the cold skin. There was no heartbeat.

Poppy's tears dropped gently onto the pillow. "Bye bye, Gran," she said. "I will always love you."

It was the saddest day of her life.

* * *

Every night, Poppy slept in Gran's bed. A small box on the mantelpiece contained her ashes. It felt as if she was still there. Poppy and her mum had chosen the box together, both of them liking its iridescent shine, the bouquet of tiny white flowers showing through a window on the lid.

Mum didn't approve of Poppy sleeping there. She didn't want to deny Poppy the time to grieve, but she wanted her to understand that Gran was old and it was her time. Gran wouldn't have wanted her to dwell on it, she said. She'd want to be remembered fondly, often in Poppy's thoughts, but she'd also want her granddaughter to move on.

Working with the animals helped, though Poppy had to avoid any talk of those who were ailing or destined to be put down — she'd be in floods of tears before she knew it. But mostly she let them love her. She cuddled and stroked and kissed them all. The physical closeness, the unlimited love they offered helped her feel whole again, filled the space where her gran had been. More than ever, she longed to take one home.

There was one little dog that had lost a leg in some kind of accident — no one knew how. He was a young mongrel with traces of many breeds in his face, his frame, his coat of many shades. He simply got on with his life, as if the rescue centre was exactly what he'd been hoping for, as if having three legs was the perfect way to be. Poppy loved him for that, for his endless joy at being alive. He adored her and was the one who stayed with her while the other dogs played, not because he couldn't keep up with them — he was perfectly capable of outrunning some of the older dogs — but he just wanted to be with her. The staff called him Beans, because he was always so full of energy.

The little dog was having trouble getting adopted. People were put off by the missing leg. Most people wanted a puppy — a youngster that could be trained from scratch. The older ones, the ones with battle scars, skin problems or other illnesses, were much harder to rehome. These were the animals that faced an uncertain future. They had to find a family or have their lives cut short. It seemed brutal, but the centre simply couldn't house animals indefinitely. There were too many coming in every month.

Playing with Beans one day, Poppy made the decision not to let him be put down. If nobody wanted him, she was going to look after him. She had the perfect job, after all — she could take him to work with her. Once she'd made that decision, of course, it was only a small step to take him home for a visit, to meet her parents and see how they felt about adopting him.

Poppy's mum knew straight away that Beans was just what Poppy needed. Someone to look after, to laugh and play with, to get her out of the house. Her dad took only a little more persuasion. As long as Poppy promised to train him properly, made sure he did no damage in the house and took full responsibility, then the little dog would be welcome.

* * *

A new phase started in Poppy's life with the arrival of Beans. He was already house-trained, but she didn't feel right letting him into Gran's room at night, so she returned to her bedroom and set up his dog bed next to hers, allowing him up for a cuddle in the mornings. Though at first he barked at passers-by and night-time noises, he soon settled down and became a member of the family.

The big difference was the walks. Poppy had enjoyed walking with Gran, but in recent years the walks had slowed and shortened, and she'd longed on occasion to get out into the countryside, away from people, cars and buildings. Now, with a dog as a reason to go further, she found new paths beyond the town, exploring the Oxfordshire countryside as she'd never done before.

When she first let Beans off the lead in an empty field, she realised it was probably the first time he'd seen such a wide expanse of grass. At the rescue centre they'd not been told his background — all Poppy knew was that he'd been brought in as a stray with a badly injured leg. He'd spent some time in the animal hospital until he'd recovered, then the rescue centre had become his new home.

They soon fell into a pattern. On days when she was working, the walks were local: the park, where they met other dogs and walkers, or the towpath beside the canal. On her days off, they followed circular walks from OS maps, or took the bus to the start of a less familiar trail. They walked in all weathers and Poppy's backpack was always ready.

Gradually, Poppy began to think of her gran without crying. Though the tears still came from time to time, the memories shifted. She stopped remembering Gran's illness and passing and started to recall the days when she was well and happy. Times when they laughed until they cried over something silly, or when they sat quietly reading on either end of the sofa. Gran's smile, her sense of humour, her joy in birds and spring flowers. Poppy's mum breathed a sigh of relief.

Yet there were at times feelings of such bleakness that Poppy wondered what she was missing. At first she put it down to grief, but as time went on, she knew it was not. She was restless. Perhaps, as her parents said, it was time to do something else with her life.

CHAPTER FOURTEEN

Daniel stared at the screen. In his inbox was a flurry of replies to his queries on the comics. The first offered him £1000 for all twelve. The second, a lot more detailed, suggested a possible range of values for each. Daniel worked his way through them, listing the titles and publication dates, the valuations for each, and the seller's details.

There was broad agreement on the less valuable editions — he wasn't going far on the proceeds from them — but for the others, the ones he knew were more special, there was little agreement. It was clear that some of them were assuming he was a novice and were trying their luck, while others gave examples of auction results for similar quality publications. It was all quite confusing.

What was interesting was that word seemed to have got around that he was looking for a buyer, because some of the names that popped up were unfamiliar and didn't seem to have any relation to the websites he'd contacted. Perhaps the collectors collaborated when they knew there were new items on the market. This made him suspicious. He didn't want to be ripped off, and there was a strong chance of that as it was all so new to him.

As he sat wondering what to do next, another email arrived.

Dear Daniel,

Thank you for submitting details of your collection of twelve comics. One of them in particular is of interest, though I was at first concerned that it might be a facsimile or a reprint.

You seem to have a first edition **Beano**, *the one dated 30 July 1938. Original issues are rare and highly collectible, though there are many reprints that aren't anything like as valuable. Yours, however, does seem to have the required elements: the right date, 28 pages (reprints often have only 24 pages), off-white newsprint paper (without brilliant white or glossy images), bound with glue, with zigzagged indentations on the top and bottom edges. There are other, less important pointers too.*

I am fairly certain that this is indeed a #1 issue of **Beano**, *in reasonable condition. Subject to closer inspections it could be worth around £4000. At auction, you may get more. I would, of course, need to view the item if you want me to make a firm offer.*

The rest of your collection, subject to inspection, could together fetch you a couple of hundred more.

Please let me know if you want to proceed. My telephone number is below if you'd like to discuss further. I look forward to hearing from you.

Best regards,
Bob Havering
Old Comics Inc.

This was the best offer he'd had, by some distance. He added the name to his list and underlined it. Now he had confirmation they were valuable — or at least one of them was. Even back in 1999, when he'd bought the comics, the *Beano* first edition would have been worth a considerable sum. Perhaps the stallholder at the sale hadn't spotted it — or had mistaken it for a reprint, as the last email suggested was perfectly possible. Maybe he had no idea how valuable his pile of old comics might have been.

It explained why Ryan's dad had been so persistent. From the state of the narrowboat, he wasn't a well-off man — this would have been a lot of money for him. For a moment, Daniel felt sorry for him, guilty that he was about to profit from something that could have made a big difference to someone's life. Perhaps even Ryan's life, though from the attitude of his father, it seemed unlikely that Ryan would have benefited.

But that line of thinking wasn't going to get him anywhere. The money was going to make a big difference to his own life, and he was going to do his utmost to make sure it was going to improve it. At the same time, he was going to find out what had happened to Ryan. If he had indeed been murdered — the word shocked him, even now — he was going to bring his father to justice.

At last — at last, something seemed to be going right in Daniel's life.

With shaking hands, he answered the last email. He reckoned that this one seemed genuine, and as far as he could tell, honest.

Hi Bob,

Thank you so much for this — that's very interesting! I've had a lot of interest from other collectors and am collating the responses. I will come back to you at the end of the process and hopefully arrange for you to see the comics in person.

Best regards,
Daniel

He felt like a child taking its first tentative steps, his legs weak and wobbly, uncertain where he would end up. But those first steps had been taken now, and though he felt light-headed, his plan looked like it could genuinely happen. That one copy of *Beano* would give him enough to get him started, and as long as he was careful, he could eke the money out for a good few weeks or even months.

The next thing was to track down *Golden Serpent*. He found the organisation that registered boats on the canals and dashed off an email to them. He decided to give them a couple of days to respond and if he hadn't heard anything by then, he would try calling them.

Parts of his plan were slotting into place. Best of all, for the first time in a long while, the memories had taken a back seat, replaced by a vision of the future.

* * *

Lauren's voice was distant, muffled.

He checked the signal on his mobile. "Can you hear me?"

"Yes, I can hear you, why?"

"You're a bit faint, that's all. Are you OK?"

"Yes, I'm good, thanks. Just got home."

"Do you want me to call back?"

"No, don't worry. How are you doing at Mum and Dad's?"

"Nothing much going on here. But listen, I've made a big decision. I haven't told them yet, but I've decided what to do." Daniel could hear the difference in his own voice, a touch of hope — excitement even.

"That's good."

"I'm planning to walk the canals for a few months, on my own. Camp, or find hostels to stay in. Get some peace, away from the computer games, decide — really decide — what I need to do to fix myself."

"Sounds like a great idea. But how are you going to manage it?" she said.

"How do you mean — money-wise?"

"Yes, are you going to get a job for a while to fund it?"

"I don't have to. It won't cost much anyway, but I think I've found a way to get some money. Do you remember those old comics I used to read: the *Beano*s and the *Dandy*s and all the others? Well, I dug some out of the attic. At least one of them could be worth something. I'm not sure how much yet, but I don't need much to get started."

"What, those tatty old comics? Who on earth would want them?"

"You'd be surprised. People pay a fortune for them. Especially first editions. And I seem to have one — a *Beano* published in 1938. It's not in perfect condition, but it seems good enough. I'm waiting for confirmation."

"Who would have thought?"

"I know. I'm pretty sure it's a good one. As soon as I've got the money, I'll be off, catch the end of spring and spend the summer walking."

"Good for you."

Though she was saying the right things, a small alarm bell sounded.

"Are you sure you're all right, Lauren?"

"I'm fine, honestly, it's just . . ." Lauren's voice faded away into nothing.

Daniel waited, but the pause lengthened. "Just what?"

"Just . . . part of me is jealous of you."

"Jealous? You — of me?" His voice squeaked with incredulity. Lauren, his successful, ambitious, confident sister, jealous of him, the mentally challenged loser brother?

"Yes, Daniel. I suppose I . . . My job is so hard, you know, and I don't have much of a life outside it. Sometimes I wish I could stop. Get away, like you're doing, have a real break. Maybe decide on my priorities. I can't do this for ever."

"You could come with me."

"Lovely idea, but there's no way, not this summer. I've got a lot more learning to do and a lot more to give before I pack it in."

"Shame. But maybe you could join me for a few days, or whatever time you can get off work? Even a weekend might give you a break."

"Now that is a good idea," Lauren said, her voice stronger now. "I'll definitely think about it. Any idea where you're heading?"

The more he talked about it, the more real it became. Now there was the prospect of his sister joining him, if only for a few days, and his idea was growing more robust by the minute.

He was on a quest to sort his life out. And he was determined to make it happen.

* * *

Thursday, 15 May. Daniel was fourteen years old, a spotty, awkward teenager. Luke and Sebastian were hanging out with him after school, playing computer games in his room when they should all have been doing their homework. Luke had a new game, *War Zombies*, and they were rolling around with laughter as they tried unsuccessfully to ward off armies of unlikely looking monsters on the small TV screen. Daniel had let them play—

The sudden buzz of his mobile swept the memory away. He scrabbled around his desk, among papers, notebooks and newspapers, and managed to drop it on the floor before grabbing it in time to swipe the green icon. It wasn't a number he recognised.

"Hello?" He hoped he hadn't cut the caller off by accident.

"It's Linda from the English Canals Association here," a woman's voice said. "Am I speaking to Daniel?"

"Yes."

"I'm calling about your email," Linda said. "You want to track down a particular canal boat, last seen nineteen years ago?"

"Well, yes." It did seem implausible, put like that.

"By the name of *Golden Serpent*?"

"Yes. I know it's a long shot."

"I don't think we can help, I'm afraid. Data Protection rules . . . I can't give you any information about ownership of individual boats, I'm afraid."

Blasted Data Protection laws. They always seemed to get in the way.

"Is there any other way I can track it down, do you know? It's quite important."

"I don't think so, I'm sorry," she said again. "*Golden Serpent*? I'm not familiar with the name. But if the boat's still in operation, it's unlikely they'll have changed the name. It's seen as bad luck, you know."

"Oh, I see—"

"Hold on." The woman's voice became distant for a moment. "What did you say?"

Daniel wasn't sure if she was talking to him.

"Just a minute," she said, more clearly. There was a rustling at the other end of the line, and a man's voice in the background. Daniel could only pick up patches of the exchange. "Down by the . . . boatyard . . . used to moor at Banbury . . ."

The line cleared and Linda returned. "My colleague seems to remember the name. He says did it have a gold snake painted on the side?"

Daniel could hardly believe it. He swapped his phone to the other hand. Before he realised it, he was standing, pacing the room. "That's it! Has he seen it recently?"

"That's all I can give you, I'm afraid."

"Can I speak to your colleague? Please, could I have a word, do you think?" This fragile link could be so important, he was desperate not to let it go.

"Uh, well it's not strictly . . . Just a minute. Hold on." There was a muffled shout, then bumps and crackles, and a man's gruff voice finally came on the line.

"Hello?"

"I understand you've seen the boat I'm trying to track down — *Golden Serpent*. The one with the snake on the side."

"Ah, yeah."

"When was this, was it recently?"

"Who wants to know?"

Taken aback a little, Daniel tried his best to sound friendly, innocent, though he didn't want to explain his reasons. The more he thought about it, the more foolish it sounded, trying to track a boat down after nineteen years. "My name's Daniel, I met someone from that boat a few years ago. I'm trying to track him down. Do you happen to know where it is?"

"As my colleague said, we're bound by Data Protection. I'm familiar with that boat, though."

"Are you able to say when you last saw it?" He had to keep the conversation going — it seemed his best chance to track it down. "That's not covered by Data Protection, surely?"

"Dunno. Few months, maybe a year. That's all I'm saying." Daniel's hopes rose. So, it was probable that the boat still existed.

"I'm very grateful," Daniel said, hoping good manners would help. "Thank you so much. Just one more thing—"

"Look, I've said all I'm going to say."

"No, it's not about the boat. I just wondered, do you know the canal network well? I'm planning a trip — a walking trip along the canals and I wondered if you could recommend where I should go."

The man cleared his throat. "Yeah, I know the canals a bit." He laughed, a deep cynical sound. "Only lived on them for forty years. Walking, you say? Well, depends what you want."

"I want to see interesting parts of the country, get a feel for what it must be like to live on a boat. Hopefully get to know some people." Daniel grimaced to himself. He was clutching at straws now, trying to keep the man talking.

But there was more scrabbling and Linda was back on the line. "Sorry, he had to go. If you're looking for a walking holiday on the canals, I suggest you visit our website, see if you can find what you need there. Well, if there's nothing more . . . Good luck with your trip."

"Thank you, thank—"

Linda had gone.

Daniel stared at his notepad. While he was talking, he'd scribbled a single word: 'Banbury'. Was it possible that *Golden Serpent* had been moored in Banbury when the man had seen it?

He opened a map. There it was, not far from Oxford. That was a stroke of luck. Even if it was a red herring and *Golden Serpent* had moved on long ago, it gave him a purpose, a place to start.

CHAPTER FIFTEEN

Daniel dreaded telling his parents what he intended to do. But telling them would ensure he carried out his plan.

He picked a quiet moment when he was able to talk to his mum alone. He leaned against a line of cupboards in the small kitchen with a mug of coffee while she fussed around him, cleaning the worktops. She moved him to one side gently as she progressed along one side of the room.

"Mum, I'm going to be off soon, so I'll be out of your hair."

His mum paused, the damp cloth hanging from her hand like a limp flag. "What do you mean, off?"

"I've been making plans. I want to take some time to decide what to do with my life. I'm going to go walking, probably until the end of the summer."

"Well, that sounds interesting." She put the cloth down and rested a hand on the worktop. "Where will you go?"

"Along the canals. I'll camp mostly, so it won't cost much. I've got enough money to start me off."

"On your own? Sounds a bit lonely to me. But it'll be peaceful, give you time to think, if that's what you need."

"It is exactly what I need, Mum. There's too much going on when I'm working, my brain can't rest. Actually, Lauren said she might join me for part of the walk, if she can get the time off work. Or even for a weekend or two."

"Lauren? Does she like walking?"

"Not really. But I think she could do with a holiday. She's finding the job quite hard." The underemphasis was deliberate. He didn't want his mum worrying about Lauren too.

"It's a big responsibility, what Lauren does." The frown lines on his mum's forehead deepened. She sat down with her now lukewarm coffee. "As for your plan, I don't know what your dad will say."

Daniel grunted.

"Don't be like that," Mum said. "You know he only wants the best for you."

"I know. He wants me to do something with my life, and that's exactly why I'm going. I want to make some decisions, sort my head out. You know I'm not the same as other people. My brain is always on, full of thoughts and memories, all the time, never stopping. I need to find a—"

What *did* he need to find? A cure? Respite? An answer? The right therapist? At once, a memory surfaced, the therapist who didn't say anything, Daniel's refusal to respond, the awkwardness, the feeling of hopelessness, despair . . . With an effort, he brought himself back to the conversation.

In his mum's face he read concern, anxiety, love, fear. He put his hand on hers across the table. "This is good, Mum. Really. This is me making a decision about my life. A decision to make some decisions, if you like. I can't go on letting things happen, hoping my head will sort itself out. I have to work it out for myself, before . . ." He paused. He was going to say "before it's too late" without even knowing what he meant. But seeing his mum flinch stopped him in his tracks. "Don't worry, Mum — I'm not going to do anything silly. That's not what I mean. I wouldn't do it, for your sake and Dad's, and Lauren's. I meant, before I've wasted any more time. Before I spend even longer in a dead-end job. That's what I mean."

His mother's face cleared a little. He was glad he'd found a way to reassure her.

The truth was a little different, however. On more than one occasion in his life he had considered a more permanent option.

* * *

"I don't think I understand." His dad ran his fingers through his hair. For the first time, Daniel realised he'd inherited the habit.

"I'm going walking, Dad. For a few weeks or months. Over the summer, anyway. Along the canals. I can manage financially, so don't worry about that. I've thought it all through. It's a kind of gap year, before I decide what to do next."

His voice petered out. He'd never confided fully in his father, and it all felt too late now.

"A gap year? At twenty-nine years old?" His tone was sceptical.

"That's exactly why I need to do this."

"But what about getting a job? You don't want to get out of the working habit, that won't help your CV."

"I know, Dad. I will get a job, once I've done this. But I've made up my mind." It seemed pointless saying more. To say that he wanted, more than anything, to find a career that inspired him. That he wanted to fall in love, create a family of his own, have a normal life. Friends, a social life. But first, he needed to get better. He wasn't right in the head, and he was going to face up to it before it was too late.

Now that his family knew, he felt energised. He would take the plunge sooner rather than later — as soon as he had the money.

In his inbox was a second wave of emails about the comics. Some were new expressions of interest, others were chasing a response about their valuations, giving Daniel more evidence that they were worth something. One or two even said they'd better any top price he was offered. He didn't trust the sources, though. They seemed to be individuals trying their luck, no website or business address, and their language bordered on pushy. He decided to follow his gut feeling and go back to Bob from Old Comics. He'd studied the website, which looked bona fide, and was reassured by the honesty of Bob's first email.

With a quick exchange of emails he arranged to meet him at Reading station, a convenient meeting place for both of them, the following day. For all the other contenders, he dashed off a standard response: *Sorry, the comics are now sold. Thanks for your interest.*

* * *

He made a list of all the things he'd need for the trip. He pored over maps online, looked for the field where the car boot sale had been held. The village of his childhood had inevitably grown since then, and he could see great swathes of new houses not far from the street where he'd grown up. With a little perseverance, he found the street their house was in, and even the house. That prompted a barrage of memories: the front garden, the sitting room — he could see again the ornaments on the mantelpiece. His dad playing football with him on the lawn. He found the field, the canal and the towpath.

Things were coming together.

Now he had the beginnings of a route. He could at least get started now. He would focus on finding *Golden Serpent* later. There would be boat people and boatyards along the way who might remember the narrowboat, and if he was lucky he might come across it.

Daniel knew in his heart that his chances of finding it after such a long time were slim. But the search would give him purpose, and he already felt better that he'd faced up to the memory that had haunted him for so long. Recognising it for what it was, acknowledging that at its core it was still a mystery, had already relieved the stress that had been building for years. If there was any chance he could discover what had happened to Ryan, that would be great. If not, he would at least have done his best. And along the way, perhaps he would learn more about himself. Who knows, he might find a new life on his travels. Anything was possible.

He looked at his packing list. At the top he'd written, *mobile*. He stared at the word until it looked unfamiliar, the letters popping out of the page. Why would he need a mobile? If he was going to do this properly, he didn't want to be part of the smartphone world. He wanted to live simply, properly simply, just for a few months. He didn't need internet access, GPS, apps to find the local pub or restaurant. He would be taking each day as it came, connecting with the world on a different level, away from roads and houses and shopping centres. Except for his mum and Lauren, there was nobody he needed to keep in touch with, and for them he would make a concession. He would ditch the smartphone for a pay-as-you go model that offered phone calls and texts, nothing more.

Every item on the list got the same treatment. Did he really need three pairs of walking trousers? He already had a pair that transformed into shorts when the lower sections of the legs were unzipped. Two, then. A single change of clothes. Rain gear was important: waterproof jacket, trousers, hat. Proper walking boots and socks. He'd have to choose them carefully to avoid getting blisters. First aid kit with blister cream and plasters. A camping mat and a bivvy bag to keep his sleeping bag dry — all of which he needed to buy. Camping equipment and the backpack would be crucial, and he didn't mind spending money on the right gear. He certainly didn't want to buy more than he absolutely had to. He would grow a beard, however messy. His hair could grow as long as it liked — he'd tie it back if it became unruly. He would become a proper nomad, a traveller, living in nature with no ties, no schedule, no stress. He would return from his adventure looking, *being* different.

As he drifted off to sleep later that night, his mind was full of visions of the future, for once replacing memories of the past. When he woke the following day, he felt more rested than he'd done for a very long time.

* * *

The journey to Oxford felt surreal. He gazed out of the window, watching the countryside stream by in a whirl of green and brown, the towns and villages punctuating the scene with greys and creams and a flash of red or yellow. The train was half-empty and he sat with his backpack upright on the seat next to him like another passenger, a stranger waiting for him to speak.

Now that he was on his way, he felt odd — like a fraud. He hadn't yet broken the tie with the old Daniel or transformed himself into the new. His boots were too new, his backpack too pristine, his face clean-shaven. When he saw his reflection in the window as the train entered a tunnel, he messed his neatly parted hair with his hand. He was in a kind of limbo, like the place between heaven and hell. It wasn't as if he believed in either, but he could find no other words to describe the feeling.

As the train rushed towards its destination, he felt the full range of emotions. Terror gripped him, his heartbeat rising. A moment later, he was elated. He almost called Lauren to tell her how much he missed her, as if he was going on a trip around the world, but held himself back. Disturbing her at work wasn't a good idea.

At one of the few stops, a woman sat down opposite him. He felt a surge of irritation but told himself to relax. The woman smiled at him, rummaged in her bag and brought out a paperback, its cover illustrated with garish colours. Within minutes she was engrossed in her book, and his mind returned to his thoughts and memories, to the drama that had unfolded before his ten-year-old self.

It had all started with those comics — the very comics that were funding his trip. He was glad he'd sold them, they were bad luck. The first-edition *Beano* had certainly stirred up some strong feelings. A couple of people had sent angry messages back, saying he couldn't possibly be getting the best price for them. One even claimed to have emailed him first, with the best offer, and was quite abusive. Noting their names, Daniel was pleased he'd followed his instincts. Bob had been lovely, a real enthusiast, and honest too. They had struck a deal, he had gone away happy and the money was in Daniel's account within days.

Ryan's dad had really wanted those comics, too. Could he really be a murderer, killing his own son and dumping his body unceremoniously in a canal, for the sake of a first-edition *Beano*? It sounded ludicrous.

If he really was a murderer, then what on earth was Daniel thinking? Doubt crept up on him like a prowling cat. What if he did find the narrowboat — what would he do then? Would he confront Ryan's father and accuse him of murder based on something he glimpsed nineteen years ago? The man would surely laugh in his face — or worse. Daniel remembered how frightened he'd been, how strong the hand was that had grabbed him by the scruff of the neck. Was he planning to put himself in danger?

CHAPTER SIXTEEN

Daniel's walk from the station did nothing to relieve the sense of strangeness. The familiar streets of his childhood looked the same, but different. They appeared smaller, less important.

The memories came rushing in . . . Daniel and Lauren as young children being walked to school by their mum, the corner shop, now converted into flats, where they'd bought sweets with their pocket money. The same pavements, with their cracked and broken stones repaired with squares of tarmac, like patches on the knees of worn trousers. The narrow streets, pitted and potholed, more run down than he remembered them. The houses seemed mostly unchanged, though there were signs of builders — skips taking up parking spaces in the road, scaffolding rising like prison gates around one or two houses. And many, many more cars than he remembered.

It was still early in the day, so he decided to walk past his childhood home, though it meant a short detour on the way to the field. Though he wanted to get on his way, it was unlikely he'd be back any time soon, and he was curious to see if his memories were accurate.

As he reached the familiar street, he had a strange sense that he was still only ten years old, walking home from school, his backpack full of books rather than camping gear. There were some changes — a new driveway here, a paved-over front garden, a porch where there'd been none — but he could easily imagine he'd been transported back in time. He crossed the street where he'd crossed it many times before and paused outside his family's old house. Someone had replaced the rickety gate, but the front garden was still there, though the houses on either side had created parking spaces from theirs. A neat circle of plants sat in the middle, with a gravel area around it, narrow flower beds on each side. The front door, which had been blue, was now a trendy shade of grey, but otherwise the house was unchanged on the outside. In the library of his mind, the memories were sliding off the shelves, rising into his mind in shoals, like tiny iridescent fish in a clear sea.

He hesitated for a few minutes, his mind brimming with images. Such moments were dreamlike. He felt the full range of emotions, each associated with a fragment of memory, pushed out by the clamour of the next, and the next. It was both enticing and exhausting, irresistible and uncontrollable.

It took him a few moments to bring himself back, but he didn't want to attract attention by loitering for too long. He dragged himself away and walked off towards the field, his heart beating loud in his temples.

This was it. He was on his way.

But by the time he reached the gate, his feelings had turned from anticipation to deep self-doubt. What on earth was he doing here? He wasn't an explorer, he'd never felt like an adventurer. He wasn't even a walker. It occurred to him that he should have done some practice walks, made sure he could manage a few miles with his backpack on without blisters or muscle strain. He'd done nothing. Again, he felt the sinking feeling in his stomach, the clenching of the muscles in his neck.

Here he was on his big adventure, and he'd messed up before he'd even started. And as for turning amateur detective and chasing a murderer who was quite possibly a figment of his overactive imagination — well, that was simply laughable.

His feet took him to the edge of the canal, where he stood for a few moments, gazing into the water. There was no one else around, the only sound a gentle breeze in the trees around him. Small birds flitted in and out of the hedge, busy searching for berries and insects. The narrow towpath disappeared around a gentle curve a few hundred yards ahead and far into the distance behind.

The image of *Golden Serpent* disappearing around the bend was as clear as day. He gazed at the spot where the bundle sank, imagining Ryan's body slowly decaying under the murky water, his bones sinking into the dark silt on the bottom. But the canal was flat and calm, refusing to give up its secrets.

He was tempted to hang around, feeding on the memory, but it wasn't the right thing to do. He had to give this journey a try. If he ended up with painful feet and sore muscles, that would be part of the experience, not an excuse to give up. There would be good days and bad days, no doubt about it. There would probably be many moments when he would wonder what on earth he was doing, but he had to keep his mind on the true reason for this journey. To find his way.

It wasn't long before he reached a lock. There were no boats and this lock wasn't big enough to warrant a keeper. Boaters had to work the locks themselves, tying up and using a lock handle to operate the gates. Daniel looked forward to seeing the locks in use, and he knew there were some popular places where the locks were stepped, creating an interesting scene for onlookers.

He adjusted his backpack, inspecting the sky. It was overcast, but no rain was forecast. He hoped it would stay that way for his first few days as a novice. The next few weeks and months would be make or break, and whichever it turned out to be, he was going to do his best to see it through.

CHAPTER SEVENTEEN

He spent the first few days quietly, allowing himself time to get used to this new, strange life. He spoke only to greet other walkers and boat people, exchanging a few pleasantries with the cashier when he went to buy food. It didn't take long for him to fall into a pleasant routine, waking early and walking for most of the day, until either he found a good spot to camp or his feet gave him blister warning signals. Luckily for him, though clouds darkened the sky, the weather stayed dry and the earth beneath his feet was firm as he trudged on, past fields and farmhouses, bridges and pubs. The banks of the canal were thick with long grass, burgeoning nettles and cow parsley, while hawthorns threw shadows across the towpath as he walked. Robins flitted from one bush to the next, keeping their distance as they heard his footsteps approaching. The blisters stayed away.

When he reached the first pub on his journey, he hesitated. It would be nice to sit and rest his limbs, watch the water with a glass of beer, even have an early lunch. But tempting though it was, he carried on. He wasn't yet ready to socialise, and he guessed from the bustle inside that the place would soon be full. That's when he remembered it was a weekend, his first on the canal. No wonder there were more boats passing him, more walkers with their dogs, families out, children trailing behind. He'd have to keep track of the weekends if he was to avoid the crowds. Thinking that made him smile — his new definition of a crowd was that he was not on his own on the towpath. It hadn't taken long for him to make that change.

Other things were changing too. Already the quiet had seeped into his spirit. To his surprise after such a short time, his brain was more settled and he was sleeping well. At the end of each day he was physically tired, in a way that he'd never experienced before, and after trying for a few minutes to read one of the few books he'd downloaded onto Lauren's old Kindle for the trip, his eyelids would droop. Sometimes he was asleep by nine in the evening, when the light had only just faded into darkness. He got into the habit of sitting at the entrance to his tent, watching as twilight tiptoed slowly across the fields, into the trees, over the water. This was when the animals would appear — a fox loping slowly past in the distance, rabbits emerging from the low bushes, a mouse scuttling away into the grass. His body was falling into a new rhythm, the rhythm of nature, of animals and plants and trees. It was strangely liberating to leave his phone at the bottom of his bag, and after the first couple of days he forgot even to check it. No TV in the evenings, no pounding music in his earphones. No computer games to stupefy his brain.

It wasn't that the memories weren't still there. They were, in droves, particularly the memory that had brought him here. But they were less defined, less urgent. He could push them away more easily, sending them back to their proper places in the library of his mind.

He needed this time away from the old Daniel. He needed this to last.

* * *

The first thing that happened to disturb his new-found calm was the rain. It came abruptly in the middle of the night, torrents of it, and he was ill-prepared. The little tent was soon saturated, raindrops thundering on the thin fabric, a stiff breeze whipping at the entrance flap, which he'd failed to secure properly. He woke to find the side of his sleeping bag wet where it was in contact with the flimsy nylon, and once he'd scrabbled about moving his possessions away from the sides of the tent, he was wide awake and cold. In the early hours of the morning, pushing the sleeping bag into his ears to drown out the din, his spirits dropped.

Unpleasant thoughts compounded his physical misery. This was going to be a disaster. He'd planned the trip badly. He was never going to find *Golden Serpent*. And at twenty-nine, he was too old for this. He should be moving up the career ladder, buying his own place, planning a family. That's what normal people did. What was he thinking? Did he really imagine he was up to this amateur detective nonsense? This whole venture was ridiculous. He was an idiot to think it would help his mental state.

At last the wind dropped. He drifted into a half-slumber. Strange images and sounds invaded his sleep, colliding with odd parodies of people he used to know. School friends gurned, an aged aunt shrieked in horror, the woman from the corner shop in Iver who had been kind to him when he was small looked at him with no eyes. He woke with a metallic taste in his mouth and a numbing fatigue that kept his body paralysed while he listened to the gentle *drip drip* from outside that punctuated the whisper of drizzle on the roof of the tent. He lay for a while, feeling the stiffness of a bad night's sleep in his limbs, then forced himself up, threw on some clothes and emerged shivering into the cold morning air.

The field he was in rose quickly away from the canal, obscuring the fence on the opposite side and whatever might be grazing there. He hoped it was empty — he didn't particularly want to contend with curious cows or sheep as he packed up his tent. Everything was sodden, clumps of grass flattened, drops falling in a stream from the leaves of the hedge beside him. It was still drizzling and he was hungry, but he decided to get going. He would stop for breakfast when the rain stopped, or find a place on the way, a tea shop where he could dry out. As he packed up his damp sleeping bag, he realised he needed more waterproof bags to deal with nights like the last one.

The light rain turned back to heavy showers as he trudged onwards, his hood shielding his face, his eyes on the ground. His waterproofs soon proved worth the extra money he'd spent on them, shrugging off the relentless water. The towpath turned to mud beneath his feet, and he noticed how different the experience of putting one foot in front of the other was when the ground was soft. The only people he saw over the next few hours were dog walkers, their heads down, their pets bedraggled and muddy. The wind whipped the water's surface into crazy whorls and lines like doodles on paper, while bushes bent their heads low against the raging gusts that lashed the fields.

At last he reached a bridge. His stomach growled with hunger and though he'd kept himself hydrated with sips from his water bottle, he knew he had to eat very soon. There was a small flight of stone steps beside the bridge, and at the top he could see what looked like a pub sign on a building a few hundred metres away. He was reluctant to pull out his map, which should have been in a waterproof bag hanging from his neck, but wasn't — so he was unsure exactly where he was and what pub he was looking at. But it could be several miles to the next one, so he headed in the direction of the sign.

The pub was closed. Not only closed but shut down. Wooden boarding was hammered into place inside the windows, the outside furniture ramshackle and rotting. Daniel's shoulders drooped. Where else could he get some food? There was no shelter on the towpath for him to stop and dry out.

A woman walked towards him on the pavement, an umbrella in one hand, a supermarket bag in the other. On her head was a yellow plastic rain hat, pulled low over her forehead. Daniel perked up. A supermarket! It might have a café attached, or at least he could buy some food to eat as he walked.

"Excuse me," he said. "Is there a café nearby, at all?"

The woman looked up at him. "You made me jump!"

"Sorry."

"Don't worry, I was on another planet," she said with a smile. "A café, here? No, nothing like that. All we have is the newsagent's, and they're not open today. Horrible day, isn't it?" She lifted her chin. "You OK? Looks like you've been on a long trek in this rain."

"I'm fine. It's just, I've made a bit of a mistake, not eating before I set out. Is there anywhere near here where I can get a sandwich and warm up a bit?" As he said it, he realised how cold he was. The lack of food was taking its toll.

"Oh no, dear." The woman shook her head. "Not here."

"Oh well, never mind." He turned back towards the canal, his feet dead weights on the hard pavement. "I'll have to keep going then. Thanks."

The woman called after him. "You could take the bus." She pointed to a bus stop across the road. An old-fashioned sign stood at the edge of the pavement. Behind it was a shelter, part-hidden by an overgrown hedge. "It's only fifteen minutes to the shopping centre."

"Shopping centre?"

"Well, there's a Tesco, and a Homebase, and some kind of shoe store. Not what you'd call a proper shopping centre, but it's useful."

Daniel looked at the bus stop. He didn't want to take a bus, but on the other hand, a bus shelter had never looked so attractive. "Great. Thank you — I'll do that. What do I ask for?"

"Just say Tesco's. That'll get you there. Buses go every hour." She checked her watch with difficulty, the shopping bag waving around her arm. "Only twenty minutes to wait."

CHAPTER EIGHTEEN

The sun was shining, the air warm and fragrant as Poppy left the house with Beans and set off towards the canal.

Each day the line of colourful narrowboats along the towpath seemed to lengthen, as if they were congregating for an event. She stopped by one where the owner was washing the roof, and asked if something was going on.

"You'd think so, wouldn't you?" the man said. "But no, it's just a good stopping place. Easy to walk to the shops and cafés from here, isn't it — there aren't many places on the canal that are so convenient. And the good weather brings the trippers out." He smiled, gesturing at a long blue boat chugging by, a website address on its side advertising its availability for rent.

Poppy was intending to walk for a couple of hours while the weather lasted. The ground was already beginning to harden underfoot after a few days of rain, and many of the boat owners were drying clothes or setting out chairs in the bright sunlight.

Leaving the boats and the town behind, she breathed in the peace of the canal and the countryside, her spirits rising. So she was dismayed when a large group of walkers approached, a sea of blue T-shirts indicating that they were in some sort of organised event. The first few passed by, nodding and smiling in greeting, and then Poppy saw how many of them there were. The trail of blue T-shirts seemed to stretch for miles. The path here was narrow and Poppy had to pause to let groups of people past.

Once most of them had gone, she asked a couple of stragglers what the event was all about.

"We're walking for the Alzheimer's Trust," the woman said. "It's called the Memory Walk. We're all walking in memory of someone we've lost."

"How lovely," Poppy said. "I've just lost my gran to Alzheimer's. Perhaps I should join you."

"Do!" they said. "You'd be very welcome."

She smiled, shaking her head. "Sadly, I'm working later. Perhaps another time."

They waved as they left, a blue snake winding into the distance.

Poppy stared after them. A seed had been sown in her head. She could walk to raise money for Alzheimer's, in memory of Gran. What better thing to do than remember her grandmother by helping others with the same terrible disease? She had holiday owing. She could easily plan something in the summer months, and Beans would love it. They could camp, or stay in hotel boats or inns. It would be an adventure, and fun.

Perhaps this was what she needed. To commemorate Gran would give her life a purpose, even for a short time.

* * *

"Are you sure you want to go on your own?" her mum said, her forehead creasing with worry. "It doesn't sound very safe. You never know, some of those canal people can be a bit strange . . ."

"Of course. I'll be fine — lots of women walk on their own. And actually, canal people are really friendly. I've never felt threatened walking the towpath."

"But you've not stayed overnight. Or walked very far from home, have you?"

"No, but the days are long in the summer, and I'll have my mobile. I can call or text you every day, to reassure you. Honestly, Mum, I thought you'd like the idea." Her mother's anxiety was dismaying. She couldn't do something like this if she knew her mum was constantly worrying about her.

"I do, I think it's a great thing to do. You're a kind, thoughtful girl, and I'm proud of you for even thinking of doing something like this."

"Mum, I'm twenty-five years old. I could be living away from home, getting up to all sorts of stuff and you wouldn't even know, so how could you worry then?"

Her mother laughed. "True. But I will know, won't I?"

"If I do this — and nothing's fixed yet — I promise I'll stay safe. You can track me on my mobile, I'll check in, I won't put myself in danger. I'll even buy a personal alarm if it makes you feel better. And I have a dangerous dog to protect me!"

"The only thing dangerous about Beans is he's a tripping hazard," her mum said. She smiled. "I can see your mind's set on it. I know you'll be sensible. It's just all those stories you read in the papers, about girls disappearing or being attacked — it's terrifying. Any mother would worry."

"I get it, Mum, believe me." Poppy hugged her mum. "But if you look at the statistics, those things happen very rarely. And you can be unlucky wherever you are, whatever you're doing."

"Well I'm grateful for mobile phones, anyway. At least we can keep in touch. If it's what you really want."

"I think it is. It'll be good for me, and I want to honour Gran in some kind of tangible way."

"Which is lovely of you. But do talk to your dad. Make sure he's comfortable with it."

Poppy sighed, giving her mum a sideways look.

"Yes, you're an adult. But you're still our daughter. Just reassure him, please."

"OK, I will."

For the first time since Gran died, Poppy felt a thrill of excitement. Though it was only going to be a short trip, she had the feeling it could be life-changing.

* * *

Dad couldn't have been more supportive. "You're a grown woman now, with your own mind," he said. "I know you'll be sensible. I think it's a grand idea."

"Mum's worried, though, Dad. You will reassure her, won't you? I really want to do this. I'll research it properly, book places to stay when I can. I'm sure I'll be fine."

"I know you will." Her dad patted her on the shoulder. "It'll be a good adventure, for a good cause. Just stay in touch."

Alone in Gran's room, Poppy lay on the bed. She could feel Gran's presence, even though it was many weeks now since she had passed away.

"What do you think, Gran?" she whispered.

It's a perfectly lovely idea. The answer rang through her mind. *A proper adventure! I'll be with you in spirit, that's for sure.*

"You always will be, Gran. I'll never forget you. You never know, if it works out, I might do it every year, to remember you."

Marvellous. You always were my favourite grandchild.

"I'm your only grandchild."

Yes, so you are. And a wonderful one, at that.

"Thank you, Gran. You're wonderful, too."

Poppy opened her eyes and stood up. She was ready to prepare for her big adventure.

CHAPTER NINETEEN

Fortified by a large tuna baguette, Daniel began to feel better. Inside his waterproofs he was dry, and now he was warming up. His tent and his bedding still needed airing, though. Tonight wouldn't be pleasant if he had to sleep in damp bedclothes.

Outside, the dark clouds seemed to have lifted a fraction, allowing the sun's warmth to filter through, and he reckoned the weather would clear up quite soon. Perhaps he'd be able to stop somewhere and spread his things over a branch or a hedge to dry before night-time.

He decided to look out for a boat hotel or an inn if it started to rain again. He might treat himself even if the weather improved. A warm bed, a proper bathroom and a good night's sleep were hugely tempting. Consulting his map, he saw that there were two pubs marked some miles away on his path northwards to Braunston. He might make it by nightfall if he started now and made good progress.

But not long after he started, he came across a narrowboat stuck across the canal, its bow clearly grounded on the far side, the stern wedged against the bank. It tilted slightly, its hull leaning towards the towpath. He knew that canals were, in general, not deep, but this boat seemed to have found a particularly shallow spot. Perhaps they'd been trying to turn round, or not noticed when the boat drifted to one side and got stuck. A woman appeared from below with a pole and started to push at the bank, while the door at the bow opened to reveal a slender lad of about fifteen, bent on pushing at the opposite bank with what looked like a broom handle.

"Can I help?" Daniel said. He couldn't walk on while they were so clearly struggling.

The woman noticed him for the first time. She was clearly upset — her hair had fallen forward over her eyes, her cheeks flushed pink. From her clothing, Daniel decided she was not a boat dweller. White trousers were not regular boating attire, or gold jewellery.

"Oh, thank you so much. We don't know what we're doing. We were trying to turn but there wasn't enough room. Stupid of us. Now we're well and truly stuck."

Daniel looked from one end of the boat to the other. It was painted dark green, with a black roof and colourful flowers painted in the traditional style on the side. "Let's see," he said. "Is that your son up the other end?"

She nodded.

"Could you get him to throw the rope to me from the front?" If the boy could get the rope to the bank, he could pull from the towpath while they pushed with their poles at either end.

The woman picked her way along the side of the boat to talk to the boy, who took the mooring line and started to swing it towards the towpath.

"Whoah, hold on." Daniel discarded his backpack and hurried towards the front of the boat. But the boy had already hurled the rope in a messy heap. It landed in the canal, a good few feet from the towpath.

"Roll it up," Daniel shouted, demonstrating with his arms. "Like this. Hold the rope with your left hand and loop it round your elbow."

The boy coiled the soggy rope around his forearm, grimacing.

"Again, that's it, until it's all taken up. Great. Now I suggest you stand up high — are you OK to stand on that box?" Daniel could see a sturdy wooden box next to the spot where the boy was standing. "Take your time. Now swing two or three times. One, two, three—"

The boy took another wild swing and the coiled rope landed in the water, a few feet closer than last time. His face fell. "I can't do it. Mum, can you come and help me?"

"I can't throw, you know I can't," the woman called from the other end of the boat.

"You can do it," Daniel said. "You were closer this time. Come on, coil it up again." He waited for the boy to gather the rope around his arm. "This time, throw it higher. I'll count you in. One, two, three!" The boy circled his arm to its full length, stepping forward and throwing high. The rope landed half in, half out of the murky water a couple of feet away from Daniel. He ran to grasp it before it snaked back into the canal.

"Perfect! There, you did it, no problem. Now, get your pole and push while I pull."

A few minutes' heaving and the boat was free. He showed the lad how to pull the boat along the side of the water with the rope, which brought the back end in line with the front. Then he helped them moor to the side, banging in stakes with a mallet.

"Thank you again," the woman said. "My husband always looked after this side of things, made it look easy. Stupid of me, really, should've made sure I learned the basics. Here, would you like a cup of tea? Piece of cake? It's the least we can do."

Daniel hesitated. The rescue operation had taken the best part of an hour already and he was keen to get going again. But the mention of cake was tempting and there was a hopeful look on the boy's face. "That would be great."

"Come aboard, then," she said, inviting him on with a swing of her arm.

* * *

He almost regretted the decision to go on board when he realised how much talking one person could do in a short space of time — in the half an hour or so he was there, the woman, Jane, barely paused for breath. He heard the entire story of her life, or at least it felt so, and he could feel the deep embarrassment of the boy, Callum. Jane had lost her husband the previous year, to cancer, when Callum was only thirteen. He was missing his father badly. Jane was doing her best to be both father and mother to him, and was determined to do all the things they would have done as a threesome. This was the first time they'd ventured out on the boat on their own.

Though Callum stayed close by and was clearly listening, he stared out at the canal the whole time his mum was talking, except for a brief exchange of looks with Daniel when her back was turned. His expression said it all, and he seemed grateful for Daniel's sympathetic shoulder shrug.

Daniel left the narrowboat with the remainder of a banana cake and a full flask of coffee. As he climbed off the boat, he remembered the question he'd promised himself he'd ask whenever he came across boaters.

"By the way, you don't happen to have seen a boat called *Golden Serpent*, do you? Dark blue, with a gold snake painted on the side — quite distinctive."

They both looked up at him from the driving platform. "I haven't noticed one like that," Jane said. "How about you, Cal?"

Callum shook his head. "No, but I can message you if I see it."

Daniel scrabbled through his bag to retrieve his mobile, and smiled at the look on the boy's face when he saw it. "I'm trying not to rely too much on technology," he said. "It's pretty basic, but I need to keep in touch with my family."

As he walked away, he wondered if he should have warned them not to approach *Golden Serpent*'s owner, or to mention Daniel's name. When they chugged slowly past him a few minutes later, giving him a wave, he almost called out to them. But it was ridiculous even to think it. It would be a miracle if they came across the boat, and even more unlikely that Ryan's father would still own it. A chance in a million, in fact — so beyond the law of averages, it wasn't worth worrying about.

He took a moment to inwardly congratulate himself on taking up Jane's offer to go on board, despite her incessant talking. He had resolved to use this summer to cure himself of the crippling shyness that had dogged him since childhood. He knew in his heart it was isolating him and creating barriers in his life. Most importantly, it was stopping him from being happy. Even at nearly thirty, he was still beset with anxiety about the simplest things: going to the shops, stopping in the street for a chat with an acquaintance, a neighbour popping by for a chat. On occasions like these, he suffered from an overwhelming feeling of uselessness, unable to conjure up even the most banal small talk. His mind would go blank, he imagined anything he said would be boring — or plain stupid — and so he'd avoid such meetings whenever possible.

The result was that he had next to no friends. Only Lauren understood his inability to socialise. Most people ended up labelling him unfriendly, stand-offish or worse. He didn't blame them. To others, he would certainly seem so.

The panic attacks could be terrifying, to the point where his fear of having one was worse than the event itself. He knew what he was experiencing was 'fear of the fear', but there was nothing he could do to help himself. When a panic attack came, it was unavoidable, unpredictable and devastating. He would break out in a sweat, his hands shaking. His breathing would go wrong, his chest contracting until he feared he couldn't take another breath, and his heart would beat so hard he could hear nothing else. The blood draining from his face, he would instinctively bend double over his knees, his legs close to collapse.

The first time it happened, he thought he was having a heart attack and was going to die. It took him days to recover from the shock. Since then, the avoidance strategy had stood him in good stead, but the fear remained. Every day was a challenge, the consequences of avoidance a huge burden. There were times when he felt stable for a few months at a time, but then, without warning, he'd be poleaxed by panic. He'd be back to where he started, unable to function, terrified of everything.

On this trip, he was determined to explore his fear. Canal people were known to be a friendly bunch, and though his experience with Ryan's dad had been the opposite, that was surely an exception.

As he walked, he chose his moments. He said hello and walked on without feeling guilty for not stopping. It was obvious he was a walker from the kit on his back. He was forced into shops only when he ran out of supplies, but he stocked up in small villages and avoided straying into the big towns. He stopped to chat to boaters — or not — without recrimination. He even had a valid question to ask them, a possible conversation-starter.

Golden Serpent had its uses, even if he never found it.

CHAPTER TWENTY

He was looking forward to reaching the countryside after a long stretch of buildings. He still had a distance to go, according to the map, but another day or so should do it.

The morning was sunny, with patches of white cloud that took the heat out of the air. He'd already discarded his jumper and was in shorts and T-shirt, enjoying the freshness on his bare skin. His beard was quite visible now, his hair unruly. Tan lines had appeared on his ankles, around his neck and on his upper arms. He was beginning to feel at home on the canals, learning how best to pitch his tent so the wind didn't catch it, how to set his sleeping bag in the most comfortable position, getting familiar with the noises of wild creatures in the night.

Each day as he walked, he focused on the present. This was a kind of homework for him. Every day he practised pushing memories away or creating new ones, denying the past its dominance in his mind. This, along with challenging himself to engage with people along the way, was how he would create a new way to survive in the world.

Some days it was hard, though, to tear himself away from the old habits. Today, he focused for the first hour or so when there was nobody around. He paused to watch a gaggle of ducks feeding along the edge of the water, spotted a kingfisher in a bush over the other side and smiled at the owner of a quirky boat with gnomes all along its roof. But as he did that, an image blossomed into his mind, of a street he'd been to as a boy, a garden filled with gnomes. Gnomes fishing in the pond, digging in the flower beds . . .

He was still absorbed in the memory when he came to an underpass, the traffic rumbling and crashing overhead, echoing in the corridor created by the mass of concrete. Ahead he was dimly aware of a man's figure, but by the time he reached the grey graffitied wall on his right, the man had disappeared and he thought nothing of it. The first he knew of any danger was a thud from his left.

He lost his balance and fell with a sickening crash, his backpack pulling him sideways. The dark shape of a man stood over him, a black cap shielding his face, long hair reaching narrow shoulders. As Daniel struggled to his feet, a vicious kick landed in his stomach, winding him. Another hit him square on the chin as he writhed in pain.

Sparks flashed in his eyes, his hand flew to his face, but a powerful hand forced his arm behind him. He struggled and yelled, his feet scrambling on the slippery grass, but to no avail. All at once his backpack was gone, a figure in dark clothes was running, and a scream of rage — a woman's voice — joined his own shouts, echoing eerily through the bleak concrete passage.

Dazed, he pushed himself to a sitting position and tried to focus, a curtain of black falling across his line of sight. There were shouts, thumps and a woman's voice again, but the words were indistinct. He hung his head between his knees, praying for the swaying, sick feeling to go, so he could run after the man and retrieve his bag.

Without it he was finished. The end of his trip, his recovery, all his plans smashed.

A hand tapped his shoulder. "You OK?" a woman said.

He made an attempt to raise his head. The sparks still flew. He groaned, letting his head drop again. "My bag . . ."

"Don't worry," the voice said. "We've got it."

A wave of relief washed over his body and his shoulders slumped. "Sorry," he whispered.

"Take as long as you like. Do you want us to call an ambulance?"

That opened his eyes. "No, definitely not," he mumbled. The pain in his jaw shot up his cheek like the worst kind of toothache. He groaned, squinting up at the woman's face, the wall behind her too bright. There was a movement behind her and a dim shape resolved itself into another head, a boy's face, vaguely familiar. It was Callum, and as the woman's face became clearer, he saw that it was Jane.

"Are you sure?" She crouched beside him. "You don't look too sharp."

"I'll be fine. No doctors, please." Daniel tried out his jaw with a still trembling hand. Nothing seemed to be broken, though the pain shot through his face. He didn't dare open his mouth more than a fraction.

"Is it your jaw?" Jane peered at his face. "I can see where you were hit, there's a nasty bruise coming. What a bastard."

Daniel sat up gingerly. His head was clearing slowly, the dim shapes around him sharpening. He still felt sick and shaky. "My bag?"

"It's here." Callum dragged it round from behind him. "I think everything's there, he didn't have time to open it up."

"Thank you so much." Daniel checked the pockets and almost wept with relief. Everything was in it. Bank cards, cash, driving licence. Map, phone. Stupid — he should at least be keeping his bank cards and phone on his person. This could have been a disaster, but for Jane and Callum.

His jaw and lip were swelling now, and though he tried, he could barely speak.

"Look, you can't carry on like this, not straight away," Jane said as they helped him up.

The world tilted for a moment, then righted itself.

"Come to the boat, it's just past the bridge." Jane took his arm. "We'll get you cleaned up and rested. Cup of tea and something to eat — that'll sort you out."

* * *

Installed in the lounge area of the boat, Daniel sat dazed, a mug of warm, sweet tea beside him.

"Callum does karate," Jane said without being asked. "Black belt."

Daniel glanced at the boy, who nodded, blushing. He barely looked strong enough to lift the teapot, let alone beat off a grown man.

"Mum was right in there, too," he said. "You should have seen her. She was scary. He ran off like a rabbit when she piled in."

Jane laughed. "I saw what was happening, realised it was you. He was a skinny piece of work — didn't frighten me."

"Could have had a knife, though," Daniel mumbled through the dull ache that had replaced the searing pain in his jaw. "You could have been hurt. Thank you for helping me."

Jane pulled open a drawer and started to rummage. "You're going to need a good supply of painkillers for that jaw." She threw a packet to Callum, who handed it over.

"I have some in my bag," Daniel said. But he didn't trust his legs to hold him up while he looked, so he popped a couple of Jane's pills onto the table. He needed to gather his strength before putting his sore lip to the mug.

"Have some more, I reckon you'll need them."

"Thanks." Daniel closed his eyes for a moment as a wave of nausea rose from his stomach.

"I don't think you should carry on walking today," Jane said, sitting beside him. "You're as white as a sheet, and look, your hands are shaking."

"Maybe. But I can't camp here." The further he got away from that bridge the better, and he needed to get going soon in case the man returned.

"Of course not. But how about you come with us for a bit? You can get some distance between you and that creep and have a rest — you'll feel better for it. You can have a lie down in Callum's cabin. We travel very slowly, but we can get you away from this area."

Daniel was about to shake his head — this trip was about walking, not boating, and the idea of being with people right now was not appealing. He found himself longing for an empty field and his sleeping bag. But he did feel terrible, and his sleeping bag was still wet from the night's storm. He glanced at Callum's face, which had lit up as he waited for Daniel's reply.

"Thank you. That's a really kind offer. Perhaps a short rest would help."

"And some food. Rest now, then we'll get some lunch when you're ready. You'll be much better in a couple of hours, apart from those bruises."

Normally he would run a mile from a bossy person like Jane. But right now, he was shaky and his confidence had taken a knock. A few hours on a boat was just what he needed.

CHAPTER TWENTY-ONE

It was strange, the day of Poppy's departure, made even more strange by the fact that the first few miles were so familiar, part of her daily walk with Beans. It was Mum's day off and she had insisted on accompanying them as far as the canal. The anticipation had rubbed off on Beans, who could barely contain his excitement as they set off, prancing and jumping as if he had eight legs rather than three.

"You don't need to see me off, Mum," Poppy said. "I'm only going for a few weeks."

"I know. It feels different, though — as if you're off to travel the world."

"Really, Mum — what are you like? I'm not getting on a plane, or even a train."

"Still, we'll miss you." Her mum took her arm as they walked.

"I know. I'll keep in touch, I promise."

When she'd told Karen at the rescue centre what she was planning, Karen had suggested she took a proper break over the summer. "You work so hard, Poppy," she said. "I've been worried about you since your Gran died. You haven't given yourself a chance to recover, you've just thrown yourself back into work — for which I'm grateful, of course. But

I think you need more time. You look pale, and you're not yourself, still. Take a month — take more. I've had plenty of offers of help over the summer holidays, from students, even trainee vets, so we'll be fine. And there'll always be a job for you here."

Poppy was taken aback — it hadn't occurred to her to ask for more time off than a week. But when she stopped to think about it, a month sounded wonderful. She had enough money to last a while and if it went particularly well, she had the little pot of money her Gran had left her. She didn't intend to touch it so soon, but it was reassuring to know it was there if she needed it.

Asking for sponsorship wasn't Poppy's strong suit. She'd felt awkward at first about raising money as part of her tribute to Gran. Though it was for an excellent cause, she still felt guilty about approaching people, even if she knew they would support her. She didn't want them to feel obliged, knowing how hard it was for some of her friends to make ends meet. But her father's work colleagues had started her off with a big pledge and even her mum's boss was happy to donate. A surprising number of people had been affected by Alzheimer's in one way or another, and she'd heard many stories of friends or relatives who'd either had the disease or had dealt with the effects of it.

She hadn't even mentioned the fundraising to Karen. Running an animal rescue was like walking a tightrope, she knew, and Karen's business depended largely on the generosity of donors and friends. But one day just before Poppy was to leave, Karen had pressed some notes into her hand and made Poppy accept them. She refused to take no for an answer.

The small figure of her mother faded into the distance as Poppy gave a final wave. Though she'd tried to make light of this trip, it was clear to them all that this was, in a way, a seminal moment. A bit like a student taking a year out — though rather late, she thought wryly, at twenty-five years old — this was a journey that could teach her a lot, take her to new experiences, places and people. She hoped it would, but that didn't mean she was leaving home for good. As she walked, Beans trotting ahead of her as usual, the guilt she felt at leaving her parents faded and a wonderful sense of anticipation took over. The future was full of possibility, and she was walking into it with Gran by her side.

Poppy was by nature friendly and gregarious, never one to hold back. She talked to everyone on the same level. She found people fascinating, wanting to understand their lives, their views on the world, their deepest secrets. Sometimes this delving into people's private worlds got her into trouble, but mostly people were charmed by her openness, her relaxed way of finding common ground. They trusted her instinctively. Poppy wasn't frightened of meeting new people or of travelling alone. She had Beans, and he was enough — the best company she could ask for, affectionate and happy.

She'd never camped before. She'd bought a cheap, pop-up tent so she didn't have to worry too much about putting it up. It was tiny but would serve the purpose, and she had a lovely warm sleeping bag, courtesy of her dad, who understood how important the weather would become to someone spending all their time outdoors. And Poppy didn't mind dirt, or sweat, or physical effort — nobody working with animals could afford to worry about those things. She'd take a shower when she had the chance, look after herself by eating properly, take care of Beans. Otherwise, she wouldn't worry too much.

As she walked away from Banbury there were fewer people around, and soon the sounds of traffic and other urban noises faded away. All she could hear was the tramp of her feet, the tinkle of Beans's tag on his collar, the birds calling and the occasional lapping of water at the edge of the canal. When a boat passed, it was an occasion. The water swished and swirled against the bank, the engine rumbled, people waved and smiled.

At her first lock, she stopped to watch a long narrowboat negotiate its way in. A man guided it at the tiller, his hand on the control, leaning out to check the boat was straight as it glided into the corridor of the lock. The woman with him hurried with a line to tether the bow, then waited at the gates to wind them open once the lock had filled. As the water level rose, the woman stooped to stroke Beans.

"On a long walk, then?" she said, indicating Poppy's big backpack.

"I expect so. I've only just started, but I'm going where my feet take me," Poppy said.

"Sounds good. For the summer? Or just for a holiday?"

"Probably the summer, or until I get fed up. But I'm doing it in memory of my Gran. She . . . died recently." She still found it hard to say the words.

"I'm so sorry. But it's lovely that you're doing something positive in her memory." The woman signalled to her boating partner and turned back to Poppy.

"She had Alzheimer's. I'm raising money for the Alzheimer's Trust."

"Brilliant, that's wonderful. If you can wait a minute, I'll give you some money."

"Oh, there's no need, honestly. I didn't mean—"

"No, I want to. My mother-in-law had the disease. It's horrible. We lost her far too early, it was heartbreaking. I insist. My husband will be happy to contribute. Wait a minute — I'll hop back on and get my purse."

Poppy waited for the boat to chug through the open gates.

The woman disappeared into the bowels of the boat. She reappeared with a ten-pound note in her hand.

Poppy was learning to be gracious when people offered her money. "That's so kind," she said. She tucked the note into the pocket of her bag she'd reserved for donations.

"Not at all. Glad to help, and good luck on your walk."

Poppy stood watching as they left, unbidden tears blurring her vision.

CHAPTER TWENTY-TWO

Daniel drifted in and out of sleep, the ache in his jaw dulled by the painkillers. On one of two small beds squeezed into Callum's tiny cabin, he watched as dappled reflections of sunlight on the water patterned the walls. The feeling of calm was overwhelming. Though he'd meant only to lie down for a few minutes until the effects of the attack wore off, the gentle rocking of the boat, the thrum of the engine and the soft light had all conspired to put him to sleep.

Consciousness returned gradually when the background sounds changed. The boat slowed, changed gear and was still for a few moments before inching forward. From his bed, Daniel could see a huge wooden gate pass by, then the blackened side of an empty lock, so close it was all but touching the boat's hull. A dull thud followed as the gates closed, then silence. He lay still, feeling the sway of the water as the lock filled, watching as the sky reappeared above. Nothing happened fast on a canal boat. The deep sense of peace was unfamiliar but comforting. He could feel his body rallying, his injuries healing.

He eased himself to a sitting position, letting his legs swing to the floor. His lower lip was horribly swollen and he could only imagine the bruising on the rest of his face. He tried standing — he was steady enough. Opening the door to the cabin, he saw another boat immediately alongside, darkening the narrow corridor that led to the kitchen. Its sides were dark blue, the paint flaking in places. He recoiled in shock as Ryan's face looked out at him from the dim interior, mouthing something. He stumbled backwards into a flimsy wall with a cry as the sharp movement jarred his injury.

When he looked again, Ryan's face had gone and all he could see was the rather ordinary interior of the other narrowboat. Its name, *Genevieve*, was painted in white towards the bow. It was too much to imagine he'd come across *Golden Serpent* by chance. His mind was playing tricks on him again.

He took the steps to the platform, where Jane stood waiting for the water to bring the boat to its new level before the gates ahead could be opened.

"Feeling any better?" She peered at his face. "Hm. Should have got some ice on that. I'll see what I can find when we get going. Here, sit on this." She indicated a wooden storage box to her left, a thin cushion perched on top.

"Much better, thanks. I dozed off." Forming the words wasn't easy with a swollen jaw and a fat lip. "It seems to have helped. I'll stand, thanks. It's nice to see what's going on."

Callum was on the towpath, holding a line to the boat. Soon they were level with him and the gates were opening. A man turned the handle with both hands, letting the boats drift gently through.

"How's the jaw?" Callum said as he jumped aboard. "Bruising up a bit."

"I haven't seen myself yet." Daniel fingered his lip. "I must look pretty ropey though. It's sore."

"Callum, let's moor just up there," Jane said. "Let's stop for lunch. Soup, perhaps?"

"Soup sounds like an excellent idea," Daniel lisped.

The soup, some kind of spiced vegetable, was perfect, though it was cool by the time he'd finished, taking only the tiniest of sips from a spoon. Every mouthful caused a jab of pain.

"Anything else?" Jane said.

"Could I possibly have a shower, please?" Daniel said. "Sorry to be so much trouble."

"No trouble at all. We're on holiday, after all, we've got plenty of time. I'd hate to think of you trying to walk on after that beating. There's no way you could have run if he'd come back."

She flicked a switch in the corridor. "Just give the water twenty minutes to warm up," she said. "I'll get you a towel."

Daniel leaned his head back against the wall of the cabin, closing his eyes for a moment. This wasn't what he'd had in mind for his trip.

* * *

"Look after yourself, Daniel!" Jane called as the narrowboat pulled away from him.

"Especially in the tunnels!" Callum added.

Daniel smiled, as far as he could, and gave them a wave. He still felt guilty that he couldn't show his gratitude properly, after all they'd done for him.

Without them, this whole venture would have come to a sudden, humiliating halt. To pick himself up and start again after such a setback would have been beyond him. He wouldn't have had the strength of character to go back, buy all the kit again, apply for new credit cards and driving licence. He would have crept back into his old life like a cockroach into a hole. Failure would have sent him spiralling down. Especially as this was supposed to be his chance to find a way through and make something of his life. Or at least come to terms with it.

In his backpack, he had Jane and Callum's mobile numbers, email and address. He would send them a thank you gift when he got back, something for the boat, perhaps — a planter of flowers, a set of traditional painted pots, a picture for the wall. He would look for something en route, and if he couldn't carry it, he'd have the shop send it.

He'd spent two days and nights with them, and by the time he'd left, they were the best of friends. Jane was kind and funny, brave and adventurous. With Daniel on board, Callum had loosened up and Daniel had seen the boy beneath the shy exterior. They'd negotiated locks together, Callum showing Daniel how to open and close the gates, pointing out the hazards and the shortcuts the seasoned boaters took for granted. They'd made good progress, and when Daniel had finally put his foot on solid ground again, he was well away from the mugger under the bridge.

Daniel had learned some valuable lessons from the experience. Not to carry all his possessions in his bag was one of them. To watch out in built-up areas and to keep his wits about him.

He'd been surprised to find travelling by canal boat so enjoyable, feeling his body revive as the countryside eased by. From the boat you could observe nature properly, hear it and feel it in the air. You could smell the water, the tang of a farmyard, the scent of wild flowers. Birdsong and the gentle lapping of water were the first sounds he'd heard in the morning. So different from before, when he'd wake to the roar of airplanes, traffic, car horns, sirens and the acrid whiff of diesel fumes. This was a new world to Daniel and he was experiencing it through heightened senses. And for once, his memory was not always centre-stage.

CHAPTER TWENTY-THREE

He wore his baseball cap with the peak pulled down low over his face to hide the bruises. He didn't want to scare anyone. Thankfully, there weren't too many people about: walkers in pairs or with their dogs. He passed by when he could with his injury away from them. The weather was on his side, the skies heavy with rain, but not giving up their load yet, the air freshening. It was a weekday, too, most children safely at school.

He was soon approaching the boatyard he'd spotted on the map. A boatyard would be his best chance to find *Golden Serpent*. The narrowboat would be old now, and if it was still on the water it would need maintenance. Over the years, something must have gone wrong with it at some point. He guessed that people who worked on boats would be seasoned canal people, familiar with both owners and boats. Someone would surely know *Golden Serpent*, with a name like that and the distinctive painting on the hull.

He approached the boatyard with trepidation, his breath quickening. He knew immediately what was happening — a panic attack. The very thought of Ryan's dad triggered a danger reaction in his brain, his body entering fight or flight mode. He paused on the towpath, pretending to be looking across the canal. He was only going to ask about the boat, and he knew the chances of finding it there were so low as to be almost impossible. But that made little difference to his body's instinctive reaction. It was out of his control.

He took great gulps of air, letting it out slowly, counting . . . ten, eleven seconds. Repeat. *There is no danger. There is no danger.* He watched a boat slide slowly past, and reminded himself of that wonderful feeling he'd had when dozing on the narrowboat, letting the gentle rhythm of the engine, the slap of the water beneath the boat take him away.

A few moments later he was heading for the boatyard, where boats of all colours and sizes were moored side by side, forming a bridge across the widened area of water, custom-created for repair and maintenance of canal craft.

At first it looked as if nobody was about. He glanced into a low wooden building with a huge open door, a workshop with an array of tools hanging on the walls, engine parts strewn over massive workbenches.

"Hello?" he called, his courage deserting him. "Is anyone here?"

A heavy footstep from behind startled him, setting his heart racing again.

"Morning." A large man in a stained blue boiler suit stood in the entrance to the workshop, wiping his hands on a rag. His receding grey hair was pulled back into a thin ponytail, and on his arms were great swirls of dark tattoos. "Can I help you?"

He sounded friendly enough. Daniel swallowed, the blood rushing to his face. "Hi, I'm Daniel." He held out his hand, and it was enveloped in a gritty, greasy paw. On the back of the hand was drawn an enormous, baleful spider. Daniel had to stop himself flinching.

"John. This is my workshop."

Aware of the man's eyes on his battered face, Daniel turned away to look through the doors at the line of boats awaiting attention.

"I'm walking the canals."

The man smiled, showing a glinting gold filling. "How's the other guy?" he said.

Daniel tried to grin, without much success. "It looks worse than it is. I was mugged, but they didn't get anything."

The man nodded, stepping over to one of the benches. "Good for you."

He didn't explain that a fifteen-year-old boy and his mum had chased his attacker off. No point in humiliating himself. "I — it's a long shot, but I'm looking for a particular narrowboat, called *Golden Serpent*. It's dark blue, with a—"

"Picture of a serpent on the side? In gold? Yeah, I know it."

Another flush, this time of fear, shot through Daniel's scalp. "You know it?"

"I've worked here my whole life, so I've seen a few boats in my time. Worked on that boat more than once. Reckon she's getting on a bit now, eh?" John picked up a screwdriver and started to tinker with what looked like part of an oven. Though it could have been part of anything, for all Daniel knew.

"Any idea where it — she — might be?"

There was a pause. Daniel waited for him to ask why he was looking for *Golden Serpent*.

"Could be anywhere, haven't seen her in maybe a couple of years. But she never seems to go too far. Oxford and the Grand Union, I reckon. Stays south. Though she may have changed hands, of course. I wouldn't know if she had."

"Did you know the owner at all? When you fixed the boat, I mean?"

The man put down his screwdriver and leaned on the workbench, eyeing Daniel as if assessing his strength. Daniel began to feel uncomfortable. He was relieved when John seemed to wake from a daydream, dug in his pocket and drew out a pair of reading glasses. They were broken on one side, giving him a lopsided, comical look.

"I met him." He went back to his tinkering.

"Sorry to ask, but a long time ago, I met his son. I'm trying to find him . . ." He tailed off, not sure how to explain why he was trying to find a boy he'd known nineteen years ago and hadn't seen since.

The man frowned. "Had a son, did he? Poor lad."

Daniel hesitated. "Why do you say that?"

"Well, I don't know why you're looking for them, but that man's a bad 'un. If he had a boy, I reckon the lad would have wanted to leave as soon as he was old enough."

"Bad in what way, can I ask?"

"In trouble with the police. Drugs. Nicking stuff. Not to be trusted, I'd say. I had the devil of a time getting paid when I fixed his boat."

The blood drained from Daniel's face. He wiped slick, sweaty palms on his trousers. "I see. Thank you."

"If you find the boat, take care." The man turned back to his work. "You don't want to get in with his sort."

"Yes — I mean no. Thank you. You don't remember his name, do you?"

"Collins. Yes, that's it, Collins. Bad sort, that one."

Collins. Daniel's search had got a little easier.

As Daniel left, John was still muttering. "Bad," he was saying. "A bad 'un, that one."

* * *

So, he hadn't been wrong about Ryan's father. Daniel wondered again what he was doing. He didn't want to risk another beating, not for the rest of his life. But Ryan's face was etched into his memory, his yells echoing as if Daniel had only just turned away. The heavy bag falling slowly, sinking into the dark water as the narrowboat slid onwards, the flash of white from a trainer. He had to find out, if only to prove to himself that the incident was real and not something his mind had conjured up to torment him.

He barely noticed his surroundings for the next few miles as his feet found their rhythm, but when he forced himself back to the present, he realised how hungry he was. Breakfast on the boat seemed hours ago and his mouth watered when he remembered the fresh bread and cheese that Jane had given him before he left.

He didn't stop for long. He wanted to get on his way while the weather was good, move on into the countryside before dark. The memory of his attacker drove him on. It would be very bad luck to get mugged a second time. A quiet field in the countryside was what he needed, as isolated as possible. Cows and sheep he could manage. People were another matter.

Daniel wondered if he could track down Ryan's dad with the little information he had. His name was Collins and he was a petty criminal who lived on a boat called *Golden Serpent* that moved around the canals in the south of England. He had a son called Ryan — or possibly lived with a boy called Ryan, who wasn't his son. If he was alive, Ryan must have gone to another school. Perhaps there was a record of him somewhere. There would have been checks on children of school age. Would schools keep records for nineteen years? Trying to find Ryan that way seemed just impossible.

But perhaps, just perhaps, he could find his father.

Daniel toyed with the idea of visiting a library, where he could get on the internet and do some searching. If Collins was a petty criminal, there was a chance he might have done some thieving or drug-dealing along his journey. The local papers might have covered the story. If so, there was a chance Daniel could find out more. But right now he was anxious to get through the built-up areas and back into the countryside. There would be more chances to get to a library or an internet café in Banbury, where he might find traces of the narrowboat and its owner. He was homing in on it now, and he'd be there in a day or two.

In the meantime, he'd ask at other boatyards, talk to people who lived on the canals. They were the most likely sources of information. The thought of talking to strangers triggered a stab of anxiety, but this was good. He needed to challenge himself. He would build his confidence by starting with small talk.

Here a long parade of narrowboats lined the towpath, many of them with tubs of flowers on the roof, bikes leaning on the sides and signs of permanence at the canal-side, including water points and rubbish bins. Some of the owners had even built small sheds beside their boats.

The boat owners were busy today. Some were cleaning — he heard the drone of a vacuum cleaner as he passed one — airing their bedding, hanging out clothes to dry. Dogs lay on the grass, wagging their tails slowly as he passed. At a boat selling coal and firewood, a man sipped coffee from a large mug, the powerful aroma making Daniel's mouth water. Daniel kept the good side of his face towards him as he approached.

"Morning," he said. "Coffee smells good."

"Want some?" the man said. "We've got plenty."

"I wasn't fishing," Daniel said. "But yes, that would be very welcome."

The man called below. "Maeve, can you pour another, please? We've got a visitor."

Daniel set his bag down, circling his arms to loosen his stiffening muscles. A woman appeared from the hatch with a steaming mug of coffee. "Yours, I think?" she said.

Daniel leaned forward to accept the mug, his feet on the verge. This was the great thing about many narrowboats. Each end of the boat, where people stood to drive or to sit, was level with the towpath, making conversation with passing walkers a natural thing to do.

"Come a long way?" the man asked. This kind of small talk was safe ground for Daniel. People were relaxed and interested, and he knew the answers. He lingered for a while, finishing his coffee, before asking about *Golden Serpent*.

"A golden snake on the side, you say? I haven't seen it, not that I remember, anyway. But there's people along here who might. Ask Fred, in the red barge with the aerial and the Union Jack — see it?"

Daniel stretched his neck to see the boat he was indicating. The Union Jack was hanging listless in the calm air, but it was just visible among the line of boats.

"He's been here years. Spends all his time watching, knows everybody. Give him a go. If he's not around, there's plenty of others to ask. Forget the hire boats — the ones with the phone numbers on the side. They won't know. Fred's your best bet."

Fred was not on board. Or at least, nobody appeared when Daniel gave a firm knock on the hatch door. Disappointed, he moved on along the line of boats, looking out for the ones that seemed well-established in their mooring places. He asked a couple of times more, but nobody had seen *Golden Serpent*.

As he walked on past the last few boats in the line, it occurred to him that in a close community like the boaters, word might get out that he was looking for Collins. Moreover, if the man at the boatyard was right, Collins might not take kindly to someone asking questions about him. Daniel tried hard not to think about the consequences of that.

CHAPTER TWENTY-FOUR

Though Poppy had camped a few times before — the odd weekend and once at a music festival — she'd only ever done it with friends who knew what to do. Camping on her own was a learning experience. Thankfully, the tent was easy to put up and anchor in the ground, but cooking on a camping stove proved a challenge at first. She managed to burn a pot after only a couple of days, and was forced to carry it with her, the carbonised food congealing into a hard crust, until she could find a proper water point where she could scrape it out with her knife. At first, she underestimated the amount of water she'd need for cooking and washing, then overestimated it and ended up carrying far too much.

Despite the teething problems, camping felt like the best way of living. She chose her overnight stopping places carefully, keeping away from prying eyes and farm animals, and with an escape route nearby, just in case. She kept close to gates and farm tracks, though not so close she was going to be spotted. Beans was always alert to the sounds of the countryside and once he'd got used to the cry of a fox at night or a rustle in the hedgerow beside the tent, he soon settled down. If there was a threat of any kind, he would make her aware, and even a small three-legged dog could create a distraction.

They slept cuddled together, Poppy's arm around Beans's warm shape, in a deep refreshing slumber, mostly undisturbed. They went to bed as the sun went down, waking at dawn. This became Poppy's favourite time of day. She'd throw on a warm jumper, unzip the tent flap and put the kettle on outside while she stretched her body and gazed at the pale light of the rising sun. She'd huddle together with Beans on a groundsheet, a blanket around her shoulders, a mug of tea clasped in her hand, watching the world wake up. She became familiar with the early bird calls, the rustle of leaves in a slight breeze, the fragrance of wild flowers as they opened.

Beans soon understood that farm animals were to be left alone. He would sit quietly beside Poppy as sheep came to investigate, watching them calmly, ready to protect her if needed. But to her relief he never chased the sheep, the cows they came across once at the edge of an empty field, or the horse who trotted up to greet them over the fence. Mice, on the other hand, he couldn't resist, but though he made valiant attempts, they were always too fast for him.

She aimed to walk every day, allowing time to shop for supplies or linger at a particularly beautiful place. She didn't want to commit to covering a certain distance — after all, this was a commemorative walk, not a competition, and she wanted to take it all in, enjoy it, and feel she could stop whenever and wherever she wanted. But after only a few days, another factor started to dictate her progress.

As a regular walker, Poppy had never had trouble with her boots or suffered pains in her feet. But she hadn't walked for so long every day, and her feet began to object. A large blister appeared on one heel, and though she'd been aware of it for an hour or so before she stopped to inspect it, she was shocked at what she saw.

She paused at a point where the towpath widened. There she found a stretch of shorter grass, punctuated with daisies and dandelions. She sat, undid her boot and peeled off her sock gently. The blister was more than an inch in diameter, angry and dark red, as if it was full of blood rather than clear fluid. This was bad. It really needed puncturing, but she hadn't brought a needle with her. It would need a plaster at the very least, and she didn't even have that — she hadn't thought to bring a first aid kit.

Cursing to herself, she inspected the inside of her boot, finding nothing there that might have caused the problem. She turned her sock inside out and checked it for lumps or thorns. Nothing. On the other foot, she found two more blisters, less alarming in colour but threatening to turn into painful sores.

Karen had warned her about this. "You'll need proper walking socks," she'd said. "Double socks might do it, but don't wear your normal ones on their own, you'll end up with blisters." What an idiot she was — if only she'd listened. She tried to get the sock back on with a square of tissue inside to protect the skin, but it was impossible. She folded a tissue inside her boot and slipped the painful heel inside. It was better than nothing, but after a rest, the blister felt worse and she knew she wouldn't get much further without treating it.

Checking the map, she saw that the next shop was a couple of miles further on. Well, she'd just have to take it easy. She could hobble there slowly and hopefully make it before it closed.

* * *

The man in the shop sucked his teeth.

"Blisters? Not good for a walker! You might need to rest those feet for a bit." He came out from behind the counter to stroke Beans.

"Do you have plasters or a dressing of some sort? Maybe antiseptic cream?"

"Might have some plasters somewhere around. But if those beggars are bad, you need a pharmacy. Get some proper blister plasters. Give me a minute, I'll have a quick look for you." He disappeared into the back of the shop.

142

"Sorry, I thought we had some, but we must have sold them," he said.

Poppy wondered what there was to be so cheerful about. She was tired. She'd felt every step of the way since she'd looked at her blisters and she really needed to treat them now. "Is there a pharmacy nearby?"

"A mile or so, maybe. You'll have to come off the canal, though."

Poppy's heart sank. This was not part of her plan.

The man gave her a sympathetic smile. "Painful, is it?"

"Very. Can you give me directions please?"

He drew her a rough map on a piece of notepaper, indicating the route through a residential area with arrows and a couple of landmarks. It didn't look too bad.

She was relieved to find the pharmacy open and empty of customers. The pharmacist, a young Asian woman with a shiny ponytail that reached to her waist, sat Poppy down and inspected her feet.

"Ooh that looks sore," she said. "Don't worry, I'll patch you up now and I'll show you how to do it for yourself. I can give you some dressings and cream to take with you."

She gently dressed the sore areas. "You must rest for at least a couple of days — you don't want to risk infection. That one on your left foot is looking pretty angry. Don't walk again until it's lost the redness, and try and give your feet some air. Oh — and don't forget these." She handed her a box of plasters. "If it doesn't get better, you must see a doctor. And a last piece of advice: if you're going to keep walking, buy some decent socks!"

Poppy left feeling much more comfortable, her feet cushioned from the worst of the rubbing in her boots, a bag of medicaments in her backpack. She headed back the short distance to the canal.

Decent socks would have to wait until her feet could take her as far as a town where she could find a camping shop. Two pairs of ordinary socks, worn together, and a good rest would have to do for the moment. It was frustrating. She hadn't put a lot of distance between herself and Banbury before this setback.

But that wasn't the point, she told herself. If she could find somewhere good to set up camp, she might enjoy a couple of days' rest, watching the comings and goings at a lock, chatting with boaters, playing with Beans. She might even treat herself to a pub meal, if there was one nearby. And she had a book to read that she'd barely started. As long as the weather held, she would be fine.

CHAPTER TWENTY-FIVE

A buzzing in his bag. Untangling himself from the straps, he fumbled in the pockets. But the buzzing stopped before he'd had the chance to answer it. A missed call from Lauren.

He looked ahead, along the towpath. Soon he'd be coming to a lock where he could stop, call Lauren back and have a drink. A break in the early evening sun would be good. His stomach growled. Perhaps he'd make it to the nearest pub for supper before setting up camp.

"How's things?"

"Good, I'm good." Her voice sounded distant, tired. Daniel imagined her arriving back at the flat, pale and exhausted, bringing a whiff of London traffic inside as she kicked off her shoes. That life seemed so far away, now. It was weird to think it wasn't that long ago that he was living the same kind of routine. "How's the traveller?"

"This is great, Lauren, you'd love it. It's so . . . different, calm. Camping's doing me good. And the weather's held, mostly."

"Whereabouts are you?"

"Coming up to Banbury. Slow progress, but I'm taking my time. Are you coming to join me?"

Lauren let out a sigh. "You know I'd love to. Maybe in a few weeks, if you're still going. I don't know — I'm so entangled with work at the moment."

"Do come. Just let me know. I'll be going all summer. But don't leave it too long, you sound like you need it now."

"You're right. I feel like I could sleep for a week." There was a pause. "And how are you really? How is that head of yours? Is the walk helping?"

Daniel hesitated. The image of his battered face in Jane and Callum's mirror returned, the harsh voice of his attacker, the vicious kick, the crunch of his jaw. The memory hadn't faded like the bruises. But there was no point alarming Lauren.

"I think it is. I'm practising mindfulness every day. It's not easy but I'm slowly getting the hang of it. I like this slow way of living, there's a lot less stress to deal with. I feel like things are . . . settling."

As he swung his bag onto his back, he thought about what she'd asked. Was this helping his head? He'd replied that things were settling, but were they, really?

There was only one way to find out. Banbury wasn't far now, and maybe, just maybe, the answer was there.

* * *

He soon started to see a series of old lift bridges, left open permanently these days. A fizz of adrenaline put him on high alert as he passed under a motorway bridge, but there was nobody around. Soon a river flanked the canal on one side, a railway on the other, while the motorway noise stayed with him for a few miles. Houses started to appear, and the canal traffic seemed suddenly to increase, as if the boats had hidden in some backwater and, at a secret signal, come together simultaneously. It looked as if the canal passed right through the centre of the town.

There were boats lining one side of the canal, stretching as far as the eye could see. Beside the modern brick of a shopping centre was a famous boatyard with a working forge and a dry dock. Daniel was hoping it might be the perfect place to ask about *Golden Serpent*. People sat in the sunshine on their boats or beside the towpath as he passed.

A few of them called to him, "Morning! Good day for a walk," or nodded to him. This would be a good place to stop for something to eat, to chat to the boaters. He could visit the library when it opened and see if the internet turned up anything on Collins.

"Bit of a bust-up?" the man at the boatyard asked. Hands blackened with oil, he tinkered with the engine of a boat at the head of a long line.

"I was mugged."

"Sorry to hear it." The man rested an elbow on the rail that ran around the boat's stern. "Not on the canal, I hope?" He looked as if he'd spent his whole life outdoors, his skin nut-brown, lines etched in his cheeks and forehead. His beard, grey and silver in patches, was so long he'd plaited the last couple of inches. His hair, thin and silver, was held back with a simple black band.

"It's OK, he didn't get anything."

The man nodded, assessing Daniel, perhaps weighing up the odds of him having started the fight. "What can I do for you?"

"I'm looking for a particular boat — an old narrowboat called *Golden Serpent*. It has, or had, a golden snake painted on the side." Every time he mentioned *Golden Serpent*, Daniel lost focus, finding himself reliving the scene from years before. Controlling it took all his energy.

The man nodded, wiping his forehead with the back of his hand. A greasy smear, combined with the beard and the hair, gave him a piratical look. "She's been around for years. Used to pass through here quite often, though I haven't seen her for a few months now."

"Would that have been last winter, then?"

The man looked at him quizzically. "I suppose it would have been. I'm wondering why you're asking, now."

Last winter. Then it was possible, if not likely, the boat was still on the canals, not scrapped or renamed. "It's a bit of a long story. Can you — would you happen to remember which direction she was headed in when you last saw her?"

"Ah, she was off northward. Can't say where she'd be headed. There's options at the next junction, you see. Could have gone Coventry way, or stayed on the Oxford to Rugby, or headed south to Northampton, London direction. What's the story?"

"I met someone who lived on it — her — a good while back. I'm trying to track him down. It's a long shot. I expect he moved on a long time ago."

"You never know with boaters. We're loyal to our canals, we are. And our community." He turned back to his work. "I wish you luck, anyway. Enjoy your walk."

On a grassy bank, Daniel pulled out a notebook and pencil. Though he wasn't great at drawing, he wanted to show people the boat and the snake symbol in case it jogged their memories. Wishing he had coloured pencils, he chose a narrowboat of a similar colour and copied the outline. The platform at the back, where the tiller sat, was easy — he knew it was level, with no drop as you got on board. A rail behind it, the name in gold lettering across the stern. Towards the bow, the golden serpent with its forked tongue and zigzag pattern. The name again. Bikes lying on their sides on the roof, logs in bags, rope and boxes.

He paused a while to watch a couple of boats passing, and was surprised by a voice.

"What have you got there?" a woman said. "Mind if I have a look?" She smiled down at him, a small woman with a kindly face. Her clothing was colourful, bohemian, a scarf tied around her hair, dungarees knotted at the shoulders. She looked like a boater.

"It's nothing, really," Daniel said, but it seemed rude not to allow her a quick look at his drawing.

She took the notebook out of his hands and he looked away, embarrassed. "It's good. So you're not drawing one of these? You're welcome to draw mine, if you want. It's the red one, three boats down. See it?" She pointed along the line of boats.

"Yes, thank you. I'm not an artist, though. It's this particular boat I'm interested in."

"I know it."

Startled, Daniel squinted up at her silhouette, half-blinded by the bright sun behind.

"It was here only a couple of months ago," she said. "Surly fellow. Keeps himself to himself. I don't know where he was heading, but he looked like a seasoned boater to me. Boat's seen better days."

Daniel's scalp tingled as the woman kept talking. He started to interrupt, to ask exactly when, if there was anyone else on the boat, but she carried on without taking breath, moving on to her own boat, her husband and how it was to live on the canals. Daniel would have been interested, but now he was laser-focused on her comments about *Golden Serpent*.

At last, she paused.

"You've seen it?" he said. "You met the owner? Is his last name Collins, do you know?"

"Now that I don't know," she said. "All I know is he's thin and bald. Scruffy-looking fellow, probably sixty, if he's a day. Bit of a loner."

"So, there's nobody else living on it?"

"Didn't see anyone. Unlikely, I'd say. Boat's full of stuff, no room for anyone else."

"Stuff?"

"Not that I've been inside, you know. But I had a quick butchers through the windows. Crammed with furniture, logs, bikes and boxes. Newspapers and comics strewn all over. Not the best-kept boat on the canals, that's for sure."

Comics. It had to be him.

"Did you happen to see which way it went?"

"He didn't stop. Too many people around here for him, I reckon. Yes, he headed north. Ask again at the junction — they'll know if he's passed on through."

"I will. Thank you."

Daniel closed his notebook. The boat had passed through quite recently, on its way north. And it tended to stay on the Oxford Canal or the Grand Union. He hoped Collins was a creature of habit, or he would never catch up with him.

CHAPTER TWENTY-SIX

There was no time to waste. He had the feeling he was closing in. Only a couple of months before, *Golden Serpent* had been seen passing through Banbury. It was as if it was calling him on, leaving him clues along its journey. This was nonsense, of course, but it gave his legs energy. His spirits rose.

Abandoning his plans to stay over in Banbury, he packed up his things and set off, past a flurry of bridges that punctuated the canal's journey through the rest of the town, under another motorway. Hills appeared to his right, and it wasn't long before houses appeared ahead, marking the next village. As he passed some stone cottages flanking the bank, a tall hedge sprang up, casting a shadow over his path. There were very few people around now, and in the space of three hours, he saw no more than one or two dog walkers and a couple of slow-moving boats on the water.

He felt jumpy. At first, he put this down to the motorway crossings, the reminders of the beating he'd endured. It wasn't surprising that the fear lingered. But here he was in the countryside, a sleepy, rural place. He turned his head a couple of times as he walked, checking the path behind him and the opposite bank where there was a clear view across a valley. Nothing there to concern him. So, what was it niggling at his senses, telling him to stay alert?

Once, when he turned, a movement in the distance set his heart thumping. But when he scrutinised the path, there was nothing. It was empty, benign, nobody trailing him. He shook his head — he was being ridiculous. The mugger wouldn't have followed him this far, surely. He was being paranoid.

To prove to himself that he was safe, he slowed his pace, then stopped and took off his backpack. It was a pleasant afternoon, with a light breeze across the water, and this seemed as good a place as any to stop for a quick cuppa. He'd learned to carry a Thermos with him every day — boiling water on a camping gas stove took far too long to want to do it often.

He watched as a moorhen bobbed along the water for a moment or two, dipped its head and disappeared. Another bird — or maybe the same one — popped up further along, then another, and he began to wonder how many of them were down there, searching for food on the bottom of the canal. He supposed it was a sign that the water was clean. Clumps of wild flowers along the towpath tumbled over the canal-side on the opposite bank and a bumblebee zoomed past him, its velvety back shining in the bright sunlight. Soon he began to feel sleepy, and a few minutes later he was dozing, his head on his backpack, his cap over his face. The anxious mood had passed.

He woke with a start. He'd fallen into a state of total relaxation, listening drowsily to the sounds of the countryside, his mind drifting. This happened to him so rarely that for a moment, he was disoriented. He grabbed for his bag as if he was drowning, his arms flailing, only registering where he was when he felt the weight and solidity of the backpack under his hand. He looked at his watch. He could hardly believe it. Though he'd only slept for a matter of minutes, it felt like an entire night's blissful sleep. Time had stretched while he lay there — it was as if he'd been in a different world entirely.

Glancing around to reassure himself that nobody had crept up on him, he packed his Thermos away and stood, slinging his backpack into its usual position on his back. There were miles to be done before he could rest again.

Soon he reached a clutch of locks that coaxed the canal water upwards, level by level. Here light woodland bordered the towpath, and he began to feel nervous again. He felt much safer with open fields on either side.

Alone in a deep cutting, he was spooked by the silence, the dark water beside him and the dense woods beyond. When a pheasant sprang from the bushes behind, its alarm call almost brought on a panic attack. He crouched for a moment, breathing deeply. He looked forward to seeing people and boats again.

The feeling that he was being watched was like a laser beam behind his heart, boring into his flesh. He quickened his step until he was half-running, and was hugely relieved when the countryside opened out and there were signs of human habitation again.

He was heading towards a major junction where the Oxford Canal met the Grand Union. Boats and people would congregate there, he was certain. Only five miles further on, the Oxford Canal branched away from the Grand Union, and at either point Daniel had a decision to take — north or south. He decided to linger at the junction, perhaps stay a few days if he could find a good spot to camp.

As he came around a bend in the waterway, there were signs of a campsite ahead, in a field bordering the canal. In the distance he could see a town on the side of a hill rising towards a distant windmill. The junction would be only a short distance further on.

At the next lock, a girl sat on a blanket watching a boat negotiating the gates. She looked around his age, with dark hair scraped into a ponytail. Her feet were bare, a dressing taped to one heel. A walker, then. Perhaps a camper? Maybe she could tell him what the campsite was like, or if there was a better place to stop further on.

He was nearing her when a movement at her side surprised him. A little dog, one back leg missing, separated itself from her side and ran to greet him, tail wagging. He bent to stroke its back. It was some kind of mongrel, scruffy and endearing, its eyes bright and friendly.

"Come here, Beans." The girl shaded her eyes against the sun. "He doesn't need you bothering him."

"No worries," Daniel said. "He's great."

"My best friend." A lock of hair escaped from the ponytail, framing one cheek. Her face was untouched by cosmetics, clear and open, with a sprinkling of freckles across the nose. Not beautiful, but — he couldn't have described why — fascinating. There was genuine warmth in her smile. He found it hard to drag his eyes away.

Beans ran back to her side and settled down. Daniel felt almost jealous. He was glad he had the sun behind him and she couldn't see his face.

"Nothing like a dog to keep you company on a long walk," she said. "I work for a rescue centre — I could find you a good one, if you're interested."

"One day, maybe." They watched as the boat passed through the lock on the other side.

"Want a sandwich?" The girl reached for a plastic food box at her side. "I've overestimated — they need eating."

"If you're sure."

"Sure I'm sure." She grinned, holding the box out to him. "Sit down, there's plenty of room. Budge up, Beans."

Daniel dropped his backpack on the ground and sat rubbing his shoulders. A groove had formed above his collarbone where the straps had been. The muscles on each side were knotted and tight.

She'd made a selection of sandwiches, each round wrapped in foil. Daniel found he didn't care what he chose, his mouth watering as the smells were released with the opening of the lid.

They sat in comfortable silence for a few moments, watching the canal as they ate.

"Water?" The girl offered him a plastic bottle.

"That's OK, I have my own," he said.

"Where have you come from? You look like a proper walker." She gestured at his bag, with its kettle and stove hanging from the back, the sleeping bag rolled into a ball at the top. He noticed her clear skin, the blue of her irises, the depth behind them striking him once again. She was perhaps a little younger than him. Her arms were tanned, the blonde hairs on her forearms catching the sun, and she wore a simple grey T-shirt and denim shorts. A pair of well-used walking boots sat beside her.

"I started a few miles out of Oxford," he said.

"How far are you going?"

He shrugged. Somehow he didn't mind her questions. "Going where my feet take me. I'm . . . taking a break."

"Cool." There was a pause as she leaned back on her elbows. "Beans and me, we're not going too far. Especially now I have the world's worst blister." She pointed at the dressing on her heel, making a rueful face. "I've got to rest it until it's hardened up. Bit of a pain, but it's nice stopping for a while to watch the world go by."

Daniel nodded, not sure how to respond. But the girl seemed not to expect an answer. She stroked her dog gently and his eyes began to close.

"Are you camping here?" Daniel said.

"I am. It's OK, actually. Normally I just find somewhere on the towpath, but as I'm staying a couple of days, maybe more, I thought it would be good to be with other people for a bit. There's only a few of us, and the tents are spread out, so you still get some privacy."

Daniel nodded. "I usually camp on the towpath, too. But I might stop a while here — I've got a couple of things to do. Mind if I join you in the field?" He felt a rush of blood to his face, but she didn't seem to notice.

"No problem at all." She hesitated. "I'm Poppy, by the way, and this is Beans."

"Daniel." He held out his hand.

She took it with surprising strength, her small hand warm and dry in his. "Nice to meet you, Daniel."

155

CHAPTER TWENTY-SEVEN

When Poppy had checked the map and found the campsite symbol, she couldn't believe her luck. The site was right next to the towpath, surrounded by farmland, the beginnings of the town visible in the distance. There was a lock, a turning point, and a bridge — all points of interest if she was going to have a quiet couple of days watching the world go by on the canal. The farmer, an old boy with a pronounced limp and a cloth cap that had seen better days, seemed pleased to see her. His grin revealed gaps in his teeth top and bottom, a gold cap glinting in the sun. A young sheepdog bounced around Beans.

The farmer said she could stay as long as she liked. Only a few tents dotted the field. She found a good place to set up and hobbled to the towpath with a blanket, some food and her book. She planned to catch the sun, doze and relax while her foot recovered.

As she sat musing about the future, Beans jumped up and ran to a walker who had approached without her noticing. He was about her age and slender, his hair wind-blown on his shoulders and a healthy-looking beard. In knee-length shorts and a T-shirt, with heavy walking boots and thick socks — she noted the socks with envy — he looked like a seasoned walker. At first, she couldn't see his eyes below the peak of a baseball cap, but when he looked up, she noticed fading bruises on one cheekbone. He bent to stroke Beans, who seemed instantly to engage with him. He must be safe, then. She trusted Beans's judgement implicitly.

The young man seemed shy at first, keeping his head down, watching the water as he spoke. But there was something about him that intrigued her: he wasn't like the other walkers she'd come across. He was on his own, for a start. She found herself wanting him to stop and talk, so she offered him a sandwich and made room for him on the blanket.

It took a while to draw Daniel out of himself. He wasn't a natural talker, but she felt comfortable with him. She was pleased when he said he was going to stay over at the same campsite.

Later, when the sun's warmth was beginning to fade, they walked over to the field together. When he left her to check in with the farmer, she said impulsively, "Do you want to join me for supper? I've got a portable barbecue and some sausages. Might be able to rustle up something to go with them."

"But — you've already given me lunch."

She shrugged and smiled, waiting for his reply.

"It sounds great. I'll bring what I've got. Where's your tent?"

"It's the blue one over by the hedge, with the hawthorn tree behind it. The smallest one in the field. Beans won't be far away."

As she limped back to her tent with Beans at her heels, she heard her mum's voice in her ear. *Be careful, you never know who you're talking to. You're far too trusting sometimes. Call me every day, won't you?*

If she was quick, she could call her mum before Daniel arrived for supper.

CHAPTER TWENTY-EIGHT

"Sometimes people just click. There's no other way to explain it." Lauren's words rang in his ears as he walked back to the field. In the days when he was desperate for a girlfriend, she'd tried to explain to him how it felt when you met someone you really liked. The 'clicking' had not happened to him throughout his teens and his young adult life, with friends or with girls. As usual, he'd turned to Lauren for advice.

He was surprised at himself for deciding to camp here. Just this morning he'd had no intention of lingering, quite the opposite. He'd decided to get to the junction as soon as he could, to investigate *Golden Serpent*.

But he'd clicked with Poppy. He couldn't understand it — they'd barely spoken, but he'd settled down next to her on the blanket and had a proper conversation. Even the silences were comfortable. All the anxiety gone, just like that. No more feeling he was being watched, no rising panic at the thought of having to converse with a stranger. There was something about her that calmed him. He felt safe around her. How odd that felt, with someone completely new.

At the farmhouse he bought wine, bread and cheese — his contribution to the barbecue. He soon spotted Beans sniffing around in the hedgerow, and it didn't take long to identify Poppy's tent. She was crouched nearby, getting the barbecue ready. He pitched his tent a little further along the line of the hedge, within striking distance of Poppy's, dug out his lamp, unfurled his sleeping bag and had a quick wash. There wasn't much he could do about his clothes or his hair, but at least he could be clean.

She hadn't mentioned a time, so he waited a few minutes before walking over. The air was still warm, the late sun bright, and they had a good hour or so of daylight left before nightfall. Poppy was sitting at one corner of a large groundsheet, the foil barbecue on a patch of level grass beside her, smoking gently.

When she smiled at him, his stomach did a tiny flip. It was the openness of her face. There was no guile, no wariness, just a generosity that shone through. In that instant, his mind did an immediate trawl of the people he knew, questioning when someone had last smiled at him in that way. Properly, without a hint of mistrust. Only pleasure to see him. He couldn't remember. Never, possibly. He wasn't the kind of person people smiled at.

These thoughts travelled like lightning through his mind in the fraction of a second it took for him to take another step towards her. But to his surprise and confusion, she saw something in his face.

"What?" she said, standing up. Her smile made him pause, and he found himself grinning back, feeling foolish and confused and happy all at the same time.

"Nothing." He handed her the bag of food and wine. "Just thinking."

"What were you thinking?" She laughed, taking the bag from his hand.

"Oh, just, this is . . . nice." He gestured vaguely at the barbecue, the tent, the field, feeling a flush creep into his cheeks. He hoped she was dazzled by the sun as she had been earlier, or maybe that the colour had got lost in his beard.

"Nice?" she said. "It's fantastic! Don't you think camping is just brilliant?"

"I — Yes," he said, sitting down. "On a day like today, it is." What he meant was, *With you, it is*.

"Had some bad days, then, have you?" She sat beside him. Beans appeared between them, touching Daniel's leg with his cold nose, his tail wagging. He settled down, his back warm on Daniel's thigh.

"I had a bit of nasty weather early on," he said. "Wind and rain. But it wasn't too bad, it was just I wasn't used to it."

Poppy opened the bag. "You got wine! Where did you rustle that up from?"

"The farmer keeps some bits and pieces, just in case."

"Hope it's a screw top, I didn't think to bring a bottle opener."

"It is indeed." He took the bottle from her hands. "Where's your cup?"

"Here." She held out a tin mug. "Let's drink to good weather and camping."

The sun was fading fast. They fell into silence as they ate, watching the moon rise as the light faded.

"So, tell me, why are you doing this walking thing?" Poppy's gaze stayed on the sky as she spoke.

Daniel followed the line of her profile with his eyes. He wanted to run his finger down her forehead, along the bridge of her nose, over the turn of her upper lip. Just to feel the shape of her, the warmth of her skin beneath his hand. He didn't know how to answer her question, but somehow he felt compelled to give her an honest reply.

To his immense surprise, he found himself describing what had brought him on the journey. Losing his job, his girlfriend and his flat in quick succession, and he went right back to the beginning. Everything came pouring out — the car boot sale, the comics, meeting Ryan. The horrifying scene when he saw the dark bag slide into the canal, the flash of white that disappeared in an instant. How he'd told no one, how it haunted him. The agonies of his teenage years, the uncontrollable memories, the fear. The taunting at school, his father's disappointment in him. The visit to the police, the silence that followed. It all came gushing out.

Poppy sat with him, watching the sky, saying nothing, glancing at his face from time to time. With anyone else, he might have worried they weren't listening or had switched off from his monologue, unsure how to stop him. But he knew Poppy was listening intently. Nothing seemed to surprise her, not even his description of the scene with Ryan's dad and the heavy sack. At one point, she moved just a fraction closer to him, and he could almost feel the warmth of her body, her heart beating beside him.

When he reached the present, the rush of words slowed to a trickle as darkness fell around them. They gazed into the dying embers, the echo of his story all around them.

Poppy took a deep breath and exhaled slowly. "Wow."

"I'm sorry, I didn't mean to . . . I've never told anybody that. Except my sister, Lauren, and I only told her a short time ago." He could hardly believe what he'd done. He'd trusted a stranger with secrets he'd kept hidden for years. All the insecurities, the fears, all the characteristics that had got him bullied and reviled at school. Only a few short weeks ago, that would have been unthinkable.

"It's OK," she said simply. She stood, and Daniel held his breath. "But I am a bit cold. Hold on, I'll just grab a jumper."

He sat bemused, rooted to the spot. It was as if he'd removed an outer layer, leaving the real Daniel, soft and vulnerable, exposed. Had he scared her off? But in the next moment, she was back beside him on the blanket, scrambling into a large sweater.

"That's quite a story," she said, drawing the sleeping Beans towards her.

He breathed again. "Have I shocked you?"

She hugged her knees, pulling the jumper down over her bare legs. "No. I'm just . . . absorbing it."

He prodded the barbecue with a stick, the glowing remains pulsing with the last flickers of heat.

"So, what will you do now?" she said.

"I suppose I'll go on looking for Collins. Ryan's dad."

"What happens if you don't find him — if you never find him?"

It was Daniel's turn to fold his arms around his knees. "That's just it. I don't know. Do you think I'm mad?" He kept his head down, because he didn't want to watch her struggle to answer him.

"No, you're not mad," she said without hesitation. "But—" He imagined her mind turning over, honing her response until it was acceptable. "Do you think it's going to solve . . . things?" she said at last.

"What, cure my brain, you mean?" he said with a grimace.

"You don't need curing."

Daniel felt a surge of gratitude.

"I think what you're looking for is — I'm not sure if this is the right word — a diagnosis. Certainty, maybe, understanding. Acknowledgement. That your brain is special, that your memories are true and correct. I don't know."

Her words comforted him like he'd never felt comfort before.

"But is finding Collins the only way to do it? Couldn't you do it anyway, without . . . I don't know, pursuing a goal that, you said it yourself, doesn't have much chance of doing what you want it to do?"

He stared at her face in the lamplight. Her hands made shapes in the shadows as she spoke, her voice gaining strength. Beans slept on, his legs twitching.

"I mean, let's assume you do find him — which is a long shot, but let's go with it for the moment. He could just deny everything. Then what do you do? Do you insist that you're right and risk getting yourself into trouble? You said yourself he was a tricky customer, and you're going to accuse him of murdering his son. He could go nuts just at the suggestion."

"I know." Daniel hung his head.

"But apart from that, I mean, the point is, even if it's true and he admits it all, which I doubt, what does that mean for you? Just that your recollection of that moment is correct. Not that your mind is special or that your memory is exceptional." She paused, as if pondering a difficult question. "I suppose what I'm asking is, do you think your plan to find this man could be more like . . . a quest to find the truth about yourself?"

CHAPTER TWENTY-NINE

He woke to grey daylight, a cool wind rustling the bushes behind the tent. Elsewhere all was quiet. He knew it was early from the quality of the light, the eerie silence of the new day. He was fully awake, his body heavy and warm, cocooned in the sleeping bag.

He practised his deep breathing, staying in the moment. He tried to keep his mind from wandering, coaxing it back each time it swerved away, focusing on his breath. When he'd first tried the exercise, years ago, he'd given up after a few weeks. Now it seemed to work a little better. Perhaps he was making progress at last.

He pondered their conversation last night. Poppy was right, of course. The search for Ryan's dad was a goal that he'd persuaded himself was the real one. But it wasn't. The real goal was the diagnosis. When she'd used the word last night, he'd been taken aback. She'd only known him for half a day and she knew what he needed better than he did.

She was unlike anyone he'd ever met. She'd let him in without a hint of reserve. When she'd talked about her grandmother, tears had gathered in her eyes as she talked. He was flattered that she trusted him, impressed with her self-awareness. Younger than him and grieving, she'd taken off on a solitary journey in her gran's memory, and now she was sharing her deepest feelings with a stranger. She was very different from him, and yet he felt he'd known her all his life.

He wondered if they could walk together for a while, if she would want his company. Somehow he was reluctant to leave her. But asking her to join him when they'd only just met seemed crazy — he'd be setting himself up for rejection.

A snuffling at the door of his tent drew him back to the present. The shadow of a paw scratching, a tiny whine.

"Hey, Beans," he said softly as he crawled towards the door on his forearms, the rest of him still in the warm sleeping bag. He unzipped a few inches for Beans to scramble through, his tail wagging, his entire body turning itself from side to side as Daniel scratched his back. When he settled down in the crook of his arm, Daniel was touched to be so trusted. They dozed together in companionable silence.

When Beans began to fidget, Daniel got dressed and took him for a wander along the canal, making sure he stayed close. It was still early, no one else around, the air fresh and fragrant with the scents of wild flowers. Birds sang and chirped, flitting along the bushes as he walked, and he was rewarded for his early start by the flash of a kingfisher darting above the water. He watched for a couple of minutes as it skimmed the bank of the canal — but it was soon away, disappearing as suddenly as it had arrived.

When they got back to the field, people were beginning to move around, smells of breakfast wafting around the campsite. Beans ran straight to Poppy's tent, where the front flaps had been folded back. Soon she appeared, squinting in the brightness of the strengthening sun. She gave Daniel a friendly wave. "You're up early! Been for a walk?"

"Beans came for a visit. It seemed only polite to offer him a morning stroll."

"You're honoured. He's taken to you." Poppy limped a little as she moved around. She opened a can of dog food and spooned some out into a small metal bowl.

"How's the foot?"

"Still sore. I was hoping it might be better today, but it looks like I'll have to be patient for at least another day. It's a bit frustrating, but I'm happy to stay here. The sun's shining, the countryside is beautiful, I've got my dog and a good book — what more could I want?"

Poppy's mood was infectious, and Daniel found himself smiling. "How about you join me for breakfast? I've got bread, and . . . um, a bit of cheese left over from yesterday."

She lifted a hand. "I raise you one pot of marmalade."

"Very civilised. Seriously, have you been carrying that with you, or did you just pick it up?"

"I bought a couple of essentials when I realised I wouldn't be walking too far. Marmalade is definitely an essential. We can do toast over the stove, if you like."

Over breakfast, cobbled together from the remains of their supplies, Poppy said, "Are you off again today?"

"I was thinking of staying another night, maybe."

"Weren't you keen to keep going, see if you can catch up with that boat?"

"*Golden Serpent*, yes. I know it's a long shot. I'm going to check, but there's no point rushing."

She nodded, crunching on a mouthful of toast. "Have another piece of toast. Oh, wait — there isn't any. Oops. Running a bit low on supplies."

"I am too. Listen, I can easily walk to the town and back from here — it's a couple of miles, max, each way. Why don't I stock up while I'm there? The farmer doesn't have much, and you're not going to want to walk in yourself."

"That would be great, thank you so much. I was wondering what to do about food. Shall we have another barbecue tonight?" Daniel felt the warmth of that word. *We*. It felt like a gift.

"Great idea," he said, trying not to sound as enthusiastic as he felt. "What do you — we — need? I'll make a list."

* * *

As he strode towards the town, he began to feel hopeful for the future. This was a new feeling for him, or at least one he couldn't remember having since childhood. Everything about this trip was new. That alone was helping to distract him, fending off the memories. He was focusing less on himself, and now he was doing something useful, helping someone out, albeit in a small way. He might even have found a new friend.

But even as he thought it, the doubts returned. Of course she wouldn't want to be friends long-term. A girl like that would have a big social circle and probably a boyfriend who wouldn't want Daniel around. She'd spend a bit of time with him while it was convenient, then they would part and go back to their separate lives. She would barely think about him, while he would be left with another memory and the dull ache of disappointment.

He thought back to their conversation and wondered again what had made him open up to her when they'd only just met. It was so unusual for him to put his trust in a stranger. But she seemed to know what he needed, to understand what he was hoping for when he had no idea himself. And she was right — he was driven by this memory. It had taken on a particular importance in his head, even while he knew he could be wrong about it. It might not solve anything. In fact, it could go the other way, and he could return from this trip with no answers, only humiliation, disappointment and the knowledge that he would never come to terms with how his mind worked.

Yet here he was, still hoping to find *Golden Serpent*. What would he do if he found it, and Ryan's dad? The only decision he could make was to play it by ear. It would all depend on the reaction he got. He'd ask after Ryan and see what happened. Collins's response would say it all. He couldn't see any further into the future than that.

Daniel approached a pub that was preparing for lunch-time guests, a young lad cleaning tables outside. Daniel wandered in to find an older man, his hair a shock of white curls, wiping down the bar. "Not quite open yet, but you're welcome to wait."

"Thanks. Actually, I was wondering if you could help me — I'm looking for a particular boat. It's called *Golden Serpent*. You wouldn't happen to know it, would you?"

"A narrowboat? They all pass through here at some point. Can't say I remember that one, though."

"It's blue, with a gold serpent painted on the side. It's been around for at least twenty years or so, so I guess it might look a bit different now. Though it has been seen in the last year or so."

"I'm not the best person to ask, to be frank. I'm stuck in here behind the bar most of the time — don't get to see too many boats." He lifted a tray of wine glasses onto the bar and started to hang them from a rack above his head. "You could ask at the boatyards. There are a couple coming up if you're heading to the junction. They're your best bet. There are lads there who've worked the boats for years. You could try the marinas too, the guys there might be able to help."

"Great, thanks a lot, I'll do that."

"Good luck."

Looking at his map, he noticed that he could easily cut through the town to the canal on the other side, where there were two boatyards and a marina. He decided to try that first, and do the shopping on the way back. No point carrying a heavy load further than he needed to, and if he was quick, he'd be back in time for Poppy to get some lunch.

The town turned out to be a gathering of scattered houses set on slopes that climbed steeply towards an ancient church, with most of the shops at the bottom. On a normal day Daniel would have climbed the hill to check out the view, but today wasn't a normal day. He didn't want to waste time.

Finding the canal again easily, he crossed a road bridge and within minutes was approaching a boatyard, where he found a small shop selling books, maps and gifts. When he said he was looking for a particular narrowboat, the woman behind the desk waved him on to a nearby workshop, and soon he spotted two men working on the deck of a narrowboat that was moored beside a pontoon.

Passing a large cruiser, he caught a glimpse of his reflection in its window. He looked like a proper traveller: dusty boots, ankles wrapped in thick walking socks, tanned legs topped by crumpled knee-length shorts. A plain grey T-shirt that had seen better days, a smattering of tea stains down the front. Long, dark curls framing a weather-beaten face half-hidden by an untrimmed beard. He almost laughed. What would his father think of him now? His backpack was empty in preparation for carrying the supplies, but he slipped it off from habit and put it beside him as he tried to catch the attention of the boatmen.

"Hi, can I ask you something?" he said awkwardly. One of the men stopped and straightened up. His grey boiler suit stretched tight over his stomach and a red flush tinged his large nose. Gold earrings lined the edge of one ear. He gave Daniel a friendly smile and a nod.

"Morning. What can I do for you?" He wiped his blackened hands on a filthy rag and pulled a packet of cigarettes from his chest pocket.

"Sorry to bother you. I'm looking for a boat called *Golden Serpent*. Would you happen to know it?"

The other man, greasy hair concealing most of his face, glanced up at Daniel briefly. He wrestled with a spanner and cursed under his breath. Tattoos crawled up his wiry arms, onto his shoulders, and down his chest, disappearing beneath a filthy vest.

"*Golden Serpent*, you say?" the first man said. "Now why would you be interested in that old pile of junk?"

"You know it then?" Daniel felt his hopes take a leap. "Has it been here recently?"

The man took a cigarette from the packet with a large finger and thumb and attached it unlit to his bottom lip. "Smoke?" He shook the packet at Daniel.

"Not for me, thanks."

The man shrugged, whisked a box of matches from the same pocket and lit the cigarette, taking deep puffs, his eyes narrowed against the smoke.

"*Golden Serpent*, let me think. I remember fixing her a couple of years ago, she needed half the engine replacing. How she keeps going, I dunno. She's been on the move for many years, that one, she needs putting out to pasture. She's old and worn out. Like her owner, eh, Dave?" He guffawed.

"Yeah." Dave glanced at Daniel and turned back to his work with a frown.

"Has she been through here since then, do you know? I'm looking for someone who used to live on her."

There was a pause while the man puffed on his cigarette, flicking the ash into the water.

"She passes through here every few months," he said at last. "Pretty sure he doesn't have a base. Is it him you're looking for — that Collins?"

"Not exactly. I used to know his son."

"Son, you say?" He sucked his teeth, shaking his head. "Not a good place for any kid to grow up — old Collins, he's not the best-natured man. There was a woman, though, a while ago. She was nice, very friendly. But I haven't seen her for a long time. Have you, Dave?"

Dave shook his head but didn't look up. "Nope." He cursed as the spanner slipped from his hand and clattered onto the deck.

"She probably left him. To be honest, I'm surprised any woman would have him. He's a grumpy old git." The man chuckled, flicking his half-smoked cigarette into the water.

"So I've heard," Daniel said. "He hasn't been here in the last few weeks, then?"

"We didn't say that." He scratched his head. "He could have passed through without me knowing. Often the travelling boats hole up on a quiet stretch — he might do that. They stop as long as they can, then move on when their time runs out. He seems to stick pretty local."

"Where's the best place for me to look, would you say?"

"I'd say I wouldn't bother if I was you." He gave Daniel a sideways glance, then shrugged. "But if you're set on finding him, I'd head on a couple of miles, onto the Grand Union. He don't like spending money, so he won't be at the marinas, I'll bet." He chuckled again.

"Why wouldn't you bother?" Daniel already knew the answer, but the way the man had said it made him curious.

"Ah, he's not good with people. Keeps himself to himself. Can get a tad awkward, I'd say. Eh, Dave?"

But Dave's back was turned, and this time there was no nod.

As Daniel walked away, he glanced back. The man called Dave had straightened up and was staring after him, a strange and not altogether pleasant look on his face.

CHAPTER THIRTY

Poppy wasn't too good at doing nothing under normal circumstances. Though she enjoyed reading, an hour or so was usually enough before she started getting twitchy. Having someone to talk to had made all the difference in the last day or so. But she was rapidly running out of supplies, so when Daniel had offered to walk into the town to get her shopping, she could have hugged him.

She'd had a peek at her bandaged heel when she woke up. It wasn't looking good. The blister had burst. The dressing was soaked with blood and pus and the area around the wound was red and angry, sore to the touch. Carefully she had applied a new dressing and eased a sock over the top. Today was not going to be a walking day, that was clear.

She reckoned it would be at least a couple of hours before Daniel returned, possibly more if he decided to investigate the boat he was searching for. She couldn't help feeling that he was on the wrong track. How was it going to solve anything, finding out the truth about a boy he'd known so many years ago? If Ryan had been murdered, then yes, he could confirm the accuracy of his memory and maybe ease his guilty feelings by going to the police. It would be hard to prove after such a long time, but at least he'd have done something to put things right. And you never knew, perhaps they'd catch a killer and put him away.

But if the boy hadn't been in that bag, Daniel's memory could still be accurate. Collins, Ryan's dad, had thrown a suspicious-looking bundle into the canal. Daniel's memory might be special, but that incident wasn't going to prove it either way.

It was so clear to Poppy that Daniel was using the incident, or his memory of it, to prove something. She had sensed from the beginning of his story that here was a person who was repressing part of himself. That must be so hard, not being able to express yourself as you really are, even to your family. It wasn't surprising he had seemed reticent at first.

His story fascinated her. To have memories so powerful that they tumble out of your mind, interrupting everything, must be both brilliant and terrible. Brilliant, because if you really could remember every single moment of your life, then all the joyous occasions could be relived over and over, in glorious detail, with all the positive emotions and sensations too. But terrible too, because the bad times were just as insistent — even more so for Daniel, given that the memory of Ryan and Collins seemed to have taken over his life. The bad memories must equally prompt all the feelings of fear, humiliation, loneliness, sadness, anger that Daniel had experienced growing up. How dreadful that must be for him.

Poppy tried to imagine some of the bad things that had happened to her coming back to haunt her again and again. There weren't very many, but reliving them when she didn't want to think about them would be unpleasant, to say the least. And her memory was nowhere near as vivid as Daniel's.

She was glad he'd confided in her and she wanted to help. She'd never heard of anyone else who struggled with this constant barrage of memories, but that meant nothing. Somewhere out there would be another person with the same problem. There was probably even a name for the condition. Perhaps it was studied by eminent scientists, studying the brain, researching diseases like Alzheimer's. She felt sure there must be someone, somewhere, who knew more about it. How strange — here she was, walking in honour of someone who couldn't remember, and she'd found someone who couldn't forget.

She sat for a moment, the image of Gran's face in her mind's eye. The pain of her loss had lessened just a little. The moments when she remembered her healthy and happy were more frequent now, the sickening dread that had settled on her in the last weeks of Gran's life was finally fading.

"What can I do to help Daniel, Gran?" she asked softly.

Be his friend, came the answer. *He needs someone to believe in him.*

"But I want to do more."

I know, Gran's voice said. *And you will. You'll find a way. You always do.*

* * *

She'd been sitting there too long. She shifted position and Beans jumped up, hopeful brown eyes on hers, tail wagging.

"OK, Beans boy. Come for a hobble round the field. Let's see if there are any other dogs for you to play with. Mum's not going to be able to take you for a proper walk today."

She scrabbled in her bag for a pair of old flip-flops. They would be easier on her bad foot. A few charity leaflets in her pocket, she set off to visit the neighbouring tents, hoping the other campers might like to donate to her cause. Even a small amount would help.

By lunchtime, she'd collected more than fifteen pounds, a lot of it in loose change. People didn't like carrying change in their pockets while they were walking, and she'd benefited from that. It was heavy, but she didn't mind. Beans had found a friend in a little spaniel, who had chased him round the field in the warm sun, and he was panting and happy, ready for another kip. She was beginning to feel hungry. She wondered how long Daniel would be, and whether it was worth finding out what the farmer had. She might be able to scrounge a few eggs from him. Otherwise there was a bit of stale bread and not much else in her food bag.

She filled the kettle from her water bottle and lit the stove. A cup of tea might fill her up enough to last until Daniel got back. Stretching out on a blanket, she opened her book and started to read.

But before long her head drooped. She dreamed of boats and dark waters rising. Rising too high. A boat bearing down on her, a man silhouetted on the stern shouting at her to get out of the way. At his feet was a bundle, and as the boat grew larger and larger, a boy's face appeared, his skin white as snow, his eyes glazed over, staring. Terrified, she tried to run, but her boots were nailed to the ground. She bent to undo the laces, but it was too late, the boat was upon her—

Something cold and wet touched her face and she woke with a start, raising her arms to protect her head. Her hand fell upon warm fur. "Oh, Beans," she said. "Thank you. What a horrible dream."

She stood up, replacing her hat, which had fallen from her face as she slept. She could just make out a figure approaching from the far end of the field. "Oh good. Look, Beans, Daniel's back. Let's see what he's got us for lunch, eh?"

* * *

"So he could be just around the corner," she said as they ate. Daniel's search for the boat seemed to be getting somewhere. Poppy wasn't sure whether to be pleased or scared for him.

"Or he could be miles away. Don't worry, I'm not counting on it. But obviously I'm going to have a look, ask at the next place. The marinas, the other boatyard, they're not far. At least I know that the boat's still on the water and the same guy owns it."

"A nasty guy who could get pretty annoyed with you."

"Yes, well . . . I know it seems crazy." He hung his head, his fingers picking at the grass beside him, and Poppy felt a rush of sympathy. In that moment she revised her opinion. Clearly this was something he felt compelled to do, and if it was so important to him, he should see it through. Even if it meant disappointment. It might mean he could move on, regardless of the outcome.

"Listen," she said. "If you can wait another day, I'll come with you." It had never been her intention to find a walking buddy. Her spontaneous offer surprised her as much as it seemed to startle Daniel.

His eyes widened. "Really? That would be—" Then he shook his head. "No, I can't ask it of you. You have other plans. This is probably a wild goose chase, and a risky one at that. I don't want to get you involved."

"Really, I mean it." She knew this was the right thing to do. He needed support, he was gentle and kind, and she could back him up. Two would be much better than one, in this kind of situation.

"I can help, honestly. He'll be less likely to behave badly with a woman around, I'm sure of it. You need somebody with you, anyway, just in case."

"But what about your walk?"

She thought for a moment. What would Gran say about this? In an instant, she knew. "My walk goes wherever I take it. I'll still be remembering Gran, no matter where I go, and collecting donations. I might be a bit slow at first, but if you can cope with my company, I'd be glad to come with you. We can decide to split up whenever we want. Come on, what do you say?"

She was glad when he nodded. This added a new dimension to her walk. She promised herself it wouldn't detract from her tribute to Gran. But it would add excitement — and Gran would approve of that.

CHAPTER THIRTY-ONE

He was astonished that she offered to help look for *Golden Serpent*. In his heart, he knew he should have done more to dissuade her, but he wanted to spend more time with her. The thought of having her walk with him, even for a short distance, was irresistible.

He stammered his thanks and did his best to persuade himself it meant nothing. She would walk with him for a little, that was all. If she changed her mind or they split after only a few hours, he would still have the pleasure of her company for a while, and that was all he could ask.

They spent the rest of the day together, taking a blanket down to the canal's edge. They talked, dozed and sat in comfortable silence, watching boats come and go. Poppy got into conversations with other walkers, while Daniel stayed in the background. He lay back on the blanket and listened, fascinated by her ability to draw people out. He tried to analyse how she did it, to learn from it, but she confounded him. It would take a lot more than a couple of conversations for him to work out what made it so easy for her to engage with people. To apply it to himself could take a lifetime.

The memory of other, failed conversations from his past elbowed their way through his mind, pushing the present away. The time when, not yet in his teens, still trusting his memory, he'd insisted on telling the English teacher she had a date wrong — it couldn't have been 7 March, because that was a Tuesday, and the event they were discussing had happened on a Saturday. It wasn't even an important date, and she'd got irritated with him for pursuing it. The other boys had laughed. His first day at work, at that horrible, dissatisfying job, when he'd tried to make conversation with the girls across the corridor, he'd stammered and dried up, the colour rushing to his face. He'd never forget the twitching of their mouths, the stifled giggles as he stumbled away.

The humiliation, the hurt. The exact smells, sounds, locations, colours. They were all still with him, like a surround-sound movie.

"Daniel, did you hear what I said? Hello? Come in, Daniel, are you with me?" Poppy's voice sent the memory spinning away. The emotions took a little longer to dissolve.

"Sorry, I — I was somewhere else." He sat up, focusing his gaze on the water.

"You definitely were. Is that what happens?"

He knew exactly what she was asking. "Yes." Pressing his chin onto his knees, he rocked a little. "You can tell how frustrating it was for my teachers. And for my parents. What were you saying?"

She smiled. "Can't remember now. Oh — yes I can. I'm hungry, and it's nearly time for supper. Shall we hobble back?"

* * *

"I'm not sure you're going to want me tagging along, you know." Poppy was sitting outside her tent, changing the dressing on her foot. "This blister is taking ages to get better."

Daniel could see the redness around her heel, spreading upwards into her calf.

"Do you want to wait another day, or two, even? I'm fine with it, if you think it'll help. Or I could come with you into the town and we could find a doctor — the farmer can probably tell us where to go. Looks to me like you might need antibiotics for that."

"I don't know." Poppy prodded the wound with a finger. "I don't want to hold you up. It is better than it was, believe me. Doesn't hurt nearly as much."

"Well that's a good sign. You won't be holding me up, so don't worry about that. I've got the whole summer to do this." The urgency to find Ryan's dad seemed to have lessened, somehow.

Poppy added an extra layer of padding to the dressing and secured it with a sticking plaster. She eased a sock on over it, then another over that.

"Sure you can get your boot on?" Daniel said.

"Should be fine — I always wear two pairs of socks. It's supposed to stop the blisters. So much for that. I won't tie it up too tightly." She replaced the boot, stood and walked a few paces around the tent. "Not too bad. Should be OK to walk today, as long as it's not too far."

Daniel pulled his map from his bag. "It really isn't. The town's two miles from here, and the place I need to get to is literally only a couple of miles further on. We don't need to do it in one day, even."

"Well, if you're sure. I would like to help you, and I'll definitely get bored if I stay here any longer."

"That's a decision, then?"

She smiled. "That's a decision."

"Let's pack up. I'll take the heavy stuff, OK?"

"If you're sure."

"Stop saying that." Daniel started back to his own tent. "And don't forget the marmalade."

Daniel's backpack was full with two people's camping equipment. Various items hung from the straps, and as he hauled the bag onto his back, he was glad they weren't planning to walk too far. He was fitter than he'd ever been, but he wasn't used to carrying a weight like this.

He'd lent Poppy one of his walking sticks — as yet unused — and with the help of this and a lighter pack,

Poppy set off with only a slight limp. It was mid-morning already as they left the field and the sun shone intermittently between bubbles of white cloud moving slowly across a pale blue sky.

"Take it easy," Daniel said. "No need to rush. You don't want to make it bad again."

After a short while they came to the pub where he'd stopped to ask about the boat. At a picnic table in the sun they shared a plate of fish and chips, washed down with pints of cider. Poppy went to pay at the bar and got into conversation with the barman, leaving him with a handful of leaflets.

She eased her leg over the bench as she sat down. "It's really heartening," she said. She showed Daniel a five-pound note and some coins she'd collected in donations. "As soon as people hear about Gran, they remember someone they know, or knew, and talk to me about them. Everyone's been touched by Alzheimer's."

They sat in silence for a few moments.

"Have you tried to find other people like you?" Poppy said, startling Daniel from a memory of his grandparents.

He frowned. "Not really. I don't know why. Lack of energy, low motivation, I suppose. Perhaps I don't believe there's anyone else like me."

"Really? Among all the billions of people in the world? I'm pretty sure you're not unique — nobody is." Poppy hesitated, deep in thought for a moment. "What about the experts? There are some pretty eminent scientists doing research into Alzheimer's. There must be specialists in all kinds of brain diseases, brain conditions, injuries. I'd be amazed if there's nobody studying brains like yours. Your brain could teach them a lot. Imagine that! You could provide a breakthrough in brain research."

"Woah, Poppy, don't get carried away." He wasn't comfortable with the way this was going.

"No, but have you ever tried to find someone?"

"What do you mean, a brain expert?"

"Exactly. An expert in memory and the human brain. I bet you there's some professor here in the UK who's getting paid good money to study brains just like yours."

"Maybe." Daniel's good humour of the morning faded. Thinking about his condition always left him with a feeling of helplessness.

"Does thinking about it bother you?" She knew without a word from him.

"It does, a bit." He nodded. "You're right, though. I need to make the effort, find someone who really understands. It's probably not even difficult. It's just—"

"Scary?"

How was Poppy able to understand him so well, already, when all his life he'd been misunderstood? Of all the people he'd known in his life — here the ranks of faces flicked through his mind's eye as if scrolling past on a computer screen — only Lauren had come close, and not even she had Poppy's prescience. He bowed his head, the peak of his hat hiding a sudden rush of feeling.

"Scary. Yes."

"I get that. It must be terrifying." She was silent for a couple of minutes. "Shall we get going?"

CHAPTER THIRTY-TWO

At first it was strange, having a walking companion. Daniel was used to being alone, and if he wasn't getting lost in his thoughts and memories, he was trying to stay in the present and appreciate his surroundings. Having Poppy beside him gave him a sense of responsibility. He couldn't drift off into his memories, or even practise his mindfulness, because it might seem rude. The simple act of walking with her ahead or behind made him stay in the present. He was aware of her, conscious of her limp, watching for signs of pain. With any other person, this might have caused him stress, but Poppy's calmness seemed to transfer itself to him. Soon he relaxed, allowing the rhythm of his steps to fall in with hers.

Even walking slowly, they soon reached their destination. The towpath skirted round the outer edge of the canal, a bridge leading to the town.

"How are you doing, Poppy?"

"Fine. Enjoying being back on the path."

"Do you want to carry on, or have a look around the village? There's supposed to be an old church and brilliant views from the top. If you fancy it, we could give it a try?"

Poppy paused for a moment to adjust her socks. "Not really — churches aren't my thing. I'm fine to carry on. We can always go back if we can't find somewhere to stop for the night." She smiled and bumped his arm with her shoulder. "Anyway, we've got a boat to find."

* * *

"You're best asking at the marinas," the man at the second boatyard said. "I've only been here a year or so. She may well have been through, but I don't remember her, sorry."

On the way out of the boatyard, Daniel again had the disquieting feeling they were being watched. He cast his eye over the boats that were moored there, but apart from a man mopping a roof, there was nobody around.

"What?" Poppy said, following his gaze.

"Nothing. Just a feeling."

"What kind of feeling?"

"It's probably nothing. Sometimes I imagine things . . . It's the anxiety."

She raised her eyebrows. "What things?"

She was nothing if not direct, which was one of the things he liked about her. But he didn't want to scare her. Nobody liked to think they were being watched. Or followed.

"Oh, you know. People looking at me. Stupid, I know."

She shook her head. "Not stupid. Oversensitive, maybe. There's nobody there, Daniel."

She was right. The boats were quiet, tilting gently in the wind, but there was no sign of anyone except the lone man with the mop.

"Come on, let's crack this." She poked him with her walking stick. "Onward!"

But as they left the yard, the feeling struck again. A shiver ran down the back of his neck. A movement in the corner of his eye made him whip round.

Nothing — only his mind playing tricks again. But however much he tried to push it from his mind, a tiny trace of the feeling remained.

A warm haze drifted over the canal as they approached the marina, a large area of water with narrowboats lined up diagonally on either side.

"Let's check them," Poppy said straight away, setting off to walk the perimeter of the marina.

Daniel felt a lurch in his gut every time he saw a boat that looked similar to *Golden Serpent*. Every other boat was blue, though the colours varied from light turquoise to dark navy. "Let's take it slowly," he said. "If it is here, I'd like to be prepared, not come across it all of a sudden."

"Sorry." She paused to let him catch up. "I'm letting my enthusiasm run away with me. Of course you don't want to bump into him. What will you say if we do find him?"

"I've been thinking about that for most of my life," he said with a grimace. "But I still don't know. I've got some vague idea of asking after Ryan. What do you think I should say?"

"We'll get a feel for what he's like when we see him. See if he's chatty."

"I think we can be pretty certain he's not, from what I've heard."

"You can't just turn up and ask about Ryan straight away. It seems a weird thing to do, especially after such a long time. Can you imagine, if he really did kill his son and dump him in the water? Even mentioning his name would get you into trouble."

"What should I say then?"

"Let me approach him first. I could stop and make some friendly remark like 'nice boat', or something, or ask how old the boat is. Then you could say you recognise the boat, ask him how long he's owned it." Poppy stopped to take a sip of water. She gazed across the line of boats. "Mention the place where you saw him, maybe remind him about the boot sale — then you can say you thought he had a boy with him. How's that?"

"Brilliant — why didn't I think of that? You may have saved me from another beating."

"Another one?"

He hadn't mentioned the mugging, what with all the drama of the story about Ryan and *Golden Serpent*. He didn't want to be the person who was always in trouble.

"A long story."

Those raised eyebrows again.

"Tell you later. Ready to roll?"

"Yes, let's get to the next marina. It's not far, right?"

"Less than a mile, I'd say. And there's another boatyard. Then I think we should think about where to stop for the night."

"Sure. I think my foot will be ready for a break by then."

"You will say if it's feeling bad, won't you?"

"Of course. It's absolutely fine at the moment — my double dressing seems to be working. And I'd rather get away from the junction before we camp. It's a bit too busy round here."

"Of course, much better to stay somewhere quiet. Let's go."

Soon they saw the signs of a boatyard, a queue of colourful craft lining the approach. There was no one around when they arrived, so they sat on a bank nearby and waited. A young lad in overalls soon appeared and unlocked the workshop. They followed him in.

"Hello," he said with a cheery smile. "My dad's not here at the moment but can I help you?"

"We're looking for a boat called *Golden Serpent*," Daniel said. "Blue, with a golden snake—"

The boy nodded. "Yep, she was here last week."

"H-here? In this boatyard?" He could barely mask his astonishment. Finding *Golden Serpent* had seemed such a crazy, far-fetched idea, he'd persuaded himself it would never happen. Or perhaps he hadn't really wanted it to happen, and now that it had, he was floored.

Mercifully, the boy carried on without noticing. "Yep. We fixed her up, but she won't last long, I reckon. He'll have to give up on her soon."

Daniel, still reeling, barely heard the question. Poppy stepped forward. "We were looking for the owner, actually. Has he moved on?"

"Limped on. She's not been looked after. Hull's very thin — going into holes. Should have been overplated years ago. After the owner, was you?" He gave Poppy a quizzical look.

"A man called Collins," she said. "Was it him?"

"I reckon," the lad said. "Still owes us for the repair. Doubt we'll see that money." He shrugged.

"Was he on his own?"

"Yep, just him. He dumped some of his junk, then took off without paying."

"Would you happen to know which way he went? We'd like to catch up with him."

"Reckon you're not the only ones. On to the Grand Union — east. Least, that's the way he was heading when he left. Won't be too hard to catch up with her, she's like an old tortoise now. Owe you money, too, does he?"

"Nothing like that. We — my friend — used to know his son. Was anyone else living on the boat?"

"Don't think so. He's a loner, that one. No sign of a family. Been around the canals for years, my dad said. Comes and goes. If you look hard enough, I reckon you'll find him."

"Thanks. You've been very helpful."

Daniel nodded at Poppy. "Shall we get on, then?"

She nodded back and smiled her thanks to the boy.

"Want me to tell him you're looking for him, if he comes by?" the lad said.

"Ah, no, that's OK. He won't remember me," Daniel said, a little too quickly. The last thing he wanted was to warn Collins that they were looking for him. "I'm sure we'll catch up with him soon."

CHAPTER THIRTY-THREE

As they walked away from the boatyard, Poppy exhaled with a whistle. She could hardly believe they were so close. This was even more exciting than she'd expected. "Wow, Daniel, we found him! He could be round the next corner!"

She glanced at Daniel's face, but his head was down, the peaked cap concealing his expression. "Daniel?"

When his eyes met hers, she stopped in her tracks. "Daniel? You look scared."

Daniel kicked at the long grass that bordered the canal. "Of course I'm scared," he said at last. "I've been frightened of this bloke for nineteen years. I've had nightmares about him, about what I saw — I've relived that scene on the boat every day for so long, I don't know what's real and what isn't any more. Now I'm about to find him, I'm terrified. I'm not a very brave person."

He was trying to smile, but Poppy detected the break in his voice, the slight tremor in the hand that pushed his cap back off his forehead. At once she felt guilty for her enthusiasm. She was treating Daniel's story like an adventure, a mystery to be solved, but it was so much more than that for him. It was a huge step that could change his life.

In that moment she saw his fragility. He was like a fragment of porcelain that could shatter into a thousand pieces at the softest touch. Her first instinct was to hug him, to tell him it was OK, she was here. But he didn't need mothering, he needed someone who believed in him, like Gran said.

"Listen," she said. "You're right to be scared, and you're brave even to think about confronting that man. But I know why you want to do it, and I do understand how important it is to you. Look, we don't have to run off and find him tonight. Why don't we take it easy, rest a bit, talk some more about how to play this. You can let it sink in, about *Golden Serpent*, gather your thoughts before going anywhere near Collins."

Daniel set off at a pace, shaking his head. "No, I need to do this now. I'm getting somewhere at last. I can't risk losing him — or more likely, my courage."

"Woah, hold up! I'll be getting another blister if you charge off like that."

Daniel stopped. "God, I'm sorry, Poppy. Wound up in my own problems again. Are you OK?"

She almost laughed at his change of expression. Anger and fear had transformed into remorse and concern in a flash.

"Of course. Don't look so worried. Listen, let's stop for a cuppa and gather ourselves. Just for a minute."

"OK." He undid the straps on his backpack. "Let's do it."

They sat gazing into the murky waters of the canal, lost in their separate thoughts. Ducks busied themselves in the reeds while a breeze doodled patterns on the water's surface. Further along, the light glistened on tiny wavelets that ran with the wind, fading into nothing as they slowed.

Poppy glanced at Daniel. He was running his hands through his hair, a gesture she'd noticed before. In most people, it would signify bafflement or tiredness, but in Daniel it was unreadable. She suspected he'd disappeared into his memory again. Perhaps he was reliving that scene, made real even for her now that they knew *Golden Serpent* existed and Collins wasn't far away.

"Tell you what," she said, trying to pull him out of his inner world, "let's carry on, gently. We'll go along the first stretch of the Grand Union to the east, see what it's like, and ask again after Collins. If it looks good for a night's stay, let's call it a day and hunker down. If not, we can come back to the junction and head north."

Daniel nodded but he looked miserable, like a confused child.

"We're homing in, Daniel." She paused, watching his expression. "But listen, you always have a choice. You don't have to do this. You can stop now, and nobody's going to judge you."

He grunted. "I am. *I'm* going to judge me. I always do."

"But why? You're not obliged to do anything about Collins, or what you suspect he might have done to Ryan. You were how old? Ten?"

He nodded.

"Exactly. A ten-year-old boy isn't responsible. Even if you witnessed a crime, you were too young to know what to do. You've carried the responsibility for years, and the responsibility wasn't yours. You did nothing wrong, Daniel."

Daniel shook his head miserably. "I could have—"

"No, you couldn't. At ten years old, you couldn't have been expected to do anything about it. And when you did do something about it, the police weren't interested."

"Logically, you're right," he said. "But unfortunately my brain disagrees. It forces me to remember it, all the time, and until I've done something to make it right, it will carry on controlling me. I have no choice."

* * *

Poppy felt nothing but sympathy for Daniel as they made their ponderous way along the hard, dry towpath. She was pretty certain this quest wouldn't have the right ending for him, but at the same time she could see why he had set so much store by it. He'd run out of options, and had begun to believe that this was his only way out.

She bit her lip as she followed him along the path. Perhaps she could do something positive to help him, to give him some peace, when he'd finished trying to search out Collins. She was convinced he could be helped, if only he could find the right people. Perhaps she could ask her Alzheimer's charity? They must have contacts — scientists, academics. At the very least, they could put her in touch with someone who might help. She promised herself to contact them as soon as she could, without telling Daniel. She could guess what his reaction would be.

Somehow she knew she had to help this man. They'd only spent a few days together but already she felt close to him. He'd confided in her, shared his deepest secrets. That was remarkable in itself. She felt humbled by the level of trust, the courage that must have taken. It showed a rare level of sensitivity. He'd voiced all his fears and anxieties. That, too, was endearing. He didn't seem concerned that he might appear weak, as some men would.

Poppy's idea of strength was different from most people's. She didn't see strength in the usual type of masculinity — fearlessness, power, pride, control, ego. Connection, emotional intelligence, humility, kindness — these were the traits that Poppy admired. Daniel seemed to have all these and more.

She looked at him now as he stopped to let a couple of walkers pass. He'd removed his hat and was gazing across the water, the wind ruffling his hair, unruly curls that reached his shoulders and fell down across his cheek, forcing him to brush them away from time to time. His body was lean and muscled, and the sun had darkened his bare skin to a warm tan. His eyes were pale blue and piercing, and when he smiled, they danced.

She wondered if she was falling for this unusual man with the wild mind. He'd made no sign that he was interested in her beyond friendship, but she felt a kind of joy in his company that could go further, if things worked out. Every moment they spent together, it seemed to grow stronger.

But now was not the time. She wanted to help him, and she would do her best. He needed a friend, and she was happy to fill that role. Then she would see what happened.

Lost in thought, she started at the buzz of her mobile in her shorts pocket. "Hi, Mum," she said, waving Daniel on. "Yes, all fine, thanks. The blister's much better today, and yes, we're walking. A bit slowly, but it's OK."

She hung back, letting Daniel drift a little further ahead. "Actually, Mum, can you do something for me please? I scribbled the name and number of the woman at the charity on the notepad in the kitchen."

There was a pause at the other end as her mum checked. "Yes, got it! It's—"

"Can you text it to me, please? I'm still walking, it's tricky to write it down just now."

"That's fine. How much have you collected?"

"I haven't counted recently. Lots of loose change, but it's growing."

"Well done you. Speak tomorrow."

"Bye, Mum. Love you."

As she slipped her phone back into her pocket, a text arrived. The next moment of privacy she had, she would make the call.

CHAPTER THIRTY-FOUR

His mind was in turmoil as they made their way from the marina through the junction. Here the two canals met and he hesitated for a moment. If they turned north, there would be locks, more marinas and another boathouse within the first mile or so, and plenty of people around. But the lad in the boathouse had reckoned Collins would head east, where the canal was quiet.

Either way, they'd still be lucky to find him. Daniel was under no illusions. Though narrowboats were slow, chugging along at a fast walking pace at most, *Golden Serpent* could be many miles away by now. Even if Collins had stayed south as they were hoping, they could keep missing him for months. But Daniel had to keep trying, and there seemed no other way of doing this. He no longer knew if this compulsion was about Ryan and a sense of duty to an abused and murdered child, or if it was about him, his need to have his memory confirmed — or a combination of the two. He just knew this was something he had to do. He probably would have run the next few miles if it hadn't been for Poppy.

They took the eastward path, which soon opened out and they were able to walk side by side. "I need to take my mind off all this," Daniel said. His eyes fell on Beans, who was trotting happily ahead. He got the feeling a dog could teach him a lot about staying in the moment. "Tell me about the rescue centre, and the dogs. Persuade me I should get one."

"With pleasure. You'll regret suggesting that," Poppy said with a grin. "There's so much to say."

"Let's start with Beans. It's brilliant, the way he gets on with things. You'd never know he'd lost a leg."

Poppy wasn't exaggerating about how much she could talk about dogs. She clearly loved working in the rescue centre, and was passionate about the animals. Daniel wondered if he could ever feel that much love for a creature. Or for a human, come to that. He barely noticed the time as the path passed underfoot smoothly, like a moving pavement.

They soon reached open countryside, the canal quiet in contrast with the activity at the junction. A line of moored boats crouched on a straight stretch of water, free of locks, barely any houses in sight. These boats looked like permanent homes, the borders of the towpath dotted with possessions. Bikes, bins, plant pots filled with bright geraniums and herbs, wheelbarrows and wooden pallets crowded the hedgerows, giving the stretch a jaunty, bohemian look. Owners busied themselves painting their doorways or tidying the outside areas, greeting them as they passed.

"Come on, let's ask," Poppy said.

"I don't know." Daniel scanned the line of boats. "Perhaps we should wait a bit."

"Come on," she said again. "No time like the present. I'll do the talking, if you like. I'd like to get some more donations anyway."

He shrugged. "Go ahead then. Thanks, Poppy. I'll just . . . skulk about in the background."

She laughed. "Skulk away."

As it turned out, Poppy got talking to a number of the owners. Hands delved into pockets, heads dipped into the interiors of boats, people reappeared with wallets or loose change in their hands. Daniel drifted away. He found a sunny patch of grass and sat watching as a large narrowboat meandered by, its driver raising his hand in a lazy wave. A lone man in ripped jeans cycled past, a hat pulled down over his face, dark greasy hair reaching his shoulders. Daniel stared at his receding back. It could have been the man from the boatyard, the taciturn one, but he couldn't be sure. He was gone in a flash.

He ran the events of yesterday through his mind. The chances of catching up with Collins weighed heavily against them. He could be very close or long gone, and there was no way of knowing. And if they kept looking, Daniel would be on guard constantly, his eyes searching the canal day and night, imagining threats from all directions. Was it really worth it?

What was the point in this search, anyway? The police hadn't believed his story last time and he couldn't think of any good reason why they should believe it now. Did he really think Ryan's dad would confess to a heinous crime — particularly to some stranger who accosted him out of the blue? Or that some kind of crucial evidence would emerge that they could take to the police, who would see sense and make an arrest? He shook his head at his own naivety. It wasn't going to happen that way, if it happened at all.

He looked back at Poppy and wondered if he was being fair to her. The last thing he wanted was to jeopardise their friendship for the sake of his crazy plan. It was a wild goose chase, at best. At worst, it was extremely dangerous.

She was talking animatedly to a couple standing in the entrance to their boat, leaning up against the hull with mugs in their hands. They were gesturing and laughing. She'd made some new friends. A moment later she came over to sit with him. He felt a fizz of energy from her.

She took a long sip from her water bottle. "That was interesting," she said. "They were all so nice. Lots of them gave me money. So generous, and they obviously didn't have much. I had to stop them giving me more!"

"That's great." He tried to sound enthusiastic, but failed.

Luckily, she didn't seem to notice. "Oh, and guess what? I've got something for you."

"Has someone seen Collins?"

"Maybe."

"C'mon, Poppy."

"OK. A couple of them said they'd seen the boat — they mentioned the snake. They were a bit vague about the driver, but it was an oldish guy, thin, with grey hair. Alone."

"That's him! It must be! When was this?"

"Yesterday."

"Yesterday — really?"

She laughed. "Yes, towards evening. Come on, let's go. With a bit of luck, we'll find him tonight."

"Just — let's sit down a minute."

Things were going too fast. His brain had survived a daily tsunami of memories for nearly twenty years, but the events of the last two days were beginning to overwhelm him. He imagined his brain becoming overloaded with data, memories bursting out like sheets of paper from a photocopier, each page dense with stories, the mind emptying itself of useless information.

"Poppy, I'm struggling a bit with this."

She glanced at him, her eyes full of empathy. "I know you are. I'm sorry. I know I'm overenthusiastic." She turned to him. "Tell me."

It took him a while to order a logical sentence. "I've started this journey thinking I want to find out the truth about Ryan. And I do, if only to settle something for myself. I need to stop thinking about it, remembering it, and I truly believe the only way to do that is to find out what really happened, once and for all. But—" He paused, unsure if he was saying it right.

"But what?"

"I know it's ridiculous, the whole thing. But I hoped it would help me work things out. Decide to get help, whatever. Find a way to live with this . . . memory thing."

"I understand that, you don't need to explain it all again." Her voice was gentle.

"I know. But since I met you, I've realised something. None of this is important. It's all stupid, frivolous, a . . . a vanity of some sort. Of course it's not going to solve anything. My brain is different from other people's, like my hair is different, or my nose. Or like some people are very tall, and others very small."

Poppy thought for a moment. "So . . . it's ruining your life?"

"Yes, but is it?" He rubbed his head. "Or am I simply making a huge thing of something other people just deal with?"

"I don't think you are. I've never even heard of anyone else with your kind of brain. Brains are very different from noses, or hair. But where is all this leading?"

"I don't know, Poppy. I've met you now, and you've shown me there are more important things, perhaps. Family, friendship. Am I sounding corny?"

She laughed. "Yep. A bit."

"Sorry, I'm not very good at expressing myself. The point is . . . The point is, Collins could be dangerous. He'll deny everything. I'll look like an idiot, and I'll probably get beaten up. I know you want to help, and I'm really happy that you do, but I don't want to get you into trouble for something that's so — oh, I don't know. Stupid."

She shook her head. "It's not stupid. I respect you for wanting to know the truth. No, I do." Daniel was shaking his head. "And I'm an adult. I made up my own mind to help you — you didn't coerce me or anything. I know Collins might be difficult, even violent. If it makes you feel better, I promise to run like hell if it gets nasty. But I'm determined to help, and when I'm determined . . ." She made a fierce face at him.

He laughed despite himself. "I know, and believe me, I'm grateful. But I'd feel terrible if anything happened to you because of me. I don't want to be the cause of harm to anyone, obviously, but especially you. I've only just met you, but I like you and I want us to be friends — as long as you want that too, of course." She nodded, opening her mouth to speak, but he interrupted. "Friends just don't put one another in danger." He sighed, picking at the grass beside him. "Listen, if we do find Collins, I want you to walk the other way. Stay where he can't see you, and leave me to it."

"But you agreed he might be less suspicious if there's a woman around."

"No buts, Poppy. I mean it. This isn't your problem, it's mine. You have to promise me, otherwise we'll have to go our separate ways."

Poppy looked at him then, her eyes searching his. "You mean it, don't you?"

"I do. I'm not doing this if it puts you in danger. Promise me."

"You must do it. So, I will promise. But I will also come to your help, if you're in trouble—" She raised a hand as Daniel started to object. "Without putting myself anywhere near danger. Believe me, I'm not keen on being beaten up, either."

They stared at each other for a moment, their faces serious, until Daniel let out a long breath. "Right. This is assuming we ever find him, of course. And that he doesn't come up behind us."

"However unlikely it all is, I'm going to be your backup. I think you should keep your phone somewhere you can grab it quickly. It's useless buried at the bottom of your bag. I'll have mine to hand too. Just in case."

"Sure." He rooted around in his bag. "You're right, I can't find it. Ah, there it is." He buttoned it into the pocket of his shorts. "Better?"

"Better. And Daniel — I want us to be friends, too. Can I be your walking companion for a while? I thought I'd like walking alone, but it's much better walking with you."

CHAPTER THIRTY-FIVE

He could barely keep a smile from his face. That she had chosen to walk with him was possibly the best thing that had happened to him, ever. So good, in fact, he forgot for a full five minutes why he was walking at all.

Before long, Poppy's mobile rang. After a couple of seconds listening intently, she left his side and wandered up and down the hedgerow, her spare hand covering her other ear to hear better. This didn't seem like a call from her mum, who she spoke to every day. When it was her mum calling, she kept on walking right beside him, and he could hear their conversation clearly. This must be something different, and from her body language, it looked important.

Figuring it was none of his business, he drifted off into memories of his own mother, a childhood scene of her gardening, on her hands and knees, him as a little boy with his own set of mini gardening tools, trying to help her. He'd had a mini spade, fork and trowel. They were painted red metal, with wooden handles, and he was so proud of them. His mother had given him a tiny patch of flower bed. They planted seeds, pansies and forget-me-nots. He remembered the fascination he'd had for the plants, running out into the garden whenever he could to check their progress, and the disappointment he'd felt when the seedlings failed. "It happens," his mum had said. "In nature, not everything will grow well. It depends on so many things."

"What things?"

"The weather is important. Plants need sun and rain to grow properly. And not too much cold. And they need to be safe. Like us — we need food and water, shelter from the weather, and someone to look after us." She'd smiled at him then, a loving look that he remembered as if it were yesterday.

A buzzing in his pocket startled him. Fumbling with the button, he failed to answer the call in time, but the screen showed an unknown number. Apart from Poppy, he'd only given this number to his parents and Lauren, so he figured it must be a mistake or a random sales call. He returned the handset to his pocket, but two minutes later it buzzed again. Someone had left a message.

"My name is Detective Constable Dunbar, from Kidlington Police. Apologies for the slow response, we've had a bit of a shake-up here and your case has been reassigned to me. I've read your recent statement and I'd like you to come in for another interview. Please call me back on this number as soon as possible."

He disconnected the call with mixed feelings. So, they wanted to follow up his statement. That was a surprise. He decided not to return the call, yet. If he could deliver the suspect to the police, then he had a much better chance of being believed.

Meanwhile Poppy had finished her call.

"Everything OK?" he said.

"Fine — you?"

"Yes, all good."

"Come on then, let's see if we can catch up with this boat."

Very soon the sun disappeared behind a large grey cloud and a breeze sprang up, bringing wildflower fragrances mingled with the heavy aroma of farmyard.

"I'm hungry," Poppy said. "Shall we stop for a quick bite before it rains?"

"Good idea. Near that bridge? Then if it starts to pour we've got a bit of shelter."

Poppy handed him a food box. "You never seem to run out of sandwiches," Daniel said. "Do you get up in the night to make them?"

"I don't, but you're right — it's a magic box," she said with a serious look. "Fresh sandwiches appear every day. Today's fillings are — look! Cheese and chutney, or cheese and tomato. Or cheese. What a selection! Oh, and I have apples."

"Perfect." He took the box from her hand, almost dropping it in the process. He saved it from spraying the contents all over the grass with a well-timed grab.

"Oh, good catch!" Poppy said. They sat on the warm grass in silence while they ate, a light breeze taking the heat from the air.

Daniel was remembering other warm days when Poppy suddenly said, "That phone call . . . I think I might have found someone who can help you."

For a heart-sinking moment, Daniel imagined another therapist, another doctor who didn't understand him. He was about to thank her, explain that he'd done all that, but she stopped him. "Wait — I think this is different from anything you've done before. There's a girl at the charity, I've got to know her a bit. Her job is to help decide what research to commission. She has to keep in touch with all the latest scientific papers, state-of-the-art studies, stuff like that, all around the world. I told her about you. I asked if she'd come across an expert in memory, your kind of memory. And she has."

"Poppy, I—"

"I knew you wouldn't want me to do this, but I had a feeling she could help, and she knew immediately who you could go to. There's a professor at Oxford University. He's one of the world's leading experts. Apparently he's really approachable. When she told him about you—"

"What?" Daniel was horrified. "Hang on a minute, you told her all about me? And she told him? How . . . ?"

"I'm good at listening, Daniel. It's not that difficult, listening to you, to understand how it must be for you. Well it wasn't for me, anyway. I hope you don't mind too much."

Daniel wasn't sure how much he minded. He was astonished that she would have taken it upon herself to go this far, so astonished he opened his mouth but shut it again. He needed time to absorb all this.

"Professor James, that's his name. You can look him up on my phone next time we get a good signal. He wants to talk to you. He's really interested, he thinks you have a particular kind of memory — he even had a name for it but I couldn't write it down and I can't remember now, but it was like a 'superior' something—"

"Shit, Poppy!" He didn't know what to think. His brain was about to explode.

"Are you angry with me?" She gave him a pleading look. "It's great news, isn't it?"

"No, I'm not angry with you. I'm just—"

"What — terrified?" She peered into his face. "You look like you've seen a ghost."

"No, I'm not terrified. I'm just . . . gobsmacked."

"But isn't this what you need? He's one of the world's leading experts — just imagine! If you can get him to confirm what you suspect, that your memory is perfect, that your brain never switches off from the flashbacks, and that your mind is completely different from anyone else's, then the police will be convinced. They'll have to be!"

He stared at her, shaking his head in amazement. "I can't believe you did this for me, Poppy. For years I've put off doing just that, thinking I'd be disappointed, that nobody would ever understand me. And you did it with one phone call."

"Are you sure you're not upset with me?"

"No, just totally taken aback." He took a deep breath. "Nobody's ever taken me that seriously, Poppy. I mean it. It's a new experience."

She laughed. "Well I listened properly, as I said. And I believed you."

"I don't know what to say. Thank you."

"And you'll contact him? Please say you will."

"I'll contact him." He owed her that, at the very least. He would have to screw up his courage, but he would do it.

"Brilliant. I'll get you his number, you can talk to him later."

Her fingers sped as she tapped out a message on her mobile, a slight frown on her clear forehead. Daniel was glad of the few moments to recover himself.

But when she looked up again, she gasped. "Oh my God, Daniel, don't look now! I said, don't!" She gestured at him not to speak.

He froze, mouthing "What?" at her. It was torture not being able to look. But he could see from her face that she'd seen something important — something on the water. He knew better than to turn when he'd been told not to. His scalp tingled with anticipation.

"Look now," she whispered, her eyes wide.

He followed her gaze, turning to stare over his right shoulder.

The stern of a narrowboat was chugging away from them. Dark blue, with gold lettering, the name spelled out in Gothic font. *Golden Serpent*.

A man steered the boat, his back to them. They could see sparse, greying hair touching the back of a black T-shirt, the skin on his arms dark with tattoos. A snake curled its inky body around his neck, the zigzag pattern on its back clearly visible as the boat drifted on.

Collins. Daniel couldn't see his face, but he would have known that tattoo anywhere. He craned his neck as the boat negotiated the narrow bridge ahead, gradually disappearing around a long curve.

"Quick!" He packed up his food with shaking hands and shouldered his backpack, helping Poppy up from the ground. "We can't lose him now. Let's go!" Without thinking, he grabbed her hand and they half-walked, half-ran along the towpath.

"Slow down, Daniel! We don't want him to turn round and see us running, that would look really suspicious. We'll catch up easily enough if we walk fast."

Daniel slowed. The first signs of a panic attack prodded at him. He let go of her hand, though she'd given him no indication that she wanted him to. But he couldn't think about that now. They were so close!

They were through the bridge and starting to follow the curve in the canal when another line of moored boats appeared ahead. But he could no longer ignore his body — something was wrong with his breathing, a spasm gripping his stomach. He stopped.

"Poppy, sorry, I need to . . ."

She turned back, seeing his distress. "It's OK," she said. "We won't miss him. Just do what you need to do."

He sank onto the grass, head between his knees, fighting to control his body. A drumming started in his temples and he closed his eyes, focusing on breathing. Everything tensed: his back, his shoulders, his fists, everything battling against him.

"Here," Poppy's voice broke through the deafening thump of his heart. "Put this on your forehead, it'll help." She placed a cool, wet cloth into his hand and guided it to his brow. He hadn't even seen her leave his side. "Try and relax your neck . . . and now your shoulders. That's it. Now unclench your hands. Keep breathing. In, and slowly out. That's it. It's OK, there's nobody around. There's plenty of time."

Conflicting emotions passed over him: embarrassment, frustration, anger at himself and the body that wouldn't obey him, worry that they'd lose Collins, fear of what might happen when they found him. It took a few moments for him to realise he was no longer shaking. His breathing had steadied, the thump of his heart lessened. He opened his eyes, raising his head cautiously.

Poppy's concerned face was inches from his, and he observed as if from afar the blue of her irises, the white of the space around them. The smooth skin of her cheek, the slight furrow of anxiety on her brow.

"I'm OK. Getting better," he managed to say. "Sorry. Panic attack. Guess you figured that one out."

She smiled and her face relaxed. "I did. Used to have them myself. No need to apologise, they're not controllable, I know that. I'll make us a cup of tea while you recover."

"No," Daniel said vehemently. Then, more softly, "No, it's OK. I can't risk missing him now. Let's go on."

Walking slowly, wary of coming across the boat unexpectedly, they approached the line of moorings ahead.

"I think I can see it," Poppy said.

"Yes, me too." Daniel focused on his breath, his step faltering. "Let's hold back for a minute, pretend we're stopping for a drink. I need to be prepared. Remember to hang back, don't go too close." Poppy nodded.

Daniel gazed along the canal. Many of the boats were quiet, their windows shaded, as if their owners were away, but one or two showed signs of life. A man stood further on at the canal's edge, smoking, and a woman sat on the roof of a boat with a book. He could just see the rear end of *Golden Serpent*, her name standing out against the dark blue of the paintwork, but there was no sign that she was occupied. Everything was calm, the only sound the birdsong in the bushes opposite and the gentle lap of water against the hulls. He took a deep breath and put his sunglasses on. From behind their shady lenses, he could watch more easily without being spotted.

"Right," he said. "I'm ready. Come on, let's do this."

He kept his head down, watching his boots as they tramped with determination towards his target, as if of their own accord.

"Wait — look," Poppy said. "There are people around on the next boat. Let's talk to them. I can ask them to donate, see if they're friendly, while you check out what's happening on *Golden Serpent*."

He nodded. Poppy went straight up to the couple who were sitting in the sun on the boat just behind *Golden Serpent*, mugs of tea in their hands.

"Hi," she said. "Lovely day."

Daniel watched her with envy. He'd never been able to do that — go up to a stranger and talk in such a relaxed and unconcerned way. It was a gift, and Poppy seemed to possess it in spades.

The couple were immediately friendly. "Well, hello, walkers," the man said. "Where are you headed?"

"Where our feet take us," Poppy said. "Enjoying the summer walking the canals."

The man nodded. "Great way to do it — good on you. Nice dog." He leaned down to give Beans a stroke.

"Do you live on the boat?"

"We do, over the summer. In winter it's not so good, gets a bit cold and damp. We've got a house in Banbury . . ."

Poppy had found common ground already. Daniel's gaze shifted to *Golden Serpent*. At the stern, ahead of them, he could see that one of the hatch doors was slightly ajar. Someone was home, and he felt a thrill of fear. He could just see movement inside, though the interior was dark, and the boat rocked a little, though there was no wind to speak of.

Poppy had started to talk about her gran and Alzheimer's, and the couple busied themselves finding money for a donation, a biscuit for Beans.

Daniel touched Poppy's sleeve. "Let's ask them."

Poppy turned to the woman, who was sitting closest to her. "Have you got to know the other owners?" She indicated *Golden Serpent*, keeping her hand low.

"A few, yes." She pointed behind their boat. "That one's empty, but the one a bit further along, see, with the solar panels, they've been here a while. Retired couple, very sociable, we've shared a few good evenings with them. Him, in the next one along—" she waved a hand towards *Golden Serpent* — "He keeps himself to himself. He's a bad-tempered so-and-so." She lowered her voice and leaned towards

Poppy. "Not like the rest of us. My husband reckons he's up to no good. Some shady characters visiting, late at night, that sort of stuff. I was a bit worried at first, but he leaves us well alone."

"Thanks for the warning. It's been lovely to talk to you. Thank you so much for donating."

"Oh, that's nothing, my dear. Happy to donate, it could happen to any of us, that Alzheimer's. Let's hope they find a cure soon."

"Indeed. Cheers, enjoy the summer."

"You too."

Daniel turned to Poppy to suggest she stay put while he approached *Golden Serpent*. But she was too quick for him.

She was already there, knocking on the trap door.

CHAPTER THIRTY-SIX

Daniel's panic attack had made her even more determined to be the one to approach Collins first. It made sense — there was no chance she'd be recognised, and she had a genuine reason to approach people. She was quick on her feet and she wasn't scared of anyone. Moreover, she was good at getting people into conversation. It was something Daniel found difficult, and it was probably the best way she could help. If she lured Collins into talking to her, she might even pose the question about Ryan herself, in a perfectly innocent way. He wouldn't be suspicious of her in the same way he might be of a man — particularly one who seemed nervous.

She leaned over and knocked on the open door of *Golden Serpent*. In a moment, a weather-beaten face stared out at her. His head was mostly bald, with patches of grey hair at the sides, his eyes faded blue and piercing. In a single glance, she took in the dark tattoo, the snake curled around his neck from front to back. She could see its fiery eyes, its jaws wide, ready to strike. She had found Collins.

Judging by the frown on his face and the set of his mouth, she wasn't welcome.

She was intensely aware of Daniel behind her. He would be horrified at what she was doing, but she was determined.

Ignoring the man's body language, she smiled and said cheerily, "Hi, I'm Poppy. I'm walking the canals in memory of my grandmother, who died recently of Alzheimer's. I wondered if you'd donate to my charity, to help other sufferers? It's a really good cause . . ."

His head began to shake as he turned to step back down into the dingy interior.

"It's not a problem if you don't want to give," she said. "Nice boat, by the way. Do you live on it permanently?"

He paused, turning back a little, and she took her opportunity to keep him from leaving. "Only — my friend and I, we were thinking it might be a good way to live. On a boat like this, on the canals. Do you move about much?"

He looked taken aback, as if people didn't normally talk to him. His voice was deep and gravelly, like a long-term smoker's. "Nah. I stays a while, moves on, comes back. Look, I—"

"How old is your boat? I bet it's seen a few places in its lifetime."

"I dunno. Look, lady, I gotta go—"

"Does your family live with you too? It must be fun for kids, living on a canal boat."

He was beginning to look annoyed. "Nah." He waved her away and turned to go once more.

"It's just, my friend thinks he recognises you."

That got his attention. He swung round and stepped up onto the platform, one heavily tattooed arm holding on to the roof of the boat. His body tensed. "What did you say?"

Poppy, at once scared and excited by his reaction, took a big step backwards, bumping into Daniel, who had come up behind her. "I said, my friend here thinks he knows you. Or at least, your son."

His reaction was immediate. He lunged forwards, his finger pointing in Poppy's face, almost touching her.

She stumbled backwards over Daniel's feet. As they righted themselves in a tangle of backpacks, arms and legs,

Collins stepped off the boat. They scrambled back a few steps, keeping their distance as far as they could.

Collins's eyes were pinpoints of black as he turned a furious gaze onto Daniel. "What did you say? What son? What the fuck do you know about me?"

CHAPTER THIRTY-SEVEN

Daniel pushed Poppy behind him with one arm, eyeing Collins, poised to run. Adrenaline rushed through him. In an instant, his heart was thumping, his breath coming in short gasps like the start of the panic attack he'd had minutes ago. But now a powerful energy coursed through his veins. He stood his ground, facing the memory that had plagued him for years. That face, that tattoo, that gravelly voice.

"Poppy, get out of here, now. Go!"

To his immense relief, Poppy didn't hesitate. She ran from his side, back in the direction they'd come from, Beans trotting at her feet.

The air eddied and settled into the void where her body had been. Daniel kept his eyes on Collins as her footsteps faded. He couldn't be sure how far she'd gone, but when he could no longer hear her, he let his breath go.

Collins stepped towards him, jaw jutting, eyes glittering. Daniel raised his hands, palms forward. A man's shout came from one side and he risked a glance, stepping back in case Collins took the opportunity to attack. A man was approaching on the towpath, still some distance away.

He focused on Collins. "Look," he said, keeping his voice level, though his entire body was trembling. "I thought

I recognised you — from a long time ago. I'm probably wrong."

"Fuck off!" Collins spat on the ground close to Daniel's feet, a great gob of spittle. His eyes were pale marbles, hard as granite, filled with hatred. "Go on, fuck off, toerag! Keep out of my business." As the sinews in his neck tightened, the snake seemed to writhe, its body growing large and threatening. He turned away and began to climb back onto his boat, one foot already on the platform. In a moment he would be gone.

Daniel had to make his move, or lose the one opportunity he had. He made as if to leave, heading in the direction Poppy had taken. Then he turned back to Collins.

"Can I ask you one question?"

Collins whipped around. "Fuck! Can't you see where you're not welcome?" He gestured furiously, flicking his hands at Daniel. "Get the fuck out of my face!"

"Where's Ryan? Did you kill him?"

There was a terrifying pause. Time seemed to slow as Daniel felt a wave of elation flow over him. He'd said it. At last, he'd summoned some courage.

But the moment was over in a heartbeat as Collins's face puckered, spittle flying from his mouth as he bared snaggled teeth at Daniel. "You fucking bastard! Come here! Fucking hellfire, I'll teach you . . ."

Collins leaped onto the towpath like a pouncing cat, wiry arms reaching for Daniel. Fear gripped him, pushing his feet forward. But his boots were almost undone, his backpack cumbersome and the thump of Collins's feet was right behind him, his rasping breath at one shoulder.

A heavy hand grabbed the bag. He squirmed, wriggling out of the straps, the pack falling with a crash right in Collins's path. A torrent of curses followed and a sickening thud split the air behind him.

He risked a glance over his shoulder — Collins lay headlong, arms and legs flailing like an upturned beetle. The man he'd seen in the distance was running towards Collins. When

Daniel turned again, just before the curve in the canal, the stranger was helping him up.

He put some space between them before he slowed down. High on a bank, a stone bridge between him and Collins, he sat heaving, wondering where Poppy was, what would happen to his backpack, whether he was safe yet. His hands shook as he retrieved his phone from his pocket and dialled Poppy's number.

It rang and rang.

He stood, consternation rising in his chest, craning his neck to see further along the canal. She must have gone on. Perhaps she was still running and didn't hear her mobile. Or perhaps she had hidden herself and was waiting for him to follow her.

But he would have passed her if she was nearby. And anyway, she would have seen him. He climbed up beside the bridge, stepped onto the road and peered over the stone wall on both sides.

There was no one to be seen, the canal stretching out in both directions, the towpath clear, no boats disturbing the still water. The road, too, was empty.

He redialled her number. No response.

He would have to abandon his bag for the moment, or at least until he'd found Poppy. There was nothing irreplaceable in it — he'd transferred his money, his debit card and his phone at the same time and they were all safe in his pocket. It would be a nuisance, no more than that. But he had to find Poppy. He was pretty sure she was safe from Collins. She must have lost the signal, or perhaps the battery was flat on her mobile. She wouldn't be far away.

But as he started back down the steep bank beside the bridge, he was horrified to see Collins and the other man on the towpath below.

He wavered, unsteady on the steep bank, uncertain which way to turn. All his instincts told him to run in the opposite direction. But concern for Poppy took over. What if they caught up with her?

He stared at their receding backs, as if their bodies could tell him what they were up to. The other man looked familiar. He was wearing a grey T-shirt and grubby jeans, a black cap on his head, nothing remarkable. Except for the dark ink stains on his hands, crawling up his arms.

A shock of recognition flashed inside Daniel. This was the man on the bike who'd passed him earlier, given him a hard look.

And this wasn't the only time he'd seen him — this was Dave, the taciturn man at the boatyard, the one with the spanner, the tattoos and the curses. He'd been there on the bank, smoking, later on. How had Daniel not realised? Perhaps he'd been following them for miles. Perhaps he was Collins's mate, his partner in crime.

With a jolt, another thought occurred to him, another recent memory clicked into place. The kick in the stomach, the vicious blow to his jaw. The dark figure standing over him, lank hair reaching skinny shoulders. Was this the man who had mugged him under the bridge? Had he been followed all this time? It would certainly explain the feeling he'd had for some time that he was being watched.

They were moving fast, with intent. Daniel had no doubt they were looking for him.

He had to find Poppy before they did. He set off after them, uncomfortably aware they'd see him if they turned. He felt exposed and vulnerable on this part of the waterway, but there was nothing for it. They wouldn't be kind to Poppy if they caught up with her.

A slight bend in the canal took them out of his sight, giving him the chance to get a little closer. He kept his eyes on the thick hedgerow to one side, in case they were lying in wait for him. But as he came round the bend, the towpath was empty. They'd reached another slow turn in the waterway, or they were hiding, ready to pounce.

His searching eyes caught sight of a scrap of blue in the hawthorn bush ahead. It could be something or nothing, a piece of litter, but as he got close he recognised it.

Poppy's headband. Maybe she'd left it as a clue for him that she'd been here, or maybe it meant nothing. She could have dropped it earlier, before they'd reached *Golden Serpent*.

As he rounded the bend, he saw that the two men had started to run. Ahead of them, he could see a figure fleeing, a small dog alongside, a bag thrown to one side. Poppy reached a low stone bridge and ducked under. A volley of barks echoed from beneath the arch as the men caught up.

Running now, Daniel's feet pounding in time with his panicked heartbeat, he saw a hand on her back, pulling at her T-shirt as she twisted away.

Collins had her in his grasp. He took her by the shoulders and rammed her head against the bridge. For one heart-stopping moment she froze, staring Collins in the eye. Then the energy seemed to seep from her body as her legs slowly bent, her eyes closed and she folded gently onto the towpath.

He yelled with every ounce of energy in his body as the men turned and started towards him.

CHAPTER THIRTY-EIGHT

Everything seemed to slow then. It was as if the path had turned to a deep mire of mud, grasping at his feet, holding him back. The air thickened in his lungs — he struggled to breathe. The scene ahead of him grew larger: the pale body on the ground, Beans at its side, the looming figures getting closer. Behind them, a boat slid into view, only yards from the spot where Poppy lay. He was dimly aware of people on the boat, movement, shouting.

Collins was the first to turn. He saw the boat, its occupants gesticulating, the yelling adding to Daniel's roars. Collins stopped in his tracks, signalling to the other man, and they pushed through the bushes at the side of the towpath.

His lungs screaming, Daniel sprinted to Poppy's side and squatted down. Beans pressed his warm body against his leg, panting.

"It's OK, buddy, it's OK now," Daniel said, stroking his back.

But it wasn't OK. Poppy was unconscious. He took her limp hand, felt for a pulse. Her eyes were closed, her face drained of colour. As his own breathing eased, he felt a heartbeat under his shaking fingers. She was alive. But as he gazed at her face, willing her eyes to open, a dark liquid seeped from the back of her head onto the sandy surface of the towpath.

"No, no. Shit . . . No . . ." He pulled his mobile from his pocket and dialled.

"Emergency, which service do you need?"

"Ambulance please — and police, urgently. My friend has a head injury, it looks bad. She was attacked."

From behind him, voices, a hand on his shoulder. "My wife's a nurse, let her see—"

Concerned faces leaned over him, a boat behind. Someone knocked a stake into the ground, a mooring rope looped around it. He stood, letting the woman crouch beside Poppy while he finished the call.

"What's your location, please?" said the voice.

"I don't know." He turned to the man beside him. "Where are we? The ambulance . . ."

"Tell them Bridge 101 on the Grand Union," the man said. "They'll track us down, don't worry."

After that, everything happened in a haze of confusion. He sank down on the grass, head between his legs, nausea rising. Someone offered him water, put a jacket around his shoulders. A blanket appeared, a pillow for Poppy's head. There would be blood on the pillowcase, dirt underneath, he thought.

A siren sounded in the distance, growing closer until at last a blue flashing light appeared above the bridge. The noise stopped abruptly.

It seemed like a long time, though afterwards he learned it was only minutes, before they had Poppy's limp body on a stretcher, wrapped warmly, a drip attached to her arm. They carried her carefully up the bank to the waiting ambulance. He wanted more than anything to go with her. He protested vehemently, saying it was all his fault, he wanted to be there when she woke up — she would need him — but the police were adamant. They wanted to take his statement first, and that of the people from the boat. He needed to go with them to the station.

216

Holding a struggling Beans in his arms, he sat helplessly as the ambulance doors closed and the vehicle sped away, the siren fading slowly into the distance.

* * *

The police station was a small seventies brick building on the main street of the village, looking plain and out of place in a line of Victorian cottages. The officer who had driven Daniel to the station led him to an interview room and offered him tea, which arrived in minutes, together with a small packet of biscuits. It wasn't much, but Daniel felt better for it.

It started off as a straightforward interview — or at least, the officer seemed to think so. He was a young man, perhaps in his twenties, slim and boyish, his cheeks still soft with the innocence of youth. He looked nervous, as if he was new to the job. Daniel doubted he'd ever had to deal with much more than the odd burglary or traffic accident in that sleepy village. He toyed with the idea of keeping it simple, not mentioning why he and Poppy had been involved in the incident, but he soon realised that was impossible.

He took a deep breath and told him he believed Poppy's attacker was a murderer.

He almost laughed at the look on the young man's face. The expression went from amusement through disbelief and scepticism — to slow realisation and panic. The constable stood up suddenly, his chair rocking alarmingly behind him. He grappled with it for a moment before righting it and placing it decisively back in its place. "I need to . . . Excuse me. I need to bring in a senior officer. Give me a moment." A rush of air entered the room as the door closed behind him.

When he returned, he was still alone. "I'm sorry to keep you, sir," he said. "There may be some delay, I'm afraid. My senior officer is on his way."

Daniel nodded. "Is there any chance of a sandwich?" he said. This was going to be a long haul and he hadn't eaten

217

since breakfast, many hours ago. Now the adrenaline had drained away, he felt weak and hungry. "Or maybe two?"

The officer hesitated, glancing at his watch. "It might have to be chips at this time of day. Would that be all right for you?"

"Chips would be perfect." His mouth watered. He would need something to fortify him. It could be a long interview — longer than even they were expecting. And he still had no idea where he was going to spend the night. "One other thing . . ."

"Sir?" The policeman, on his way out of the door, stopped mid-stride. He seemed resigned to satisfying another request.

"I'm sorry to bother you with this, but I have nowhere to stay tonight. I lost my bag, with my tent, you see, when it all kicked off. We were camping on the canals, on a hiking trip. I assume I'm not under arrest?" The officer shook his head. "If I'm not going to be here for the whole night — which I hope I'm not — I'll have to find somewhere soon."

"I see." By the look on the officer's face, it was clear that he didn't see at all. Walking the canals didn't seem a pastime he was familiar with. "There's a bed and breakfast just down the road. I can see if they have a room, if you'd like?" He looked dubious, as if it was beyond the call of duty, but Daniel seized on the suggestion before he could change his mind.

"That sounds perfect," he said. "Thank you."

It was more than an hour before the senior officer arrived, the young policeman following him into the room. He was a large man, dressed casually, with a businesslike demeanour. He introduced himself as Detective Inspector Stevens. He wasted no time in getting started.

"I understand you've made a serious allegation against this man Collins," he said. "Please start at the beginning."

Daniel, feeling stronger after his meal, had taken the chance to order his thoughts. "You may want to contact Kidlington police," he said. "They can confirm I've made this allegation formally before. They took a statement from me a few weeks ago."

The detective nodded at the young officer, who left the room.

Daniel took a deep breath. "My memory is different from other people's," he said. "When it's to do with my life, I remember everything, in perfect detail."

CHAPTER THIRTY-NINE

"What do you mean, everything?" the detective said as they waited for the constable to return to the room. Daniel hoped the Kidlington police would be helpful.

"What I mean is, I have a perfect memory. I remember everything that's happened in my life since I was ten. And the memories are exact. If you were to give me a date, any date from maybe ten years ago, I could tell you exactly what I was doing on that day, every minute of the day. What I was wearing, who I saw, what the weather was like, what I had for lunch. In minute detail. It's hard to describe, and I know it's probably hard to believe, but I promise you, I'm not making it up."

"I see," the detective said, his face unreadable. He made a note on his pad. "And do you have anything to corroborate this assertion? It would be hard for anyone to check the accuracy of your memories, wouldn't it?"

Daniel sighed, shaking his head. "You're right, of course. All I can say is, it's true."

The detective leaned back in his seat, assessing Daniel's face. "OK, we'll assume you do have a perfect memory. We may have to find a way to judge that, if what you have to tell us warrants it. You want to report an incident, I believe."

"Y—Yes, I do." Daniel could feel the nervous tension rising with every word the detective said. From the man's expression, he was trying to be patient, but Daniel guessed he was wondering why he'd been dragged to the station for a nutcase who imagined he saw a murder nineteen years ago. "I—"

"Let's just wait for my colleague."

As if on cue, a knock at the door interrupted him and the young police officer put his head around the door. "Sir, could I have a word, please?"

The detective stepped out into the corridor, leaving the door ajar. Daniel could hear their muttered conversation quite clearly.

"Sir, Kidlington station have confirmed the allegation. They've been trying to contact him. They've found, er—" he paused for a moment — "a specialist cognitive interviewer to talk to him. Sounds like they're taking him seriously, sir. They'd like to talk to you."

The door closed. The sound of their footsteps faded.

Daniel had no idea what kind of specialist interviewer they might have found, but it sounded like he was in for some kind of psychological assessment. Would he be prepared to go through that, with someone he didn't know, in a stressful environment like a police station?

Maybe he would have to, but he cringed at the thought of being assessed by anyone, let alone a police interviewer. He wasn't about to trust the police with his fragile mind. He'd need to be sure that the interviewer had the right background, or risk being pushed over the brink into a very dark place. He'd seen many psychologists and therapists in the past, some of them highly experienced, but none had come across anything like his memory. Despite all their training, they'd had no idea what to do with him. It had been immensely disappointing and utterly depressing. He wasn't sure he wanted to put himself through that again, particularly now, when his ultimate goal was to find a way to live with his condition.

But how could he persuade them that he was telling the truth if he wasn't prepared to undergo their 'specialist' interview? It would look unhelpful — suspicious, even. He was damned if he was and damned if he wasn't. A vicious circle.

He had to do this. Somehow he had to find a way. He owed Poppy — and ultimately Ryan — to get this done. Poppy could have died because he was trying to prove something, or she could have suffered brain damage for all he knew. He fervently hoped not — but if he didn't have the courage to see this through, it would all have been for nothing. She trusted him, believed in him, and she wanted Ryan's story to be told.

He couldn't let her down. She had even found him the perfect person to help. That was it! If he could get hold of Professor James, and the professor agreed that he had perfect recall, it would surely give him ultimate credibility. They'd have to believe him then.

He was suddenly filled with nervous energy. He needed to contact the professor as soon as possible — as soon as this interview was over — speak to him before the police put him in front of the specialist interviewer. He'd ask him to do an assessment before the police had a chance. The professor would have a much better chance of persuading them. He might even be an expert witness for him, if the case went to trial.

By the time the door reopened, he was ready for them.

The detective cleared his throat, referring to his notepad. "We've confirmed what you've told us with colleagues in Kidlington. They've been trying to contact you to conduct an interview with a Tier Three specialist cognitive interviewer."

Daniel raised his eyebrows.

"I'll explain what that means," the detective said. "This is a serious allegation — I'm sure you know that. We're duty-bound to investigate it. But as such a long period of time has passed since the incident, we have to be absolutely certain of the facts. If the case goes to court, a witness who is purporting to recall events from many years ago is vulnerable to challenge from the defence. So it's vital that the methods we use to elicit the information are proven and will stand up in court. If you agree to this interview, your mind will be probed using psychological techniques to mine the information. The interview will be recorded and the contents written down as a witness statement. You'll be required to sign that. Both tape and witness statement would be available in court."

At the term 'psychological techniques', Daniel winced. It was as he'd expected. They would 'probe', possibly without any reference to his medical background. He would be laying himself open to a serious threat to his mental health.

"I do want to pursue this," he said. "But I'd have to be really sure that any interviewer undertaking any kind of psychological assessment on me had the right qualifications and the full background on my condition. I'm fragile, mentally. I suffer from anxiety and depression. I have to be sure . . ." His voice trailed away. He had no confidence that either of these characters would have any idea what he was talking about. He'd always seen the police as unsympathetic, alpha-male types. Any sign of weakness, fragile emotions, could result in mirth rather than compassion. He wasn't prepared to put himself in that kind of position.

But the older detective was unfazed. "I understand. We can provide you with his experience and qualifications, of course. Kidlington have said that they can refer the interviewer to us, if that suits you better. It can all be done here. Obviously, we don't know his availability, but it could be very soon. And if Collins is a suspect and is on the move, we need to act quickly."

"OK. But I have a suggestion . . ."

* * *

"Daniel, so good to speak to you," Professor James said, his voice deep and resonant. "I'm so sorry I couldn't talk earlier. I have a very full schedule. But I'm excited to hear more about you."

Daniel wiped a sweaty hand on his shorts. He was alarmed to find he was shaking, though he was alone on the towpath, sitting on a ramshackle bench close to the town. He was clutching the mobile so hard his hand hurt and he swapped it to the other hand, making a conscious effort to relax his shoulders. He took a deep breath.

"Professor James, thank you for agreeing to talk to me. I've got myself into a pretty complicated situation here, and I need your help, rather urgently in fact. I understand you study memory."

"Indeed — it's an important part of what I do. I'm a clinical neuropsychologist. I have interests in a number of areas to do with memory and the human brain. I very much hope I can be of some assistance. But first, let me say, I know very little about you, only that you seem to have an unusual memory. Perhaps you could explain what you think makes it unique. Take your time."

Daniel tried to order his thoughts. It was crucial that he explained himself well, and yet, despite all his looking inward, all his efforts to understand his brain, he never found it easy to describe. But, he told himself, this man, of all people, might have sufficient knowledge and understanding to diagnose his condition.

"I'll do my best," he said. "This is so important. I'm very nervous."

"No need to be at all," the professor said. "We're just having an initial chat."

"Right." Daniel took a deep breath. "I'm just going to say this, then, and hope it makes some kind of sense. I don't — can't — forget anything, even the smallest, most insignificant thing, that's ever happened to me."

CHAPTER FORTY

"Are you family?" the nurse asked. "Visiting time was over long since." Her eyes took in his dishevelled state, the dusty boots, Poppy's battered bag on his back.

"I'm her brother," he lied. "We were hiking on the canal when she was attacked."

She raised an eyebrow. "We wondered. She has nothing with her, no bag, just a phone and her credit cards."

"This is hers, I brought it for her. Can I see her now?"

She nodded. "She's resting. Just for a short while, OK? She has a bad concussion and she needs to sleep. We'll be keeping her in overnight and probably tomorrow. This way."

She led him to a room with four beds. One of them was curtained off, the others occupied by sleeping shapes. It was late. The police had kept him waiting, the interview stopping and starting, and when at last he'd left the station, he'd stopped to call the professor before coming here. The call had been long and exhausting. He felt wrung out and on edge, self-conscious about his grubby clothes and his unruly hair. It was hours since he'd eaten.

The nurse lifted a curtain for him to duck through. "Ten minutes," she said. "I'll come and fetch you."

Poppy was in a patterned hospital gown, propped up on an array of pillows, looking different without her usual T-shirt. Her eyes were closed, her breathing regular as she slept. Bandages swathed her head, the wound a lump of dressing at the back. He could see her hair had been shaved at the spot, grey scalp showing at the edges. It seemed the tan on her face had already faded, as if she'd been out of the sun for days, in contrast with her arms, which were a warm brown against the white linen.

He pulled up a chair, taking care not to make a sound, and sat very close, his head on a level with hers. Her eyes opened slowly and she stared into his eyes for a moment with a look of confusion. Confusion turned to terror and she flinched away, grimacing in pain. "No, no! Get away from me!"

Daniel drew back. "It's OK, Poppy, it's only me. Daniel — remember? I'm not going to hurt you, I came to see how you were."

Poppy's eyes were still wide with fear. "I don't know you — leave me alone!"

A nurse, hearing Poppy's raised voice, hurried to her side. "It's OK, it's only your brother. Now don't get upset, no one's trying to hurt you. You've got a concussion, it's normal not to remember at first." She took Poppy's hand, feeling for her pulse.

"But I don't know him! Make him go! Please!"

Daniel hesitated, but the nurse indicated with her head that he needed to leave. Seeing Poppy's distress, he turned reluctantly and walked away. The nurse followed him to the door. "Try not to worry," she said. "She's scared and confused now. That's not unusual with a concussion. Give her time. She'll be better tomorrow, I'm sure."

Daniel's voice shook as he replied. "I understand. Could you give her a message, please? If she remembers and asks about her dog, Beans, he's fine and is being looked after. He's with the boat people who helped us."

The boat owners had offered to keep Beans overnight, saying they were dog owners themselves and would be happy

226

to help. The police wanted to take their statements in the morning, so they'd moored up beside the bridge. Daniel had promised to collect him the next day.

The nurse nodded and Daniel left, his feelings in turmoil. As he glanced back, he saw that Poppy was staring after him, biting her lip, fear and confusion still written in her eyes.

* * *

As he made his way to the bed and breakfast, he was overwhelmed with guilt. He should never have allowed her to help. He'd known she wouldn't be able to resist — she would help anyone, willingly and enthusiastically. She was innocent and kind, and yet he'd put her in terrible danger. Why had he done that to the one person who seemed to understand him, who looked out for him? What was he thinking? How could he have been so careless? She was the last person in the world he wanted to hurt.

What if her memory never returned? The thought made him nauseous. He was a fucking idiot! He shouted it out loud in a quiet street, where it echoed eerily back at him. A couple walking past on the opposite pavement paused and stared, then hurried on, as if fearing he was drunk or worse.

It was all his fault. He'd knowingly put Poppy in danger and now her life could be changed for ever because of him. As he climbed the stairs to his room he could think only that he'd ruined his own chances in life and probably Poppy's, too.

That night he lay awake, fully dressed, for hours, staring at the ceiling, allowing the worst scenes of his life to torment him, over and over.

* * *

Numb from a night with no sleep, he sat for a while in the breakfast room with a mug of tea, wondering what he should

227

do next. Poppy was his first priority. He would drop by the hospital first thing to ask how she was. He didn't expect to see her, he simply needed to reassure himself that she was still alive and, hopefully, doing better.

At some point he would have to collect Beans from the boat owners, and go back for his bag. He'd abandoned it not far from *Golden Serpent*. Though the boat would almost certainly be gone, the thought of going back there wasn't a pleasant one.

At the hospital, a kind nurse told him Poppy had had a good night and had eaten a little of her breakfast. She was sleeping and the nurse advised against trying to see her for a while, until she was less confused.

There was nothing else to do but walk back along the canal to retrieve his bag. Perhaps one of the other boaters had picked it up, or maybe it was still there, abandoned in the hedgerow.

It took him a while to get back to the bridge where Poppy had been injured. There was no sign of the drama of the previous day, no blood on the wall, no evidence of a scuffle. The canal was flat and calm, the wild- flowers opening to the day, insects beginning to emerge. The boat belonging to the people who had helped him was still there, though they'd taken it a few metres further along, away from the bridge. All was quiet on board as he passed, blinds closed over the windows, no sign of movement.

He reached the spot where *Golden Serpent* had been sooner than he expected. Collins and his mate must have been only a few hundred yards from it when they had caught up with Poppy. He recognised the adjacent boats from the day before, particularly the one that had been next in line to *Golden Serpent*, the empty space on the bank telling the story. Collins had gone, most likely soon after the attack. He wouldn't have wanted to stay and face the police, that was for sure.

Daniel surveyed the towpath on either side of the gap. His backpack was nowhere to be seen. He rummaged around in the hedge for a while, walked a little further on in case someone had hidden it for safety, but there was no sign of it. Disappointed but not surprised, he turned to retrace his steps.

"Hey, just a minute," a man's voice came from behind him. It was the boat moored next to the gap where *Golden Serpent* had been. Daniel turned to see his bag held high. "Looking for this?"

"Ah, yes! Thank you — I'm glad to see it."

The man, bare-chested and dishevelled, looked as if he'd just woken up. "We heard what happened," he said. "Took off like a speedboat, she did." He nodded at the empty water where *Golden Serpent* had been moored. "The old guy was in a heck of a hurry, and his mate, too. Stuck his bike on the top and off they went. Scarpered before the police could get to them."

"Did they follow him, do you know?"

"They were talking on the radio, you know, so I expect they were planning to cut him off at the next lock, or maybe a bridge. You can't get much speed up in these things. Not the best of escape vehicles!" He guffawed at his joke and turned to go back into the boat. "Good luck to you, and your girl. I hope she's OK."

Thanking him again, Daniel turned to go, reassured by the familiar weight of his pack on his back. The man's words rang in his ears. *You and your girl.*

The weight of responsibility sat heavily on his shoulders. He was going to make sure Poppy was OK. It meant giving up this mad escapade, but that didn't seem to matter any more.

CHAPTER FORTY-ONE

Poppy was unnerved by the feeling of the unfamiliar bed when she awoke, the hospital sheets pinning her body to the bed, holding her captive. She pushed herself up onto the pillows and tried hauling the sheets from a different position, but they were anchored too well. Her mind was blank, her head throbbed alarmingly and a heavy weight sat deep in her stomach. She stopped struggling and examined that feeling. It was fear, and from the fear, confusion grew. Why was she here? How did she get injured?

A groan escaped from her throat. Immediately a nurse stuck her head around the curtain, startling her.

"You're awake again." The nurse pushed the curtains back to reveal the rest of the room. Fluorescent lighting gave the walls and floor a glossy sheen. Poppy blinked in the glare, peering for the first time at the room where she'd spent the night. Inert shapes occupied the other beds, clumps of hair on pristine white pillows the only part of them showing. It was all very strange.

Again? Had she been awake earlier? She tried to think, but there was nothing in her memory to connect her with this place. Panic gripped her by the throat and she struggled to sit upright, swallowing painfully.

"It's OK, try not to move too much." The nurse gently pushed her back onto the pillows. "You have a concussion, you need to take it easy. Here, have a sip." She offered a plastic glass with a straw to Poppy.

Poppy sipped automatically and handed the glass back. "Oh God — I can't remember anything. What's going on?" Tears pricked at her eyes and she wiped them away with the back of her hand.

The nurse looked at her with kind eyes. "It's normal with a concussion, not to remember. Try not to worry, it'll probably all come back. But you must rest."

Poppy lay back, already exhausted. "But what happened to me?" she said, fingering her head, where there was, inexplicably, a missing patch of hair.

"You have a nasty head injury, a bad concussion. The consultant will be round later, we'll know more then."

She could remember who she was — that was reassuring. Her parents, her grandmother, she could remember them. And she could remember that her gran was gone. The sadness hit her anew. Her home, she remembered that. But beyond that, only fog. Nothing.

She swallowed and sat up, ignoring the warning thump from her head. Panic rose in her throat. "Oh, God, I can't remember what I was doing, before this. Where I was . . . I remember my mum and dad, my name, my parents' house . . . But the rest is gone!"

She looked around the room, for anything to remind her, a trigger to her past, but there was nothing. She grabbed the nurse's hand. "I've lost my memory! What's happened to me?"

The nurse retrieved her hand, settling her back against the pillows. "It's OK, don't get yourself all upset. Temporary amnesia. Try not to worry, it often happens with a concussion. Rest, give yourself some time."

Poppy wasn't reassured. "Will it come back?"

"Usually. Best to rest and let it settle. I'll mention it to the doctor, and you can talk to her when she comes round."

Usually. It felt like avoidance of the truth. Or maybe the nurse just didn't know. She forced herself to breathe slowly, but the panic was still there. And the empty space where her memories used to be.

The nurse held her wrist, checking her pulse against a watch. "Anyway, you look much better than you did when you came in. Does it hurt?"

"A . . . a little."

The nurse leaned over, touching the dressing gently. "It's looking good."

"How long will I be here?"

"Depends what the doctor says. She'll be doing her rounds this morning, so we'll know more after that."

Poppy lay back, grief taking hold of her. She didn't know what she'd lost, but losing the past — even the recent past — seemed no less than calamitous.

The nurse took pity on her. "Listen, you'll be fine. You're young and healthy. Worrying won't help you get your memory back. Rest as much as you can, and don't be too impatient to get out of here. An injury like yours needs a bit of time."

"Do I have stitches?" Poppy wondered how bad the damage was.

"You do. We'll have a look at the wound a bit later. The dressing will need changing after the doctor's examined you." The nurse took the chart from the bottom of the bed and a pen from her pocket. "Is your brother coming back later?"

"My brother?" This was worse than she thought. She felt the blood drain from her face. A brother? Where were her memories of him? She couldn't even remember his name. Or his face. "How — what?"

The nurse glanced up. "Are you OK? You look as if you've seen a ghost."

"I'm OK. But my brother?"

"Yes, he came to visit you last night. You don't remember that, either? Well, you were probably very sleepy with the painkillers. I'm sure he'll be back again today."

"But—"

Poppy was about to say she didn't remember a thing about having a brother. But as she opened her mouth to speak, she realised it might be someone else who'd visited. She had a vague recollection of someone beside her bed last night . . . A man. She'd sent him away, the nurse had helped her. What if the man meant her harm? What if she was being stalked?

Her hand flew to her mouth. "How did I get hurt? Was it a man?" She grabbed the nurse's hand. "Was I attacked?"

"Stay calm, everything's all right. You're safe here." The nurse pressed a buzzer by Poppy's bed.

"No, you don't understand. I don't have a brother — I have absolutely no recollection of ever having one. The man who came, he could have been trying to hurt me—"

Another nurse came rushing in and the two nurses had a whispered conversation as Poppy gazed in panic from face to face. "Help me, I think I'm in danger."

"Please don't upset yourself. We'll have a word with the police and make sure you're safe. We're just going to give you a mild sedative to help you rest, OK?"

"No, no, you don't get it, he's not my brother—" But the needle had already gone in. Everything was turning soft, misty.

She dropped off to the sounds of the hospital ward: voices, footsteps, doors banging, a phone ringing.

* * *

The nurse with the kind eyes was behind the desk as Daniel approached. She smiled and nodded at him. "I guess you're here to see Poppy." She came round the desk. "Let's sit down over here."

He followed her to some chairs lining the corridor a little further down. She sat, smoothing her skirt, and hesitated. "Poppy's still very confused. It's still early days. It'll take a while for her memory to return, as you know."

Daniel nodded. "I understand."

"But—" The nurse hesitated again. "She remembers who she is, and her family, which is a good sign. Her home, she remembers that. But not . . . a brother." She glanced at Daniel's face, as if watching for his reaction.

"Ah. She doesn't have a brother. Not as far as I know, anyway. I made that up. I lied to get in here to see her. I'm a friend. We met on the canals and we were walking together when it happened. I'm sorry."

The nurse nodded. "It's OK. Fortunately for you, the police confirmed that you're a friend, and not a threat to Poppy. And it's not the first time someone's pretended to be family to visit somebody. But it has confused her unnecessarily, I'm afraid. She thought you might be her attacker."

Daniel stared at her. "Oh God, that's terrible . . . It's all my fault." Everything he did seemed to cause more damage. He dropped his head into his hands. Perhaps he should call a halt to all this, contact Poppy's parents, make sure she went home. Then get out of her life.

The nurse put a hand on his arm. "Don't blame yourself. The person to blame is the one who attacked her, not you."

"All I want is for her to get better. But I just seem to make things worse."

"I know. Just be patient. She needs a little more time. Then I'm sure you can help her recover."

* * *

As things turned out, Daniel found himself on a train to Oxford the next day. He almost didn't go. His obsession with Collins seemed ridiculous now, after all that had happened. It was only when he remembered that Collins had put Poppy in hospital that he decided to see it through. She deserved justice, even if he couldn't prove that Ryan did too.

He'd needed to push quite hard to get the police to agree. There had been more pauses while they left the room at the police station, more note-taking and some head-scratching, but he'd got his way in the end. He knew they had enough to arrest Collins on the assault charge and they were not going to let go of that. But the murder charge was clearly of a higher order for them, and they were reluctant to delay. Eventually they agreed that the specialist interviewer would be prepared and on alert while Daniel pursued Professor James.

He sat gazing out of a window, unseeing, as the train swayed across the countryside. He felt battered and bruised by the events of the last few days, as if he was the one who'd been beaten up. The worst thing was the fear. Of course, he'd been scared of Collins — terrified for Poppy when she was hurt — but this was a different kind of fear. It was a gamble, opening himself up to Professor James. However eminent a scientist he was, however experienced with all kinds of unusual, injured or underdeveloped brains, he was still an unknown.

Daniel had warmed to him on the call. He'd listened patiently, without interrupting, only asking questions when he didn't understand something. Nonetheless, this was a huge risk. He may not believe him, he may use standard tests on him that would lead to nothing. He might probe too deeply. That was possible, and what Daniel feared more than anything else. Too little, and nothing would come of it. Too much, and Daniel's overloaded, fragile mind could easily break down.

But he needn't have worried. They met in Professor James's comfortable office, where Daniel sat on a large sofa to one side of the desk, with the professor taking a matching armchair. He started by pouring coffee. The professor was friendly and relaxed, and Daniel soon felt the anxiety seep away. Much of the time was spent talking, the professor asking questions, Daniel responding as best he could, though there was nothing too taxing. Then the professor talked a little about neuropsychology, his area of expertise, explaining that he focused largely on brain disorders or injuries.

At last he addressed the subject of an assessment. "I'd like to carry out a series of tests on your brain. Ideally, this would take some time, and develop into a longer-term study, depending on the results, of course. However, given the urgency to prove to the police that your autobiographical memory — your memories of your own experiences — is absolutely accurate, I'm proposing we do some fairly simple diagnostic tests today, to allow me to prepare a report that will, hopefully, help you."

Daniel nodded, a flush of relief spreading from his stomach. "Thank you. I'm so grateful. This is what I was hoping — praying — for."

"I must warn you, these tests have been designed to measure degrees of impairment, not to measure how much above the norm your abilities might be. If I had longer, I would design a special set of cognitive tests for you, specifically to measure your recall of autobiographical events. However, what we're doing today should be enough to persuade the police to take your memory of the event seriously if, as I think is the case, you have a highly superior autobiographical memory. That's the term we use for a mind like yours."

Highly superior autobiographical memory. Daniel repeated it to himself. The words themselves were comforting. It was like stepping into a warm bath. His scalp tingled, his shoulders dropped, he closed his eyes and said the words silently to himself, over and over. He was alarmed to find himself close to tears.

In another room, where an assistant entered data silently into a computer, Professor James put him through a gruelling series of tests. Time seemed to run so fast in places he could barely keep up, but slowed almost to a stop in others. Some of the tests were familiar, some frustrating, some entirely new to him. At one point, the professor made a point of focusing on Daniel's recall of the dates of well-known events during his lifetime: the death of a well-known figure, a huge volcanic eruption, a terrorist attack. Then he zoned in on local events, happenings in Daniel's childhood that could be checked on the internet — school term dates, carnivals, Christmas events.

Daniel knew the date and the day of the week of every event that he'd attended or known about from the age of ten. He answered confidently and one hundred per cent accurately. He knew this because the assistant nodded each time he was right.

When at last they were done, they returned to the professor's room. Daniel could hardly sit still while he waited for the preliminary results. He tried to prepare himself for disappointment, but he couldn't, he was too full of hope for the right outcome.

"I won't keep you in suspense any longer," Professor James said. "Clearly these tests are preliminary. But the results are incontrovertible. Your memory is extremely strong — far above the norm — in some areas."

"Some areas?" Daniel didn't know whether to be relieved or alarmed.

"Don't be concerned. This is entirely compatible with what we know about highly superior autobiographical memory. I am convinced that your recall abilities are different, by some distance, from most people's, and I'm prepared to confirm that in my report. I'll write up the results for the police straight away. However, if you agree, I'd like to invite you for more tests. I must say I'm extremely excited by these results. There's a lot more work that could be done to investigate your particular type of brain. It could prove extremely valuable to our research studies."

"I'd be glad to. Thank you, Professor James, I really appreciate what you've done." He hesitated. "Actually, there's something else you might be able to help me with."

The professor looked up from his notes.

"My friend — the girl I was walking with — she's in hospital with a concussion after a nasty knock to the head. She's forgotten pretty much everything about her life. She's terrified, and I am too, that it might be permanent. I'd really appreciate your thoughts."

CHAPTER FORTY-TWO

Beans stayed close to his side as he climbed the side stairs at the hospital. As agreed, the nurse met him at the door, one finger to her lips. "I'll be in big trouble if Matron finds out," she said. "Let's hope nobody lets on."

They walked along the corridor towards the ward.

"I don't want you to get into trouble," Daniel said.

"It's not so bad. Sometimes we have comfort dogs come in to help patients. Though normally I'd have to get Matron's permission. Just this once . . ." She smiled and bent to give Beans a stroke. "He's a lovely little chap. What happened to his leg?"

"Nobody knows. He's a rescue dog — we don't know much about his background."

"Doesn't seem to bother him. Sometimes I wish humans were a bit more like dogs. They do live in the moment, don't they?"

"This one does, for sure."

Beans had picked up the atmosphere of secrecy and a hint of excitement. He pulled on the lead as they approached Poppy's ward, and Daniel picked him up, hiding him in his jumper as they passed the other beds.

"Let me go in first," the nurse whispered. "We don't want to give her a shock. I'll tell her she has a special visitor."

After a few minutes, the nurse returned to the door, beckoning Daniel to go in. She drew the curtains around the bed.

Poppy gazed at them in surprise. "What's going on?" she said, once the nurse had gone.

Daniel pulled his jumper up and Beans wriggled free, straight into Poppy's arms.

"Oh, you beauty!" She nuzzled him as he tried to lick every part of her face. "Of course I remember you — how could I not? You're the best, Beans. Come here, settle down." She looked up at Daniel, tears in her eyes.

"I know you're not my brother now," she said. "That threw me a bit, I must say."

"Yes, sorry." Daniel hung back, ready to be asked to leave.

"The nurse also told me you're a friend, and you helped me when I was attacked. So I need to thank you for that — and for bringing Beans in." She kissed the top of Beans's head.

Daniel hesitated by the curtain, not sure if he was welcome, but Poppy waved him in. "It's OK, you can sit down, I'm not scared of you any more. Though I still don't remember you. How did you manage to smuggle Beans in?"

"I'm good friends with the nurse now. Found out she was a dog lover. I persuaded her that if you saw Beans, you might recover your memory. I went to see the professor, the one you found . . . It's a long story, but he suggested it. And we knew it wouldn't do any harm. Luckily, the nurse agreed."

"It has already done me so much good." Poppy's arms were around the little dog as he gazed into her face. "And do you know what?"

"What?"

"I can remember the rescue centre — where I found him. I work there, don't I?"

* * *

239

Poppy listened intently to Daniel's story, her eyes wide, following his every word. Beans slept peacefully at her side.

"Is anything coming back to you?" he said, worried he was overdoing it.

"Not really, though it all has a strange, familiar ring to it. Keep going."

"I'm not tiring you out?"

"I'll tell you when — if — I've had enough."

Even leaving out the most dramatic details of the confrontation with Collins, the story took a while to tell. Poppy seemed surprised by some of it, accepting of other parts. He took it gently when he mentioned why she was walking. He didn't want her to be upset all over again by the news of her grandmother's death. But she nodded and waited for him to continue.

By the time he'd finished, she looked tired and not a little confused. He offered to call her parents but she was adamant that he shouldn't.

"No," she said. "They'll only worry. And they'll want me to go home, and I don't want to. Sounds like I'd miss the next instalment!"

By the time he left, the blue smudges under her eyes seemed darker, the skin on her face almost translucent in the harsh light of the hospital room. Daniel's stomach twisted with guilt.

* * *

Despite his concern, in the morning she was sitting up, her eyes bright, the colour returned to her skin. She smiled when she saw him. "I'm so glad you came back," she said.

Daniel fished in his backpack, retrieving a packet of biscuits, a bag of grapes and some apples. He handed them over, feeling awkward, waving away her thanks. "Of course I came back. It's the least I could do, since I put you here."

"Stop saying that," she said. "From what you said, I made my own choices."

"How's the head?"

"No pain — probably because of the drugs. The doc said the wound is looking good. No infection, and it's healing well."

"That's great."

She sighed. "It is, but they won't let me go for a few days more, until I've retrieved a bit more of my memory."

"Anything happening with that?"

"Well, after everything you told me, I felt very confused. A bit scared, if I'm honest. It's a horrible feeling, forgetting what's only just happened, and hearing it from someone else. But I feel a bit stronger now. I'm chasing fleeting images around my brain every so often. Nothing solid, but there's something there."

"Good! That's got to be positive. You do look a lot better."

"But I'm very, very bored." She surveyed the room with a guilty look to make sure nobody could hear. "I've got nothing to do but sleep. I've finished my book, and all the books I've found here are really not my thing. Romance, mostly."

Daniel fished in his bag again. "I wasn't sure you'd be up to it, but there's a charity shop round the corner . . ." He put the two paperbacks on the bed. "I found these — thought they might be similar to the one you've just finished."

"Daniel, you're a star!" She turned the books over to read the back covers. "They look perfect. You are kind."

He shook his head. "Just feeling guilty about you. Don't overdo it, will you? I don't want to be the reason for a setback as well as everything else."

"I won't, I promise."

"Oh, and I brought some cards, in case you were up to a game or two."

They played rummy until the nurses came round, indicating that Daniel should go.

"Come back as soon as you can?" Poppy said.

"I'll be in the queue waiting for visiting time to start," he said. "Sleep well, and let that brain rest."

* * *

The following day when the doctor came on her rounds, Poppy said she was beginning to remember things, like her dog — though she stopped short of saying she'd seen him. That nurse had been very good to her.

"Well, all seems good," the doctor said. "Those stitches will disappear in a couple of days, and your hair will grow back before you know it. I'm happy with your progress. It seems like you're recovering your memory quite well now. Don't expect too much of it, though. It can take some time to get back to where you were. You still need to rest. Peace and quiet will help you get better. All being well, I'll discharge you tomorrow."

Daniel, listening from the other side of the curtain, turned away to hide his tears.

"Brilliant," Poppy said, and he could hear the smile in her voice.

CHAPTER FORTY-THREE

Not far from the village, Daniel found a campsite in a quiet meadow. Some friendly campers — a family of four, a couple on a walking holiday — spotted him looking and assured him that it was a good place to stay. They directed him to the farm where he could reserve spaces.

As he walked, he realised with some surprise how relaxed he'd felt, talking to those people, those strangers. Only a few weeks ago, that would have been a big challenge. Despite all that had happened, he seemed to be finding his way, and he felt a moment of unfamiliar hope as he went to collect Poppy from the hospital.

They pitched their tents right next to each other, talking quietly into the cool of the evening through the thin fabric of the tent walls.

"You know what, Daniel?" Poppy said. "Losing my memory, even for a short time, has helped me understand what Gran went through. I was terrified. She must have been, too, but she never said anything."

"I was really scared for you. It must be awful to lose your memory — like the ground has been taken from under your feet. Imagine if you can't remember whole chunks of your life. Makes you realise what a terrible, frightening disease Alzheimer's is."

"Our memories are us, really, aren't they? Without memories, however much we've adapted them to suit us, we lose something of ourselves. When I couldn't remember anything, I had this massive feeling of loss. It was like I was grieving."

Daniel pondered this for a while. It was true, his memory did define him. Would he want to change it, if he had the chance? Probably not. However difficult it was to live with, it shaped his entire being.

Daniel fell asleep to the sound of Beans's snores. Poppy had drifted off mid-sentence a few moments earlier.

When he woke, it was still early. His limbs were heavy in his sleeping bag, his brain quiet for once. The sense of comfort that the diagnosis had brought was still there, along with something else. A sense of . . . liberation. Now he knew his memory wasn't tricking him. He'd been vindicated, and that was a good feeling. Empowerment, too. The word 'superior' in the diagnosis was sinking in. He wasn't mad, or delusional, or even mentally ill. His memory was superior. That felt good.

He drifted for a while until his mobile buzzed.

"Inspector Barker here, Murder Squad."

Daniel sat up, aware of Beans stirring in the next door tent.

"We haven't spoken before. I'm in charge of the case involving Ryan Collins and his father. I'm calling to inform you that we'll be carrying out a search of the canal in the area you described, starting this morning. Someone will let you know if we find anything. You don't need to do anything, but just make sure we can contact you."

"Y-Yes, of course," Daniel said.

The call came to an abrupt end.

He stared for a moment at his mobile. "Poppy?"

"I'm here," came her muffled voice from the tent to his left. "Who was it?"

"The Murder Squad."

"What?" Instantly there were sounds of scuffling and scrabbling. Daniel leaned forward to unzip his tent, and Beans leaped in, covering his face with licks. He was swiftly followed by Poppy, who crawled right into the tiny space, folding herself into a ball.

"They're going to drag the canal — where I saw Collins drop the bundle." Daniel said. "I can hardly believe it."

"They are? That's amazing."

"It will be if they find something."

"They'll find something. You have a Greatly Super-Duper Memory, remember?"

"It could all be nothing, though. The trainers could have been just a pair Collins wanted to get rid of. I could have imagined they were attached to Ryan's legs at the time. However good my memory is, I didn't see more than that. To a small boy, it just looked like there was a body in the bundle. It'll be deeply embarrassing if I was wrong all the time."

"I get that. But he denied having a son, didn't he? In which case, what happened to Ryan?"

"I don't know. Maybe he wasn't his son at all. There could be another explanation." Daniel started to worry about the outcome of the police search. Would they arrest a person who'd sent them on a wild goose chase? He didn't dare think about the consequences of being wrong. Another thing that could send him into a deep spiral.

But Poppy was determined. "Look, Daniel," she said. "You know there was a boy on board and you saw them struggling with each other. You know his name was Ryan and he said he lived on the boat. Those are facts. So, what happened to him? You have to admit Collins has 'dodgy' written all over him. Now we know for sure he's violent, too. I'm convinced you're right, I really am."

"Thanks, Poppy."

Daniel felt a surge of affection for her. She was completely certain of his story. He just wished he shared her confidence.

After breakfast, they wandered down to the canal, Beans trotting ahead of them. Narrowboats were dotted along the towpath, some locked up and quiet, one or two with doors open, the aroma of bacon drifting across the canal.

Ahead of them was a dark green boat, traditionally decorated with painted flowers.

"Just a minute." Daniel stopped. "That looks like Jane's boat. It is!"

Callum's head appeared as he climbed the steps to the platform. His face broke into a grin when he saw Daniel.

"Mum!" He bent down to call into the living space within. "Daniel's here!"

They soon sat with mugs of tea on the roof, Beans on Poppy's lap.

"You changed your minds, then," Daniel said. "Last time I saw you, you were off in the other direction."

"I was worried about turning round, so when we found a turning point, we doubled back. It's more interesting in this direction anyway," Jane said. "I'm so glad to see you. It's obviously going better for you now." She nodded at Poppy and Beans.

Daniel smiled. "It's been great walking with Poppy. I'm not so sure she would say the same about me though." He gave Poppy a crooked smile. "We've had some dramas, thanks to me."

"Nothing like a bit of drama to make things interesting," Jane said. "Come on, tell us."

He kept the story short, but still their eyes widened.

"Wow," Callum said. He hesitated. "The guy who mugged you — was he one of them?"

"I think he was. Collins's mate. I think he was following me. Someone must have told Collins I was looking for him and he sent him to check me out. But at the time, I had no idea."

"You were quite shaken up," Jane said. "No reason to think it wasn't an ordinary mugging. Nasty, but nothing to link it to Collins at the time."

"Where is he now, then?" Callum asked. "Did the police catch him?"

"Not as far as we know," Daniel said.

"So he could still be around?"

"He disappeared pretty quickly when the boaters arrived on the scene. He must know the police are after him. I expect he'll disappear for a good while."

"Hm." Jane looked worried. "Sounds like a real low-life. Aren't you worried he'll come after you again?"

Daniel paused. He glanced at Poppy's face. She'd gone quiet. She nodded, biting her lip. Collins knew Daniel suspected him of killing Ryan — and could identify him. If it was true, he was still in danger.

"I suppose so. But it would be crazy to come back here when the police are looking for him, surely."

"Sounds like he *is* crazy."

* * *

"Should we get away from here, just in case?" Poppy said.

They were back at the campsite. The light was fading, the air still warm, and they were waiting for the sunset, sitting outside their tents with Beans.

Daniel could feel the tension in her voice. The last thing he wanted was to risk her safety again. "I think we should. We can tell the police where we are. Or—" A thought occurred to him. "You could go on, if they don't want me to stray too far. I don't want to be the reason your walk is cut short. I've got all the time in the world, but you've got a job to get back to."

Poppy nudged his arm. "Don't be silly, Daniel. We're in this together now. Collins has to answer to both of us. Anyway, two are safer than one."

At that moment, as if on cue, Daniel's mobile buzzed. He pulled it from his pocket and glanced at the screen before connecting, mouthing "Police" to Poppy. She moved closer, angling her head to catch the conversation.

"Daniel, it's DI Stevens. We've got some news for you. A team has been searching the canal at the spot you identified — and they've found human remains."

Daniel's stomach did a cartwheel. He stood transfixed, open-mouthed, shocked into silence. Poppy's eyes were wide. For a moment he was unable to speak. But Poppy was hopping up and down, urging him to respond. "Say something, Daniel!" she whispered, as the voice in his ear said, "Are you still there?"

"I'm still here, just . . . a little . . . taken aback. Is it Ryan? Is it a boy?"

"I can't disclose the details at the moment — we're waiting for the pathologist to examine the remains. As you can imagine, it's just a few bones."

The image of a schoolboy toy, a plastic skeleton hanging from the ceiling in his childhood bedroom, popped into Daniel's mind. He shook his head to rid himself of the picture. This was a person they were talking about, not a plastic effigy.

"When will you know?"

"We've requested the report urgently. I imagine a couple of days. I'll call you when I know more."

Daniel disconnected the call. A strange mixture of feelings washed over him. Cautious relief, that he'd been right all along. Guilt — the guilt of his ten-year-old self at not saving Ryan. Fear, that they would never catch Collins. And concern for Poppy, that until they did, she might be in danger.

"They found human remains," he said, though Poppy had clearly understood from his side of the conversation. "They can't confirm yet that it's Ryan."

"You were right, Daniel." She gripped his arm. "You were right, all along."

* * *

Daniel woke to the sound of Beans barking within inches of his head. He was immediately awake. He grabbed his mobile.

Three in the morning and still dark outside. His heart began to thump — something was going on.

In one movement he was out of his sleeping bag, glad he'd slept in his shorts.

"Poppy?" he whispered.

"I'm here," she replied, to his relief. "What's going on? Shall I let Beans out?"

The barking got louder, more hysterical, as if whatever had woken him was getting closer. "Yes, let him out," Daniel said. "You stay there, Poppy, I'm going with him."

Grabbing a torch, he unzipped his tent, making no effort to be quiet. If it was a fox, it would run off. If it was a person — he daren't think about Collins — then the barking might make him hesitate.

All this ran through his head in an instant as his eyes became accustomed to the dark. Outside, an eerie moonlight turned everything to shades of grey and silver. Beans was at his feet, barking into the gloom behind the tent.

Daniel turned to investigate, imagining a fox retreating into the hedge, but as he moved, a wiry arm snaked around his neck, choking him. He shouted, wrestling with the arm, but a leg clamped around his own and he landed on his back with a painful crunch. The awkward fall dislodged the arm around his neck and he was able to scramble to his feet, avoiding the kicks being aimed at his body.

He stood facing the man he'd feared all his life, his heart beating out of his chest. But he was suddenly aware that he was taller than Collins, broader too. He was no longer a terrified boy of ten. He could tackle this man — he must, because Poppy was only a few feet away.

"Poppy, run!"

He stepped forward, holding the torch high, ready to tackle his nemesis. He was dimly aware of a scrabbling in the tent beside his, the sound of running feet. For an instant, the older man hesitated, a look of surprise flitting across his face, but then he was on him, wiry arms gripping Daniel's, legs kicking, aiming to trip or maim.

"Fucking toerag!" Collins growled. "Nobody puts the pigs onto me!"

Rage took hold of Daniel. "You murdered your own son!" he yelled.

He pulled his arm away and aimed a blow at Collins's head with the torch. Collins blocked it and grabbed at his throat, holding him from behind. Daniel kicked and writhed, but the arm held strong. Unable to breathe, he began to panic. He had to win this fight, or Poppy would be next. He kicked and struggled, scrabbling at his neck, but Collins held firm.

Dimly, he saw Ryan's tortured face, a sickly grey in the moonlight. His lips moved, he was trying to say something. But Daniel was losing consciousness and Ryan's face was beginning to fade. He mustn't let go, he must keep fighting — but the fog was gathering, the darkness falling . . .

A scream echoed from nearby, galvanising Daniel's weakening body. With one last burst of energy, he whipped his head back. A satisfying crunch, a deep grunt from behind, and he was free. Cool air in his throat. He stumbled, retching, gasping for breath. Collins was on the ground, holding his face. Daniel rushed to him and rolled him onto his front, bending one tattooed arm hard against his shoulder.

A slim figure appeared from nowhere, strong hands grasping Collins's arm and wrenching it from Daniel's grip.

"I've got him," Callum said. "You get Poppy."

Daniel jumped to his feet, adrenaline rushing through his body. He stumbled in the direction of the scream. "Poppy!"

Torchlights flashed, confusing him for a moment. Thumps and grunts came from ahead. Then, through the moonlight, Poppy's figure emerged, walking towards him. Behind her, torchlight illuminated a figure, prostrate on the grass. Four people in various states of dress sat solidly, each pinning a limb to the ground.

"Everything's under control," Poppy said. "The police will be pleased with us. Seems we've got them both."

* * *

Callum had been awake playing games on his mobile, they learned later. He'd heard sounds on the towpath and watched as two shadowy figures passed, heading for the camping field. Guessing it was Collins and his mate, he'd slipped off the boat and followed them to the camp. Unsuspecting, the two men had skirted round all the tents until Beans gave Daniel and Poppy away. Collins had waited for Daniel to appear, then pounced.

Collins's mate, acting as lookout, had hung back. Poppy had run straight into him. But by then, the other campers were alerted. Before he had a chance to do any harm, they'd grabbed him and sat on him.

When the police arrived a short time later, they were surprised to find the two safely trussed up, guarded by a circle of campers sharing hot chocolate and a bottle of whisky.

CHAPTER FORTY-FOUR

Two weeks later, Daniel waited in the familiar interview room at the station, his foot tapping a quiet rhythm on the grubby carpet. DI Stevens soon arrived, accompanied by a uniformed officer Daniel hadn't met before and two others in plain clothes. They sat without introduction or explanation.

The detective held a report in his hand, but didn't open it. He shook Daniel's hand warmly and sat down with a smile.

"Right," he said. "I'll get straight to the point."

"OK . . ." Daniel said warily.

"You're aware that we found human remains at the spot you identified."

"I am."

"And you're also aware that we found two different sets of human remains."

"I — No, I didn't know. What — Who? Was Collins a serial murderer?"

"It appears from the report that one set of remains belonged to a male around the age of the boy you met. We believe it to be Ryan. Obviously, a lot of time has passed since the body of this boy entered the water, so identification is difficult. But it does match up with your timeline and your description of events, and we're doing our best to retrieve

DNA, or find another way to prove his identity, like dental and medical records, although that's proving tricky. He didn't seem to be registered anywhere nearby. We're checking records at your old school, as well as other schools on the canal network."

"Right," Daniel said when the detective paused.

"At the moment, however, we're scratching our heads a little over the second set of remains, a female. Do you remember anything — anything at all — that could indicate anyone else present on the boat at the time you saw Ryan, either that afternoon or the evening when you saw Collins dump the bundle?"

Daniel shook his head.

"Any sign of a female presence on the boat at all? Flower arrangements, clothes, shoes, a woman's bike, perhaps?"

He'd been ten years old, a child, excited to see a boat, yes, but not looking for clues. It wouldn't have occurred to him to notice signs of a female. He shook his head again. "Maybe. I was just a boy. I looked around the boat, but I wouldn't be able to say if there were signs of a woman — I'm sorry."

There was a pause as DI Stevens made a note.

"But, can I ask, do you think the body was Ryan's mother?"

The detective sighed. "It's hard to say. We were hoping you might be able to shed some light. It could be, though, in which case our man is in even deeper trouble. We've got a long and tricky task ahead of us to gather evidence."

Daniel left the station in a state of shock. He couldn't stop thinking that he'd met a multiple murderer at the age of ten — and actually gone back to find him, taking himself and Poppy right into the mouth of danger.

* * *

"That's incredible!" Lauren said, when she'd recovered from the shock. She'd called to find out how he was getting on, and they were still on the call an hour later. "But well done you. You stuck to your guns and you were vindicated. I'm so impressed! How are you feeling now?"

Daniel, perched on a log at the edge of a field while Poppy and Beans played ball, asked himself the same question. "Different. Better. Sometimes disbelieving. Sometimes I think it'll still all go wrong and they'll discover that the bodies had nothing to do with Collins. But then I think, what are the chances? Two bodies in exactly the spot I identified, nineteen years on?" He shook his head. "They had to take me seriously."

"You should write it all down, Daniel," Lauren said. "It would make such an interesting story."

"Perhaps I will. But I can't do much about it yet. They're still gathering evidence, though they're making good progress now. They've confirmed the other body was Ryan's mother. She'd been on benefits so they were able to track her down, even though she wasn't married to Collins."

"Was it DNA that identified them?"

"I'm not entirely sure. I don't know if DNA lasts that long, even in bones. We'll find out eventually. What's certain is that Collins will go to prison for a very, very long time."

"Can they prove he killed them?"

"Cause of death for the mother was strangulation, it seems. And poor Ryan had a blow to the head. Collins is claiming he fell down the steps and banged his head. All he did was dispose of the body, according to him. He capitulated straight away when they told him they had DNA evidence, even though I don't think they did at the time. I think it'll be hard to prove, but they've got him for some pretty serious crimes anyway."

"Sounds like a very nasty character. And you found him! I'm proud of you, Daniel. And Mum and Dad will be too. Can't wait to see their faces when you tell them."

"We'll see about that, but thank you. I'm just relieved it's over — until the court case, anyway. I've no idea how long it'll be before that comes up."

"What now, then?" Lauren said. "Any more adventures planned?"

"Very funny. No, we're hoping for a few more days of sun, moving on. We'll take it gently, give Poppy time to recuperate. Then she has to get back to Banbury." He watched as Poppy, laughing, bent to give Beans a hug. He bounced around as if he was on springs, oblivious to the space where his fourth leg used to be. His rose-pink tongue dangled, his eyes bright and expectant as Poppy threw the ball.

"Will you see her again?"

Daniel lowered his voice. "Are you kidding me? I'm not going to let her out of my sight. She's the best thing that's ever happened to me, Lauren." The catch in his voice gave him away, he knew. But he meant it, and he wanted Lauren to know how important Poppy was to him.

He ended the call, his mind drifting back to the root of all this. The car boot sale, the comics. *Golden Serpent*, Ryan, Collins. The dark waters of the canal at dusk, silver ripples reflecting the rising moon. His ten-year-old self, a small boy, terrified, running as fast as he could across an empty field.

Looking back on it, that stretch of canal had provided the perfect hiding place for Collins. Hidden behind dense hedges, low trees casting their shadows, no houses in sight. The police had remarked on that section of water being deeper than was typical. All it took was a little bit of weight to keep the bodies submerged and the flat-bottomed narrowboats would have passed over the decomposing remains safely, barely stirring the silt that would gradually cover them over the years.

The police found records of Ryan's mother, though nobody had reported her missing. It had taken a long and detailed search, but eventually they had tracked her down. It seemed she'd had no family apart from Ryan, and friends would have been in short supply with a partner like Collins. People had probably thought she'd left Collins, and when Ryan disappeared, that he'd gone to join her.

It took them a little longer to track down records of Ryan, who — it turned out — was registered under his mother's last name. The police were convinced Collins had murdered Ryan's mother and cut his own son's life tragically short. With the help of the latest forensic science, they were optimistic of the right result.

"I wonder if there'll be a funeral for Ryan and his mum," Poppy mused. "What do they do about old cases? People who disappeared years ago? I've never really thought about it before."

"It would be a bit weird if you had. But if there is a funeral, I'd like to go."

"Me too. I almost feel like I knew Ryan, too. As long as Collins won't be there."

Daniel snorted. "I think he'll be otherwise occupied."

There was a pause. "Shall we make tracks?" Poppy said. "Sure."

As they gathered up their belongings, Daniel's phone rang again. Poppy raised her eyebrows. "Popular today."

Glancing at the screen, Daniel recognised the Oxford number.

"Prof James here, Daniel." His voice was confident, friendly. "Have I caught you at a bad time?"

Daniel smiled at Poppy. "No, not at all."

"I've got good news for you. At least I hope it is."

"OK . . ." He didn't want any more shocks.

"We've got funding for the research I told you about. It's more than we hoped."

"That's great," Daniel said. He hoped the professor wouldn't spot the cautious note in his voice.

"It is. I'd like you to help us with it, Daniel. Your brain — well, we'll never find another one like it. It would help us enormously if you'll agree to join us on a series of long-term studies. I'd like to meet up with you, together with a couple of colleagues, so we can take you through it."

"Do I need to decide now?"

"Of course not. Come and talk to us, hear what it's all about, then make up your mind. You're right to be cautious, it'll be a big commitment."

Daniel didn't need to think for long. He trusted this man, who'd already given him so much support. "I'll meet you, of course. I want to help, I just . . ."

"It's OK, Daniel. There are many things you need to consider. I'm pretty confident we can reassure you, though."

"Thank you. But I want to complete my walk first. It's important to me."

"Of course. We have plenty of work ahead of us. When will you be ready to fix a date?"

"A month, maybe?"

"That's perfect. Oh, and Daniel, I almost forgot to say, we can pay you. It won't be a fortune, but it will help."

"Thanks, Professor, I'll be in touch."

Turning slowly to Poppy, Daniel held out his hand.

"Come here," he said. "I've got something to tell you."

THE END

ACKNOWLEDGEMENTS

The inspiration for my stories comes from anywhere or anything — a chance meeting, an image, a fragment of conversation. For *Perfect Witness*, it was a newspaper article about a woman with a highly superior autobiographical memory. This led to further research into memory and helped me create the character that became Daniel.

Many thanks to Professor Martin Conway, Director of the Centre for Memory and Law (City University of London), for sparing the time to share his expert understanding of autobiographical memory.

I've spent many hours on the English canals, enjoying the peace, the scenery and the wildlife. They have provided the perfect setting for this book. This story is loosely based on the canals of Oxfordshire and beyond, but it is fiction, so destinations, descriptions and distances are not exact. Thanks go to the Canal & River Trust for its excellent information and advice; to Sara Kitcatt for her endless fund of knowledge about life on the canals; to Gordon and Whitney for allowing me to borrow their dog's name — Beans.

As always I'm eternally grateful to my lovely first readers, Judy Jones, Caroline Plumptre and the Scribblers; and of course the delightful team at Joffe Books.

And to my readers, thank you all for reading!